Allegiance

by

Marilee Brothers

The Soul Seekers Series

Allegiance

Cover Art by *Kim Mendoza*

The Wild Rose Press, Inc.
PO Box 708
Adams Basin, NY 14410-0708
Visit us at www.thewildrosepress.com

Publishing History
First Fantasy Rose Edition, 2017
Print ISBN 978-1-5092-1203-3
Digital ISBN 978-1-5092-1204-0

The Soul Seekers Series
Published in the United States of America

Mick fights a grin

but continues to ignore me and directs his comment to Billy. "Guess it's no secret I'd like to spend time with Mel. Just wanted to make sure it's okay with you."

I can't believe this. Twice in one night. First, Darrell wants to know if I'm up for grabs. Now, Mick is asking Billy if I'm on the auction block.

Billy also acts like I'm invisible. "Are you saying you want to date Mel? I'm not sure how I feel about that. She might not be ready to…"

"Stop!" I yell. "Do you see me? I'm right here. In this room. And the two of you are acting like mongrels fighting over a steak bone. Let's get one thing crystal clear. I'm nobody's steak bone. All I want is for both of you to leave so I can heat up a bowl of noodles in the microwave, take a shower, and go to bed in a man-free environment. Got it?"

Since they're both obtuse, I look around the room for something to throw. Finding no missiles, I settle for the broom propped in the corner of the room. I grab it like a baseball bat and begin swinging it at both men. "Out, get out!"

They both run for the door. Mick is laughing his butt off. Billy keeps looking over his shoulder, saying, "Wait, wait, we need to talk."

I slam the door and lock it, thankful I'm alone.

Praise for Marilee Brothers

"This book totally surprised me, with twists and turns I didn't see coming...a touch of humor and great characters...the start of a really good series. I can't wait to read Book #2."

~Patricia Lewin, Author

~*~

"*AFFLICTION* was a clever little mystery, romance with an aspect of the supernatural thrown in for good measure. I'm really curious what life will bring to Mel next."

~ What's Beyond Forks?

~*~

"...loved the stepfather, and...his brother as he leads a motorcycle gang...I will read more from this author."

~Shannon B, Netgalley

~*~

"...Very interesting...Loved the ending of the story but hopefully there's more...with Mel and Billy..."

~Paula DeBoer, Netgalley

~*~

"...an interesting book. I like the main character...the author made her a strong independent woman...I am interested...to find out what happens with Destiny and everyone else."

~Danielle Montgomery

Dedication

To my wonderful, supportive husband,
thank you being my number one fan.
You always have my back.

Chapter One

Billy asleep is a feast for the senses. The sheet covers only the lower half of his body. One arm, bicep prominently displayed, is tucked behind his head. I breathe in his familiar scent. Motorcycle leathers. Gasoline. Minty toothpaste. His chest rises and falls with gentle exhalations. Thin cords from his ear buds snake across the pillow and attach to his cell phone on the bedside table. Music helps keep his nightmares at bay.

I reach out a hand, tempted to slide a finger along the springy auburn fuzz bisecting the center of his muscular chest and trace it to where it terminates, south of the thin, cotton sheet. I stop short of touching him. He worked late last night and needs his rest.

I stand next to the bed and gaze down at him. His eyelids twitch but do not open. Is he dreaming? About what? What I really need to know is about whom? Especially when I notice the bulge stirring to life beneath the sheet. You'd better be dreaming about me, buddy boy.

I lean down to drop a chaste farewell kiss on his forehead. A split second later, I'm flat on my back, pinned to the bed and Billy the Kid grins down at me like a naughty little boy. He rips out his ear buds and pulls the cord free until the music washes over us. It's a rock and roll tune, a blast from the past.

"Hey, baby," he says. "Wanna dance?"

Before I can form an answer, I'm swept off the bed and twirled around until I'm dizzy and laughing uncontrollably.

He sets me on the floor and pulls me tight against his body. "You sneaking out on me, Minnie Mouse?

I manage a weak, breathless protest. "I'm supposed to meet Steve at 9:30 a.m. I need to get going."

He cups my face between his palms and brushes his lips across mine. "You sure about that?"

"Well, um…"

My body says bring it on.

My brain chimes in, *promptness is overrated.*

****

As I've done every day for the last few months, I drive slowly past the home of Eddie Morgan, the lying bastard who traded his baby daughter for a shiny new pick-up and, more than likely, murdered his wife, Dani. She was my best friend and the reason I now live in 3 Peaks, Oregon. What do I hope to see? Eddie in handcuffs as a couple of muscular cops perp walk him to their cruiser. Instead, I jam on the brakes and lower the driver's side window.

Scuzbag Eddie is pounding a For Sale by Owner sign into the patchy, neglected lawn of his front yard. I make no attempt to conceal myself. Actually, I want him to know I'm stalking him. A tad over five feet tall, I don't appear intimidating. But Eddie knows—and I know—looks can be deceiving. I've been labeled a nosy bitch along with other choice words. Sticks and stones. It's the result that counts.

Eddie glances over his shoulder, flips me off and returns to his task. For all of approximately two seconds, I try to decide whether or not to fire off a new zinger.

"Hey, Eddie, you moving away? I'll miss our little visits."

He turns and bristles, hands on his hips. "Leave me the fuck alone or I'll call the cops."

I flash a big, toothy, fake smile. "Great idea. I'll wait around until they get here—see if they have any new evidence linking you to Dani's death. Sound good?"

His shoulders slump and he whines, "What's your problem, Mel? I didn't kill my wife. I loved Dani."

This strikes me as so preposterous, I don't bother to answer. I zip up the window, pull away from the curb and reach for my cell phone. Fortunately I have my Homeland Security buddy, Mick, on speed dial. Creeping down the residential street, I wait for him to answer. Or not. After three rings, I hear him growl, "Now what, Mel?"

"Eddie is selling his house. Maybe he's leaving town. You need to nail him right now."

"Tell me something I don't know, something you haven't nagged me about every day for friggin' forever."

Like I said, sticks and stones. "I know he's guilty as homemade sin. Since when is it legal to sell your child?"

A heavy, exasperated sigh zips through the cell towers and blasts my left ear. "Look, Mel, we both know Eddie's a creep, but he claimed he couldn't care for the baby after his wife died and the Rockwells legally adopted her."

I bite my lip to keep from swearing at him. "We

both know how that turned out. Come on, Mick, how much time and effort has your agency put into investigating that rat bastard Eddie? Time's running out. Just saying."

He sighs again. "I work for Homeland Security. Though I fervently wish we had the manpower to devote to your friend's case, a little issue called terrorism seems to be taking up all our time. Eddie Morgan is a local problem. As I've told you many times before, your best bet is the 3 Peaks Police Department."

"Oh, yeah, I'm real popular with them."

Because of my actions—even though they were for the greater good—one of 3 Peaks P.D.'s top officials had seen fit to blow his brains out with his service revolver.

"What about lover boy? Can't he help you?"

"Billy's only been on the force a short time. I don't want to push it right now."

"Hmmm."

"Alrighty then, catch you later, my former friend, Mick."

His boom of laughter causes me to pull the phone away from my ear. Still, I clearly hear his words. "And I'll catch you the next time I'm in Bend. How about dinner?"

"I have a boyfriend."

He says, "Do you?" and clicks off.

Well, damn. Mick has a knack for zeroing in on a person's weakness. Like, when you have a rough spot on the edge of a molar and your tongue can't leave it alone.

William Henry McCarty, aka Billy the Kid, successfully completed counseling for the PTSD he suffered while serving in the Middle East. He's now a detective with the 3 Peaks Police Department. Unfortunately, the job throws him into daily contact with his former girlfriend, evil temptress Candy Talbot, the blonde beauty who, in my humble opinion, has but one goal: to get Billy back into her bed.

As if my life isn't complicated enough, Billy and I have another little problem—namely, my ability to read souls. He knows I can tell if he's lying when I look directly into his eyes. And lately he's been avoiding my gaze. Did he actually look into my eyes this morning? I think about it and decide he didn't. Granted, I couldn't have cared less at the time. Billy is very good at distracting me.

My poor brain is on overload, so I decide to think about it later, especially when I notice my car is running on fumes. Yes, Honor Melanie Sullivan now has a car. It's a relatively new development and a relatively old car. An ancient, mustard-colored Toyota Tercel, it came complete with a multitude of dings and scratches. Despite one hundred and seventy-five thousand miles on the odometer, she runs like a top. Because of the disgusting color, I got her on the cheap. Billy calls her Old Yeller. Wanting to stay on her good side, I call her Buttercup.

My next goal is enough money for the first and last months' deposit on an apartment of my own. For now, I'm still living in unit Number Ten at Nick's Place, a combination sports bar and motel where I earn my keep waiting tables. I no longer have to clean rooms since I insist upon Nick withholding part of my salary for the room rental.

Praying I'll make it before the engine sputters and

quits from fuel deprivation, I cruise slowly to my favorite mini market with the cheapest gas in town. The Gas and Grub. Despite the Americanized name, the Gas and Grub is owned by a Muslim family named Ayoob. The patriarch of the family, Bibi, runs the place assisted by his wife, Saarah, multiple sons, daughters, nieces, nephews and cousins. Today, I am greeted by Yasmin, Bibi's daughter, whose luminous sherry-colored eyes reflect the purity of her soul. When I hand my credit card across the counter, she smiles. "Hello, my friend. So nice to see you again."

"Good to see you too, Yasmin. Love the streak in your hair. Very cool."

Most of Yasmin's brown hair is covered with the headscarf befitting a woman of her faith. But some loose tendrils have slipped from the scarf revealing the honey-colored streak.

She leans across the counter and whispers, "Papa does not like it, but what is done is done."

I offer her my fist to bump. She runs my credit card, glances out the window and freezes. I follow her gaze and see a white heavy-duty pickup with the Rockin' R Ranch logo on the door. A man with a cowboy hat sits behind the wheel. A lanky young guy wearing a backwards ball cap jumps out of the passenger side and begins filling the tank. He turns until his back to the driver and peers through the window of the mini mart. He spots Yasmin and gives her a quick grin. I get the impression of gleaming white teeth in a handsome tanned face. Color rises in Yasmin's cheeks.

"He's a cutie pie." I say. "You know him?"

Yasmin's eyes widen and her face pales. She signals me by jerking her head to the left. Bibi rises up from behind a display of potato chips where, hidden from view, he'd been stocking shelves.

Oops.

Eyes narrowed with suspicion, he joins Yasmin behind the counter. "I'll take care of this," he says, pointing at the pick-up. "You finish what I was doing."

"Yes, Papa," Yasmin says. With downcast eyes, she hurries to obey him.

I follow her and whisper, "Sorry. I hope you're not in trouble."

When she lifts her gaze to mine, I see her eyes brim with tears. "It's complicated. Papa is what you call old school."

I feel Bibi's gaze drilling into the back of my head. I scribble my cell phone number on the gas receipt and hand it to her. "Call if you want to talk."

She stuffs the receipt into a pocket and whispers, "Tell Riley hi from Yasmin."

I map out my route to Buttercup so I can check out the Rockin' R Ranch pick-up truck. Beneath its logo, I spot the words Red Ridge, Oregon. The man in the driver's seat wears dark sunglasses, but I'm picking up what he's sending. It's the old I'm checking you out vibe. Guess I'm right because as I draw closer, he tips his hat to me. Nice to know chivalry is not dead. I walk past his open window. He leans out and hollers, "Hey, Riley, check the air in the left rear tire."

I slow down as the kid replaces the gas nozzle in the receptacle. I murmur, "Yasmin says, 'Hi.'" He glances over at me, and I get the full force of his mega watt smile. He sobers quickly. "Her dad's inside…right?"

"Yep." I keep on walking. Thanks to me, Yasmin

is now in trouble. Better not risk getting Riley in hot water too. I rev up Buttercup, gaze into the rearview mirror and shake a warning finger at the image of myself staring back. "You will not, I repeat not, become the conduit between two star-crossed lovers. Do you hear me?"

My head nods in agreement.

My heart says we'll see.

Chapter Two

I'm still fuming about Eddie as I stomp up a flight of stairs and into the office I share with my bio dad. The name of our business is CyberSecure Plus and located in downtown 3 Peaks. We share the second floor with two other businesses, McMillan Management (no clue what they manage) and a company called Confidential Inquiries run by a woman named Louise Goodhart.

Strangely, the idea for CyberSecure Plus came from Homeland Security agent, Mick. Yes, that Mick. He told us there were a multitude of businesses, including law enforcement, who would happily fork over money to find out if someone is lying. And, yes, we can tell when someone is lying. With one hundred percent certainty. Our business does not advertise. We depend on word of mouth across law enforcement agencies, legal firms, and offices whose specialty is screening future employees.

My newly discovered, newly out-of-the-closet father, Estafan (Steve) Delgado, is sitting behind his desk. I don't bother with pleasantries. Instead, I place my hands on my hips and announce, "Asshole Eddie has his house up for sale and Mick won't help me."

Unperturbed, Steve glances over the top of his newspaper and points at a table holding the coffee maker. I perk up when I spot a carton of assorted doughnuts. We haven't known each other long, but Steve knows what makes me happy. I fill a mug with black coffee, grab a maple bar, and plop down on the wheeled office chair parked against the wall.

He watches me slurp coffee and inhale my pastry before he says, "Let it go, Melanie. Too much time has passed. Sometimes the bad guys win."

The CyberSecure part of the business is owned by Steve. I'm not actually sure what he does, but it involves software designed to keep one's online personal information safe from hackers. Because of our shared experience helping solve a human trafficking/baby-selling scheme, we took Mick's advice and launched the Plus part, which is, in the truest sense of the word, unique. I know of no other like it. We briefly considered calling it CyberSecure and Stuff, but Steve said we wouldn't be taken seriously with Stuff in the title.

Still seated, I scoot across the floor until my knees are pressed against the front of Steve's desk. "I can't let it go. What if he moves to Timbuktu or Antarctica? If he killed Dani and gets away with it, what will stop him from doing it again? Why am I the only one who cares?"

"He was questioned by detectives from the police department. Correct?"

I nod. "Briefly. They were more interested in the high profile lawyers and doctors caught in the net. Eddie got lost in the shuffle."

Steve folds the newspaper into precise thirds, sets it on the desk and fixes me with his intense gaze. "You are sure Eddie is lying?"

"Yes, I've looked into his beady little eyes a

number of times."

"You asked if he killed his wife?"

I pause and think about his question. "Not in so many words. When Dani died, I didn't know how to detect a lie. Not until you taught me."

My father and I are soul readers or, more accurately, soul seekers. As referenced earlier, we have the ability to gaze into a person's eyes and discover what resides in his/her soul, be it evil, slightly shady, or pure as the driven snow. It can be exhilarating, liberating, tantalizing, terrifying, and, at times, makes you want to give up on the human race. Steve has more experience at reading souls than I do. It's still hard for me to maintain eye contact when I peek into a soul and see something so vile it scares the crap out of me.

I chug the last of my coffee and toss the cardboard cup into the trash. "I know one thing for sure. He's lying about Dani's death. He won't look at me when he talks about her. He gets all shifty and weird. He acts guilty."

"Acting guilty is a far cry from confessing guilt." Steve leans across his desk. "What exactly do you plan to do?"

I squirm in my chair. "Prove he killed her, of course."

"How?"

I lift my hands. "Not sure at the moment, but I'll think of something."

Steve's brow furrows as he gazes at me. "I know this is important to you, but perhaps you need a diversion. I have a job for you if you want it."

"Sure, why not? For an employment agency?"

Steve is the epitome of tact, and good at reading

souls. He's been welcomed by the law enforcement community, and consequently picked up a number of hostage negotiator gigs. As for me, the not-so-tactful partner? I get to stare into the eyes of candidates seeking jobs as live-in nannies or night auditors at local motels. Yes, chauvinism is alive and well among law enforcement types.

The following is a direct quote from my former friend Mick. "Mel, you're a girl. We don't want to put you in harm's way," the comment cleverly disguised as caring and protective, never fails to tick me off.

Steve suppresses a smile, opens a desk drawer, pulls out a manila folder, and hands it to me. The neatly labeled tab on the folder definitely piques my interest. Louise Goodhart.

I jab a thumb over my shoulder toward the hall and the office next to ours. "Are we talking about Confidential Inquiries Louise?"

"Yes, *mi hija*, we are talking about her."

I open the file folder and find it empty. "So, what does our formidable neighbor with the trustworthy name require of us?"

"You think she's formidable?"

"Yes, her sculpted biceps alone make me feel guilty about neglecting my push-ups."

Louise Goodhart is a woman of indeterminate age. She's tall, lean, and fit with short dark hair going gray and pale blue eyes worthy of a soul seeker.

Steve says, "Louise has a new client, a woman with a somewhat troubled past."

"Troubled how?"

"A few years ago, she was involved in a law suit against a local dentist, and it had a less than satisfactory conclusion."

Sometimes Steve is a bit too tactful. I stifle an impatient sigh. "For her or for the dentist?"

"Apparently, the trial was quite sensational and garnered the interest of the press. In the end, the dentist was cleared of all charges. The woman was discredited and labeled a liar."

"And now?" I prompt.

"Now, she says her optometrist is getting up close and personal."

"Sounds like a nut job. Is Louise seriously considering taking the case?"

"That's where we come in," Steve says. "She's accepted a retainer from the woman but hasn't deposited the check. Louise specifically asked for you. She'll introduce you as her assistant who needs more information. If you determine the woman is lying, Louise will politely decline and return the check."

Steve frowns and drums the fingers of his right hand on his desk top, a gesture I know well. He has something else on his mind. I wait for it.

"Like you," he says, lifting his gaze to mine. "I wondered why Louise would take such a case. When I questioned her, she said there was something in the woman's demeanor—she called it an air of desperation—and it gave her pause. She specifically came to Louise because she's certain no one will believe her because of her past. So, if the woman is telling the truth…" Steve's voice trails off.

I finish the sentence. "Louise gets to nail a perve optometrist."

"Right," he says. "So, what do you think?"

"Sure, I'll give it a whirl."

Despite my previous rant, I'm grateful for the opportunity to earn a bit of extra cash. It's just a matter of time before I'm an upstanding, tax-paying, apartment renting, car-owning citizen of 3 Peaks, Oregon. In the meantime, I'll keep my day job at Nick's.

Chapter Three

A couple of days pass before my appointment with Louise Goodhart's client, a woman named Rebecca Porter.

In the meantime, I'm having serious doubts about my relationship with Billy. After our previous early morning interlude, Billy has been more absent than present, claiming a heavy workload. Could be the truth. I hope it's the truth.

Unwilling to play the role of needy girlfriend, I choose not to hound him with phone calls and texts. If our relationship is doomed, so be it. I don't like the uncertainty, but try to dwell on the positives in my life. I'm alive and well. No small matter after my near death experience a few months ago. My mother, Sandra, though nosey and annoying, loves me. My stepfather, Abel, insists on calling me by my true name, Honor, a name I'm attempting to live up to. My bio father, Steve, respects me enough to make me his business partner, even though my contribution, money-wise, is on the negative side.

As I approach Goodhart's office, I attempt to clear my mind of boyfriend issues. I need to gather my wits and focus on the matter at hand, namely the contents of Rebecca Porter's soul. I'm ten minutes early for our appointment, armed with a notebook and a list of questions suggested by Goodhart.

Goodhart greets me at the door, her eagle-eyed gaze flicking over my attire, black tights, crisp, white shirt and ballerina flats. It's as dressed up as I get. She gives me a little nod of approval and waves me over to small table with two chairs. "You have the questions I gave you?"

I assure her I do, take a seat, and check out my surroundings. The basic design of her office is identical to ours, but much more sterile. Chilly, in fact. A large metal desk dominates the room abutted by a three-drawer file cabinet. No pictures on the wall and, sadly, no coffee or pastries.

Our office is quite the opposite. It exudes warmth, thanks to Steve who added an area rug, fresh flowers, and colorful works of art from his native Spain. Having a gay father who's into interior decorating is one of the perks I forgot to mention earlier.

Goodhart props her right bun against the desk and taps the toe of one sensible shoe against the floor. I get the impression she's uncomfortable. It's not my job to put her at ease, so I wait.

Her eyes bore into me. Finally, she says, "You'll be able to tell if she's lying?"

I'm thinking, it's a little late to be asking, but nod.

"For sure?"

"Yes, Steve and I can detect a lie. One hundred per cent."

"What else?"

"It depends," I say.

I'm never quite sure what a soul will reveal. It's best not to make promises I can't keep. "If she's trying to hide something, there's usually a sign, but I won't know until our interaction. It also depends on whether or not she maintains eye contact with me. If she doesn't, there's a limit to what I'll be able to read."

"So, I might be paying you for nothing."

I'm getting a little pissed at Louise Goodhart who is not living up to her surname. I stare into her eyes and see suspicion in her icy gray soul. I push away from the table and stand. "We can call it off if you want."

A flush rises in her pale cheeks. She flaps a hand. "No, no, I want to proceed. Sorry if I've offended you. It's hard for me to overcome my natural suspicion of things with no logical explanation."

"Tell me about it." The corners of my mouth quirk up in a smile I can't hold back. I plop down in the chair again. "Imagine what's it's like for me."

"Not good?"

I shrug. "Different every time. It can be downright scary or incredibly beautiful, not to mention everything in between."

"Does it ever mess up your personal life?"

I think about Billy and roll my eyes. "Of course it does. Everybody lies. Sometimes it's better not to know."

Before she can quiz me further, the office door opens wide enough to allow a woman's head to poke through. The head is crowned with a corona of frizzy light brown curls, not unlike a dandelion gone to seed. Her hazel eyes protrude slightly (good for my line of work) and her gaze scans the office, coming to rest on Goodhart before darting to me. She steps into the office, tottering slightly on three-inch heels. A turquoise silk blouse is tucked into tapered jeans that cling to her thin legs like a second skin. Her complexion is pasty. I wonder if she is ill or simply doesn't like the outdoors.

Goodhart springs away from her desk. "Rebecca, please come in. I'd like you to meet my assistant, Marilyn."

After a brief pause I remember I'm Marilyn and rise. Goodhart escorts the woman to the table. I extend my hand to shake and give her what I hope is a reassuring smile. I receive no smile in return. She settles into the chair across from me, clasps her hands together and places them on the table. Glancing up at Goodhart, she says, "Not sure why this is necessary. I already told you what happened. Are you going to help me or not?" Her voice carries a tinge of irritation.

"As I explained in my phone call," Goodhart says, "This is merely a formality. I've always found it's beneficial to have a second opinion." She points at me. "Marilyn is extremely sharp and sometimes picks up on specific details I may have missed, details that will help me help you. Make sense?"

I nod encouragingly, even though I'm thinking, *Good one, Louise. You've obviously developed an impressive line of bullshit.*

The important thing, though, is Rebecca's reaction and she totally buys it. "Well, okay, if you think it will help."

Goodhart excuses herself, tells Rebecca she'll be in touch and exits the office.

I open my notebook and scan the list of questions from Goodhart, most of which I won't be asking. I have my own method and no way will I say, "Are you telling me the truth?" I close the notebook and lean back in my chair. "Tell me about yourself."

Rebecca blinks rapidly. "Didn't Louise fill you in?

About what happened at the trial?"

"She mentioned you'd had a previous issue. Nothing more. I'd like to hear it from you."

She squeezes her hands together so tightly her knuckles turn white. Instead of looking at me, she stares down at her hands. "Here's the abbreviated version. I was sexually assaulted by a dentist. I went to the authorities. He was arrested. We went to court. He lied. The jury believed him. They didn't believe me. End of story."

I close the notebook and lean across the table, taking care not to touch her. "So he lied and got off. Then everybody assumed you were the liar. I'm so sorry."

Then, she does what I hoped she would do. She looks up at me. "Exactly. I was the victim. He was the guilty party and got away with it."

My peek into her eyes reveals a pink soul with streaks of gray. The gray tells me she is either depressed or lacks energy. Maybe both. Two tiny spots of red throb along one border, possibly a sign of pent up aggression. More importantly, I don't see the brilliant flash of light indicating the person is lying his/her ass off. Still, I have to make sure.

I formulate my next question carefully. "Surely you weren't the only one he assaulted. No other women came forward?"

She flushes, grips the edge of the table and stares into my eyes. "His specialty is sedation dentistry. I'm sure I'm not the only victim. Maybe they don't remember. But I do. Maybe I'm more resistant to whatever drug he uses because I remember him unzipping my pants and…"

She stops, swipes at her eyes, and takes a shaky breath. "Ancient history," she says.

There's no doubt in my mind she's telling the truth. The truth doesn't always set you free. Sometimes it makes you sick.

I give her a moment to compose herself before asking, "And the optometrist?"

She explains to me what he did. Explicitly. Again, I see no indication of a lie.

"What do you want Louise to do?"

"Help me prove it, of course."

"And then...?

"Then, I'll put the son of a bitch out of business."

That's when I see it. The dark, amorphous blob flitting across her soul like a wind-driven cloud. She's not lying, but she's hiding something.

We finish up and I walk her to the door. I need to talk to Steve, get a firm understanding on what I'd seen in Rebecca's soul before I write my report. As I trot down the hall toward CyberSecure Plus, my cell phone vibrates. It's Kendra, Billy's sister and my best friend in 3 Peaks.

She says, "Rat bastard Eddie Morgan is having a yard sale starting tomorrow morning. We're going. I'll pick you up at seven."

She clicks off before I can answer. I stare at the screen. Shall I call her back? Make an excuse? Knowing Kendra, I'd be wasting my breath. She'll blow it off and turn up promptly at seven. And maybe, just maybe, she might have some inside info on my missing-in-action boyfriend, Billy.

Chapter Four

A fist pounding on the door of Number Ten at 6:45 in the a.m. rouses me—after working at Nick's until well after midnight. Groaning, I stagger from my bed and open the door.

Kendra thrusts a super-sized cup of coffee in my hand and peers around me, her focus on the bed "Is Billy here?"

"Haven't seen him for a few days."

She follows me into Number Ten and plops down on the end of the bed. "Hmmm. What's going on with him?"

I collapse next to her and slurp some coffee, wishing I could inject it directly into my veins. "I hoped you could tell me."

She grabs my hand and squeezes. "No worries. I'm on the case. Stay tuned. Breaking news at five."

In spite of my fatigue, I snicker. Even though she woke me from a deep, dreamless sleep, it's impossible to stay mad at Kendra. No matter what happens with Billy, she and I will always be best buds.

"Where are the kiddos?" I ask.

Kendra has two little boys. She and her husband, Craig, are currently in the process of adopting Destiny, Dani's daughter. Destiny's so-called father is, of course, loser Eddie Morgan.

"Craig is holding down the fort. Didn't think it

would be a good idea to bring Destiny with us, although it might be fun to see asshole Eddie's reaction."

She nudges me off the bed. "Get dressed. We've got places to go, things to do."

I grab jeans and a T-shirt and head for the bathroom. "Like what? Looking for a murder weapon? A hammer with blood and hair stuck to it?"

The instant I say the words, I feel sick. I loved Dani like a sister, and I want to scrub the image of her untimely death from my mind.

When Kendra doesn't answer, I peek around the bathroom door. She's dabbing at her eyes with a tissue. She glances up at me. "Sorry. Sometimes I can't believe she's gone."

A couple of steps later, I'm sitting next to her, and we rock together in our shared misery. "Me neither."

Joined in grief, we spend a couple of minutes blubbering. Finally, Kendra pushes me away. "We've gotta get him, Mel. Pinky promise you won't give up."

I extend my little finger and twist it around hers. "You know I won't."

When we arrive at Eddie's, his street is already lined with the cars of early bird shoppers hoping to grab the good stuff.

Before I exit the car, I say, "How do you want to do this?"

Kendra shrugs. "Play it by ear. At the very least, we can put the fear of God into him."

"Like avenging angels," I say as we bump fists.

We're making our way down the sidewalk when I notice an elderly gentleman watering petunias in the front yard of the house across the street from Eddie's.

I grab Kendra's arm. "Let's go talk to him. Maybe

he knew Dani."

Kendra shakes me off. She's totally focused on Eddie and is not to be deterred. "Go ahead. I'm on it."

I scamper across the street and try to think of an opener to get the old guy talking. Flowers? Or maybe the traffic jam cluttering up his street? Turns out I don't need either one. I pause next to his yard and give him what I hope is a winsome smile.

He straightens up and looks me over. His blue eyes are rheumy with age, but his smile is genuine. "Well, hello there, young lady. I suppose you're here for the yard sale. Along with all the others."

I take a tentative step closer and decide to go with the truth. "Actually, I was wondering if you knew Dani." I tip my head toward Eddie's house. "She was my best friend, and she died right after I moved here from California."

His expression hardens as he gazes across the street at Eddie who's loading a baby crib into the back of a pickup parked in front of his house. "Hell, yes, I knew Dani. And her beautiful baby, too."

He folds him arms across his chest and stares down at me. His teeth are stained brown from chewing tobacco, but when I look into his soul, I like what I see. This is a man I can trust. However, I keep silent while he tries to decide whether or not he can trust me.

Apparently, I pass the test, because he points at the front porch spanning the width of his old but immaculately maintained house. Two Appalachian rockers sit side by side, protected from the weather by an overhanging roof. "I could use a sit down. Let's you and me chat a while."

Without waiting for an answer, he turns and strides

toward the house. I trot behind him; amazed I can barely keep up with a man of his advanced years.

He points at one of the rockers. "You sit there. It was my wife, Ellen's. She's gone now. Just like Dani."

I thank him and settle into the chair. The cushion lining the wooden rocker still holds the shape of his wife's body and encircles my body in a welcoming fashion,

He extends his hand. "I'm Hank Peterson. Lived here for forty years. Seen a lot of young folks come and go."

His grip is firm even though his skin is freckled with age spots and his knuckles swollen with arthritis.

"Nice to meet you, Mr. Peterson. My name is Melanie Sullivan, but most people call me Mel."

"And I'm Hank, not Mr. Peterson," he says. "Why did you ask me about Dani?"

"What do you think of her husband, Eddie?"

He stands, places his hands on the porch railing and spits a stream of tobacco juice into the juniper bushes lining the front of the house. He turns to me and winks. "That's what I think of Eddie Morgan."

He plops back into his chair. "Why do you ask?"

I choose my words carefully. "Do you know about his connection with the Rockwells and what happened when they got arrested?"

He blinks rapidly and glares at me. "I know you young people don't believe in newspapers, but I do. I read the paper every morning. And yes, I know the Rockwells ended up with Destiny. I'd sure like to know what happened to her after they got arrested. She was an angel, just like her mother. Couldn't ask for a better neighbor than Dani. After my wife died, Dani brought me food every day and stayed to visit. "

After my blubbering episode with Kendra, my tears are still close to the surface. A few of them spill over and trickle down my cheeks. I wipe them away. He listens carefully as I describe Kendra and Craig's effort to add Destiny to their family. "Would you like to see her?"

"Absolutely."

I promise I'll try to arrange it. We rock in companionable silence for a long moment. Finally, I say, "What did you hear about Dani's death?"

Hank folds his arms across his chest and stares into middle space. "They say she fell, hit her head, and died in the hospital."

"Eddie said she was painting the bathroom and she hit her head on the tub. Apparently, she fell off the ladder."

Hank's head swivels toward me, his eyes wide with surprise. "Fell off the ladder? They didn't own a ladder. She was going to borrow mine."

"Maybe they bought one."

"No way. She asked me about it the day before the accident."

"You sure about that? The time line I mean?"

He gives me his frowny face. "Young lady. Mel. I know I'm old, but I still have all my faculties. Plus, I keep a journal. Every day, I write down details about the weather, my interaction with others, and what I've accomplished. It's important, you know. To accomplish at least one task each day."

I can't believe it. I've managed to make contact with a veritable font of information. And, he has the journal to prove it.

I lift out of the rocker and shake his hand again. "Thank you so much, Hank. My friend and I are trying to prove Eddie had a hand in Dani's death, and your journal might be very important. And please, don't share this information with anyone unless I tell you it's okay. I'll be in touch."

He stands. "So, what's next?"

"I'm going to Eddie's yard sale and make sure there's no ladder in his garage."

"I heard he got a job in Idaho starting next month."

I blow out a sigh. "Well, damn. Guess we need to do something fast."

"Let me know if I can help. And, bring Destiny by for a visit."

I wave my goodbye and trot across the street and spot Eddie casting furtive glances at Kendra. He's on the move, making sure there's a crowd of people between the two of them. Wait 'til he sees who else has joined the party.

While he's focused on Kendra, I stifle an evil chuckle and head for a table piled high with pink baby clothes.

"Sir," I call in a shrill, not to be ignored tone. "These clothes have very little wear. Are they brand new?"

Eddie whirls around and meets my gaze. It takes a moment for his brain to collate the data. When it does, his eyes flare with alarm, his upper lip curls back like a feral cat, and he backs slowly away, narrowly missing an elderly woman with a walker who barks, "Watch it, young man!"

Kendra and I skirt around the edge of the crowd. I fill her in on what I've learned from Hank. We check out the garage and determine there are no ladders for sale.

Our work here is done.

Chapter Five

We talk about options on the drive home and agree they are limited.

"Billy," Kendra says. "He's our only connection to law enforcement."

"Not sure what he can do. He's new on the force. Besides, you can't bring a guy in for questioning because he doesn't own a ladder."

"There's got to be a way. Eddie's not that bright. Maybe they could tell him new evidence has been uncovered, implicating him in Dani's death."

"Then, he shows up with his lawyer and says, 'What evidence?'"

I blow out an exasperated breath and pound a fist on my knee. "Damn it! All I want is the opportunity to look into the big bastard's eyes and see if he's lying."

Kendra reaches over and squeezes my hand. "It will still be a dead end unless he suddenly decides to confess. Not gonna happen."

"We still have to try. And time is running out. If he killed Dani and thinks he got away with it, he might move to Idaho and do it again. Avenging angels…right?"

Kendra nods. Frustrated and out of solutions, we ride in silence until we reach Number Ten. Billy is standing in the open doorway; his Harley parked beneath my front window.

Kendra looks over at me, gives me a wink. "Shall we double team him or would you rather use your seductive skills?"

Even though I'm still a little pissed off at Billy, I grin. "How about both? Plan A and Plan B."

We bump fists and climb out of the car.

Billy wraps one arm around Kendra, the other around me and pulls us in for a bear hug. "How are my girls? What mischief have you been up to so early in the morning?"

Kendra pushes him away. I snuggle a little closer. Never too soon to start working on my seductive skills. We step into Number Ten and close the door. He drops a kiss on top of my head, points at the rumpled bed and the trail of clothes leading to the bathroom. "Looks like you left in a hurry."

"Trust Billy to zero in on the bed," Kendra mutters. She pulls out one of the two chairs next to a small table, the sum total of my furniture. "Sit."

Billy gives her a half-assed salute, turns the chair backward and straddles it. "What can I do for you, little sis?"

Kendra takes the other chair. I perch on the bed. We both start talking a mile a minute, our outrage growing as we relate the ladder story. Finally, he lifts a hand. "Hold it. And you want me to do what?"

"Look into it, of course. Was Eddie ever questioned about Dani's death?" I say.

"I doubt it. At the time, there was no reason to. He called 911. Said his wife fell and hit her head. Apparently the docs found nothing suspicious. So now, you're telling me he didn't own a ladder. Pretty easy to come up with a cover story. He'd say he borrowed one from a buddy and returned it."

Kendra leans across the table and pokes a finger in Billy's chest. "You're a smart guy. I bet you can figure out a way to talk to Eddie, even if it's not official. Just make sure Mel's with you so..." her voice trails off.

Billy shoots me a quick glance. "So Mel can do her thing."

Do I detect a trace of bitterness in his tone? Or am I being a hypersensitive, needy bitch? Only time will tell.

Kendra stands. "You got it. She'll be able to tell if he's lying."

I cringe inwardly, knowing this is the very issue looming large in my relationship with Billy.

He says, "And do what? Charge him with murder on the basis of what Minnie sees in his soul? There's a little thing called proof."

With a snort of disgust, Kendra heads for the door. "First things first, brother. You do your part, we'll do ours."

Huh? I'm not sure what she means, but nod enthusiastically anyway. I lock the door and walk over to Billy. It's time for Plan B.

I press my body against the back of the chair he's straddling. I stroke his face with both hands, taking care to avoid his gaze. Now is not the time to talk, to ferret out the truth. Instead, I focus on his sensual mouth and softly feather my lips across his. His hands slide around my body, cupping my butt, his fingers probing and caressing. A shiver of anticipation crawls down my spine and settles deep in my belly. I catch my breath, wrap my arms around his neck and lean into the kiss.

Breathing hard, Billy pulls away. "Hang on."

He stands, kicks the chair away, and lifts me up, pressing me against his body. My legs encircle his waist, and I hang on tight as he walks us to the bed. Flat on my back with Billy above me, I reach for the fastener on my jeans. His hand is already there, deftly unbuttoning my pants and sliding beneath my panties. I groan with pleasure as his lips follow the path of his hand, trailing kisses along the tender skin of my belly.

Eager to feel his naked body against mine, I push him away and try to squirm out of my jeans, only to get them hung up on my running shoes. My ankles are bound together. I struggle to a sitting position and reach for the shoes.

Billy chuckles and uses his body to pin me to the bed. His mouth brushes against my ear. He whispers, "You have a dilemma, Minnie. Handcuffs for the feet. Looks like you're at my mercy. Hmm, whatever do you suppose I should do in this situation?"

He clamps his hands around my hips and slides down my body, his silken tongue leaving a trail of heat, igniting a fire begging to be quenched.

I manage to gasp out an answer, "Not much fun for you."

He lifts his head stares directly into my eyes. The fire I see burning in his soul each time we make love burns brightly. "Making you happy makes me happy."

The honesty I see in his soul chases away my doubts. For the moment.

"Besides," he murmurs. "My turn will come."

Guess I didn't realize how much my body missed his. I lose myself in the sensation of his mouth hot against me, unable to think, unable to breathe, unable to move until I'm borne away on waves of pleasure.

I remain in my happy place while Billy kneels, removes my shoes and releases me from my denim prison. Our clothing ends up in a tangled mess on the floor. At some level I'm aware he's slipped on a condom. Then, his body covers mine and we rock together in a rhythm as ancient as the history of mankind.

Later, as we snuggle together half asleep, I realize I've lost my focus. I've never been good at using my feminine wiles for trickery. Is it too late now? Worth a try.

I give Billy's neck a little nip. He rouses from his somnolence and pulls me closer. "Again, you insatiable wench?"

"Nope, just wondering where Eddie Morgan hangs out now. It's sure not at Nick's. Guess he doesn't want to run into me."

He pulls me on top of his body and ruffles my hair with one big hand. "Wondered when we were going to get around to Eddie."

I feel a flush rise in my cheeks. Guess my seductive skills could use a bit of tuning up. "Sorry, Billy. I can't let it go."

His chest rises and falls in a deep sigh. "Tell you what. I'll check it out and let you know. Will that work?"

"Oh, yeah, that will work," I say. "Making you happy, makes me happy."

And, I proceeded to make him happy. Again.

Chapter Six

I'm standing in the shower. A stream of hot water pounds the top of my skull. My brain is swimming in confusion. Before Billy left to go to the Vet's Center for a meeting, he said Candy Talbot has a new boyfriend. Yes, the very same Candy who I had pegged as my rival for Billy's affection. She now has a rich lawyer boyfriend and, according to Billy, is madly in love.

Part of me is relieved. The other part is still fretting, since I can clearly see Billy is troubled. The only time he's fully present is when we make love. The rest of the time, his glances are fleeting, as if he's afraid I'll see something he'd rather keep hidden. Therefore, I tiptoe around the issue, taking care not to rock the boat. I can't be myself. I feel like we're living a lie, and it's making me crazy.

I hop out of the shower, throw on some clothes, and fire up Buttercup. Steve and I have an 11:00 a.m. meeting with Louise Goodhart concerning her client, Rebecca Porter. I glance at the time on my cell phone and stomp on the accelerator. Time wise, I'm cutting it close. Louise does not look like the type who tolerates tardiness.

By the time I park the car and dash up the stairs to the CyberSecure office, it's 11:05. I'm overheated and breathing hard. I burst through the door and find Steve and Louise sipping tea from the delicate china cups I'm afraid to use for fear of breakage. Give me a sturdy mug filled with strong, black coffee, and I'm a happy camper.

"Ah, here she is," Steve says with a smile.

Goodhart's cool glance appraises my frazzled appearance, and I feel my face heat up. It's like she knows exactly why I'm late. Thank you, Billy.

"Sorry." I pull up a chair. "Heavy traffic."

I can see Louise doesn't buy this, but Steve waves a dismissive hand. "No problem."

He slides a folder across the desk to Goodhart. "Melanie and I conferred, after her meeting with your client. Here are the results."

She takes her time, tracing the words down the page with her pointer finger. When she's done, her frosty gaze swings over to me. "So, bottom line, she's not lying about the optometrist? "

"She's not lying."

She frowns at me. "But you mention seeing something else. Therefore, you can't be one hundred percent sure, can you?"

Steve clears his throat. I sense he's about to jump in and rescue me. No way.

"I am absolutely, one hundred percent certain she's not lying about the doctor and his inappropriate behavior. The other issue is harder to explain."

I glance over at Steve who gives me a barely perceptible nod, his way of telling me to go for it.

"Steve and I have seen this phenomenon before. A fleeting image darts across the soul, indicating the person has a secret he or she would rather not share. Something is bothering Rebecca, something she wants

34

to keep hidden."

"Maybe she's hiding the fact she's lying."

"No," I insist. "We're talking about two separate issues."

She looks at Steve. "Do you agree?"

"Absolutely. Of course, it's your decision about what to do with the information. It's not for us to say."

Goodhart sets the report on Steve's desk and sighs. "Yes, you're right. My decision."

She drums her fingers on the desktop and considers her options for at least a full minute. Finally she turns to me and her lips curl upward in a brief, humorless smile. "I believe I'll take her case on one condition."

Steve and I wait her out.

She rises and stabs a finger in my direction. "I need further proof. Therefore, I think it would be advantageous to have another opinion. Melanie, perhaps you're in need of an eye exam."

Even though I'm wondering why I'm the chosen one, not Louise who wastes no time leaving our office, I reluctantly make an appointment with Dr. Dirk Hoffman for the following week. Billable hours. I need the money, plus, I'll be getting a free eye exam. Bring it on, Dr. Hoffman!

Before I head out, Steve says, "Don't forget about lunch tomorrow."

"There's no way I can ever forget my birthday," I say. "Thanks to my mother."

Steve grins. "So, you'll be getting a phone call?"

"Oh, yeah. Every year I hear the same story. A detailed description of her long, agonizing labor, the delivery, and how I was kicking and screaming like I didn't want to be born and…" I take a shaky breath and stare at the floor before continuing. "Not Hope though. Sandra swears Hope was born smiling."

Memories of my twin sister who died at age six always had the same result—me fighting back tears, which is why I do my best to keep thoughts of her at bay. I swipe at my eyes and turn toward the door.

"Don't you think it's about time you deal with your sister's death?"

My anger flares. I stop and spin around, ready to tear into him. How dare he pass judgment about the worst day of my life? When it happened, he was living in Spain and seemingly unaware of our existence.

My anger fades when I see what he's holding, cradling in his hands like it's a fragile, exquisite treasure. I know exactly what he's seeing since I have the original photograph. It was our sixth birthday. A smiling Hope squints into the camera with a gap-toothed smile. I stand next to her, mugging for the camera. Our hands are joined. With her free hand, Hope grips the string attached to the red helium balloon floating above her. Mine is blue. Our birthday tradition. Red balloon for Hope. Blue balloon for Honor. Obviously, the tradition died along with Hope.

At a rare loss for words, I mutter, "See ya tomorrow," and flee the premises.

I crank up Buttercup and pull out onto the busy street, trying to push Steve's words from my mind, but the thoughts gather strength and swirl through my consciousness like dust bunnies formed by lingering doubt. Damn it, maybe Steve's right.

My parking slot in front of Number Ten is not available. This happens frequently. When motel dwellers can't locate a parking place next to their own rooms, they take mine. No biggie. But, this is different. A huge Mexican man sporting an impressive Fu Manchu mustache is sitting behind the wheel of a shiny, black vintage car. The man in the driver's seat is my Uncle Paco, a slightly shady gangbanger I usually see astride a Harley along with his fellow members of the Los Habañeros motorcycle club. As I pull in next to him, he steps out of the car, pulls a blue kerchief from the pocket of his leather vest and flicks a tiny speck of dust from the car's gleaming surface.

"Wow, Unc, you bought a car?"

He folds his arms across his massive chest and glares down at me. "Car? You think this is just a car?"

I try not to snicker. "Looks like a car to me."

He gestures at the object in question. "This…is a classic muscle car. *The* classic muscle car. A 1964 Pontiac GTO." He pats the long, long hood and then wipes the fingerprints away with the kerchief. "I'll have you know this can go from zero to sixty in six point six seconds."

I try to look duly impressed. "What happened to the bike?"

"Still got it. But, think about it, girl. You can't drive a baby around on a Harley. Not safe."

The light bulb clicks on in my overloaded brain. "Oh, right. Aida and the baby. So, does that mean you're sticking around for a while?"

Aida, a beautiful young woman from Kazakhstan, was brought to this country under false pretenses, sedated, and impregnated by evil people who planned to sell her baby to the highest bidder. Fortunately, the baby-selling ring was busted before her little girl was born. Strangely, Aida and my uncle bonded. Big time. I wonder if Paco has given up his gypsy life-style to be with Aida.

Paco jams his hands in the pocket of his baggy jeans and gazes over the top of my head. "Well, um, yeah, we'll see how it goes. You know, her problems with immigration and all." He pulls a small box from his right pocket. "Think she'll like this?"

He pops the box open with his thumb, revealing a sparkling diamond ring of at least two carats.

I gasp in surprise. "Oh my God, Paco. You? Married? Are you sure?"

His brows draw together in a fierce scowl. "Nobody. I mean nobody, will be taking my girls away. Got it?"

I nod vigorously. "Got it."

He shoves the ring box back in his pocket. "Just wanted you to know. See ya around."

Speechless with shock, I raise a hand in farewell.

Paco climbs behind the wheel, turns on the ignition, and revs the powerful motor, a blissful smile blooming on his face. He puts it in gear, backs out of my parking space, and using restraint, pulls slowly out into the street without a backward glance.

Wow. Did not see that coming.

Chapter Seven

The call came as I stepped out of the shower. I wrapped a towel around my dripping body, perched on the edge of the bed, and chirped, "Hi, Mom."

I was greeted with a deep voice responding, "*Feliz Cumpleaños, mi precioso.*"

Not Sandra. My stepfather, Abel, the man who'd raised me as his own child. Abel speaks perfect English, but when he's emotional, he reverts to Spanish. There's something about his native language that always gets to me. The words roll off his tongue like poetry set to music.

Sweet Abel. He's a successful businessman, but prefers to spread the gospel in an eighteen-wheeler known as the Godmobile. It's interior is outfitted with pews and an altar. Abel loves to travel to truck stops, preaching the gospel. It's his true calling and, as an ordained minister, he has performed a number of weddings in the Godmobile.

Before I can respond, Abel and my mother begin singing a loud, off-key version of Happy Birthday.

When I sense it's winding down, I say, "Hey, thanks, you two. I…"

Abel says, "I'll say goodbye now and let your mother talk."

"Hi, Sweetie," Sandra begins. "Can't believe you're twenty-three. Seems like just yesterday when I went into labor and…"

While she reminisces, I set the phone down, dash into the bathroom, and snag my robe from the back of the door. By the time my nakedness is covered, and I pick up the phone, she's reached the part where I appear (and we say this part in unison) "kicking and screaming as if I didn't want to be born."

When she pauses for breath, I thank her and wait for the interrogation.

"Is Billy taking you out to dinner?"

"I'm working tonight. Actually, he doesn't know it's my birthday."

Sandra gasps. "He never asked you? Maybe I should call him."

"Not a good idea. I don't know his birthday either."

"What's wrong with you people? You are still seeing Billy, aren't you?"

"Yeah, but his job keeps him pretty busy."

With a disapproving cluck, she says, "You're not telling me something. Mothers know these things. Maybe I should…"

"Guess what?" I interrupt, not wanting to hear the rest, which would likely involve her appearing on my doorstep sometime within the next twenty-four hours. "Steve has a special birthday lunch planned for me."

A long silence ensues. Finally, she says, "Well, it's a nice gesture. Too bad he wasn't around for the actual birth twenty-three years ago."

Yes, my mother is bitter, and she has every right to be. Steve impregnated her with twins and then abandoned her. He had issues, not the least of which was his sexual preference. I was able to forgive him. Sandra can't.

Our conversation winds down after that bombshell. Before we say goodbye, I make her promise not to call Billy. She reluctantly agrees, promising she'll catch a ride on one of Abel's trucks very soon and not to be surprised if she pops in for a visit.

I decide to file that bit of information under, Things to worry about later.

I arrive at CyberSecure Plus promptly at one. Being European, Steve does not fancy eating lunch at noon. The caterers are just leaving. The office has been transformed into an elegant restaurant. A pale pink linin tablecloth covers a round table. The centerpiece is a glass bowl of white roses. Two places are set with gold-trimmed china plates, ornate silverware and champagne flutes. On a separate table, I see an assortment of cold cuts, champagne in an ice bucket and crusty rolls on a silver bread tray. The aroma of fresh-baked bread wafts across the room and my stomach emits an embarrassing rumble of anticipation.

"Happy Birthday, *mi hija*," Steve says. He flips the sign on the door to closed and waves me into a chair. A chair with a blue balloon tied to the back.

He settles into the chair across from me, which leaves one chair unoccupied. The chair with the red balloon.

I suspect I know what's going on but decide to play dumb. "Are we expecting someone else?"

But Steve is not buying what I'm selling. He covers my hand with his. "It's her birthday, too. Always has been. Always will be. That's why we're doing this here. In the office."

I stubbornly cling to my ignorance. "And, what are we doing?"

He gives me a quick, knowing smile and pats my hand. "We're celebrating your birthday, of course. Yours and Hope's. Your mother said you always wanted the blue balloons and Hope preferred the red."

He rises and fills our champagne flutes with a deft hand. "Let's get started."

It's then I realize I don't know a great deal about my bio dad. Apparently he has an agenda, which pisses me off. Still, part of me is intrigued. I can't very well stomp out of the office when he's obviously gone to a great deal of trouble and expense planning my surprise. I decide to be a grown-up and roll with it.

We clink glasses. He toasts my birthday in English. We drain our glasses. He re-fills them, we clink again and he toasts my birthday in Spanish. We guzzle it down.

"One more time," Steve says, beaming at me.

He fills the glasses, we clink and he says, "*Buon Compleanno.*"

"Not Spanish," I say, taking a tiny sip.

"My mother was Italian. Now, drink it down. It's bad luck to take only a small taste."

I obey but wonder if Steve is trying to get me drunk. If so, why? Fortunately, Steve has run out of foreign birthday wishes and serves lunch.

"Cake and coffee later," Steve announces after we've eaten our fill. He pushes his empty plate to one side and folds his hands on the tabletop. "Now, let's talk about Hope."

I don't like the feeling of his gaze boring into me, so I look over the top of his head. "Maybe I don't want to talk about Hope."

He leans back in his chair and sighs. "Honor.

Melanie. Mel. I'm not doing this out of morbid curiosity. You and I have a unique relationship, and I'm not talking about father-daughter. As far as I know, we're the only two people in the world who can read each other's souls. Several months ago, you looked into mine and discovered I had a secret, a secret I have now come to terms with. Do you remember what I saw in your soul?"

I glance into his eyes and see nothing but compassion. "You said I was the girl with the rainbow soul."

"And the second time?"

"When I was trying to figure out what to do about Aida and the others?"

He nods.

"The colors were fading and bleeding into each other because I was under stress."

"Do you want to know what I see now?"

I shrug. "I guess you'll tell me whether I want to know or not."

He chuckles. "Yes, it's true. But whether or not you want to act on it is ultimately up to you."

I lift my hands. "Go for it."

He captures my hands in his. "The first time I read your soul, I told you about the jagged black line bisecting the blue spectrum. I believe it indicates the trauma you experienced when Hope was killed. There were also some anger issues."

"And now?"

"The jagged black line is now a chasm, almost completely covering the blue prism which now looks as if it's merely a border for the black."

I know the color blue in a soul is usually a good

thing, indicating a keen intellect, calmness, and trust in others. So, if mine is shrinking…

He releases my hands. "As you know, soul reading is somewhat iffy. However, I have seen this phenomenon before and have a fairly good idea what's going on. But first, will you answer some questions for me?"

Part of me wants to run for the door. The other part is curious. I feign nonchalance. "Sure, fire away."

"You told me your ability to read souls didn't manifest itself until after your sister was killed. Correct?"

I nod.

"And since that terrible moment, you've done your best to drive Hope from your mind because you feel as if you caused her death."

"I did cause her death. If I hadn't thrown the ball over her head into the street, she'd still be alive."

He leans forward, resting his arms on the table. I'm unable to look away from his powerful gaze.

He says, "Did your mother ever tell the two of you to stop and look both ways before you went into the street?"

"Of course she did. Constantly. She always said stop, look, and listen."

"So Hope knew better than to run out into the street after the ball."

Outraged, I grip the edge of the table, not willing to believe what I'm hearing. "Are you saying it was Hope's fault she got hit by a car? I was the one who threw the ball." My voice is squeaky with pent-up anger.

"What I'm saying, *mi hija*, is you've been carrying

a heavy load of guilt all these years. Did you ever think Hope might like to carry some of your burden? Maybe Hope was the one with the soul-reading ability. Maybe after she died, this is her way of being part of your life, of guiding you, helping you. And, what have you done?"

He slams an open hand on the table causing the delicate china plates to jump and rattle. He stabs a finger at my chest. "You've closed yourself off to her. You've shut her out. You've allowed guilt and bitterness to hold her at bay."

My eyes fill with tears. "But, she's dead," I wail.

"Her physical body may be dead, but her soul is very much alive."

I stare at him for a long moment. "I don't believe you. If her soul were alive, I'd know it. We were inseparable."

"Are you willing to listen to what I have to say and give it a try?"

I take a deep breath and rein in my anger. Steve is trying to help me. What's my alternative? Become increasingly angry and bitter until I've erased a part of my soul? Unwilling to trust my voice, I nod again.

Steve reaches into his pocket and pulls out a small white box. He hands it to me. "All I ask is that you keep an open heart."

I lift the lid. Nestled in the cotton is a sterling silver necklace with two hearts suspended from a chain. The hearts are open and linked together. I swallow hard and glance up at Steve. "Thank you. It's beautiful."

"May I?" He takes the necklace from me and fastens it around my neck. The chain feels warm against my skin. The open hearts sway back and forth and then settles against the icy fist of resistance surrounding my living, beating heart.

Steve places his palms against my cheeks. "Please, my dear, open your heart and allow your soul to heal. Feel your sister's presence. If not for yourself, do it for her. Her soul is unsettled. You're the only one who can make it right. Hope and Honor belong together."

My tears are flowing in earnest now. Unchecked, they gush from my eyes as if released from a high-pressure hose. Sobs follow. Steve wipes my face with a cloth napkin and folds me into his embrace, gently patting my back. When my sobbing fit subsides into hiccups, he places a finger under my chin and tilts my head back until I'm gazing into his eyes.

"Tell me what you see."

I am familiar with Steve's soul, having peered into it many times at his request. It had settled into a sameness, indicating he is pretty much content with the manner in which his life is unfolding. This time is different. It was like someone photo-shopped his soul and enhanced it. Not only are the colors brighter, little bursts of light bounce around like a cricket on speed, illuminating different spectrums. It's hard to explain to a non-soul reader. On impulse, I cup the open-heart necklace in my hand and watch as the burst of light flutters and settles cozily onto a light pink section of Steve's soul. I've never seen that particular shade of pink in Steve's soul, but I've seen it other souls, almost exclusively in the souls of women holding babies. I've seen it many times in Kendra's soul when she's holding one of her little boys and Dani's baby girl, Destiny. As a shade of red, pink is a powerful color. The color of a parent's love. Survival of the species.

I blink hard and look away from Steve's gaze for a moment. When I trust my voice, I say, "I see love for your child."

He grips my hands and smiles. "And now, you have an ability I don't have. You are not only to read souls, but also the thoughts and feelings contained in the soul."

"No way," I say.

"Way," he answers.

Chapter Eight

After birthday cake (chocolate with raspberry filling) and three cups of coffee, Steve determines I am safe to drive despite our multiple champagne toasts. His test includes a heel-toe walk across the length of the office as well as my reciting the alphabet backward. This is not easy, even when a person is sober.

The aftermath of my father's emotional birthday bash leaves me unsettled. What do I want? I want Billy's muscular arms around my body. I want to feel his heart beating against mine. I want to drive unwelcome thoughts from my mind with pure pleasure. I want it badly. I drive aimlessly, trying to remember if Billy is working today. He works four ten-hour days, followed by two days off. Since his days off are on a rotating basis and mine are as well, I have a hard time keeping track.

I never know when to expect Billy to pop into Number Ten. But, I don't go to Billy's house unless I'm invited. It was something my mother drummed into me. "You don't just drop in on people, Mel. You call first. What if they're in the midst of something embarrassing?" (When I was little, I always asked, "What?") Or, she'd continue, "Maybe they're having a bad day and don't want company."

Should I call first? Oh, what the hell, girl, go for it.

I pull up in front of the neat, little bungalow

formerly occupied by Billy and Kendra's widowed mother. Several years ago, she'd attended a high school reunion and met up with an old boyfriend. They carried on a long-distance romance for over a year before the gentleman showed up in a humongous motorhome and said, "Let's have some fun." She loaded up her personal belongings, grabbed the cat, and gave Billy the keys to the castle. Every Sunday evening, she calls her kids and updates them on her itinerary.

But wait, there's a strange car parked in the driveway, a late model Jeep Cherokee with a pink decal on the back window inscribed with the words "Backwoods Princess."

I know it's not Kendra's car. She drives a kid-friendly minivan. I scan my mind for further possibilities as I step out of Buttercup and approach the front door. I cross Candy Talbot off my list since she drives a pick-up. The drapes are closed. My hopeful heart takes a dive.

I reach for the doorknob and then change my mind. Instead, I rap my knuckles against the door three times and twist the knob. It's locked. In spite of advice to the contrary, Billy doesn't lock his door when he's home. When I said, half teasing but not entirely, "You're hoping someone will break into your house so you can shoot him," he grinned and replied, "You know me too well."

But, do I?

I'm filled with a sense of dread when I hear muffled voices and footsteps. The drapes part and Billy peers out to see who's on his porch. We lock gazes. His eyes widen in surprise like I'm the last person he expects to see hanging around the 'hood.

He releases the drapes, throws the door open and forces a smile. "Hey, Minnie. What's up?"

I look past him and see her. The Backwoods Princess. She's lounging on the couch with her feet up on the coffee table, a longneck beer bottle in her right hand. She sees me and lifts the beer in greeting. I'm not close enough to read her soul, but I know enough about women to read her expression. It says, "I'm the new girl in Billy the Kid's life."

Billy is shifting his weight from one foot to the other and staring at the floor. "Come on in and meet Haley. Former military like me. We went through the academy together. We're just, um, comparing notes, ya know?"

Oh, yeah, I know how that goes. Starts with a few beers and then things get real friendly. Has it only been a few days since Billy was in my bed? What is he, a super man?

I'm still frozen in the doorway, not sure which way to jump. I'm staring at Haley who sets her beer down and is now approaching the door with an ingratiating smile. She's a bit taller than me and curvaceous. With a practiced head toss, she flips her shiny brown hair until it drapes across her left shoulder. Her eyes are green. Like a cat. There's a strip of artificially tanned skin between her teensy white V-neck tee and the jeans riding low on her hips. A gold ring pierces her belly button.

She holds out her right hand. "Hi, I'm Haley McFadden. And you are...?"

I look over at Billy who seems to have lost his ability to speak.

I decide not to hold back. I take her hand and give

it a little squeeze. "I'm Mel, Billy's girlfriend. Guess he didn't tell you about me."

Her eyes widen and both of us fix Billy with an accusatory gaze.

I'm thinking, Okay, question answered, you two-timing son of a bitch. I have no idea what Haley is thinking,

I say, "Nice to meet you, Haley. Have a nice life."

I spin around and head for Buttercup, too angry to cry. Billy follows me to the car. I slide into the driver's seat. Billy grabs the door before I can close it. "We need to talk."

Although every fiber of my being is screaming, *Flee*, I say, "I'm listening."

He puts a hand on my shoulder. I shrug it off.

"Okay, I get it. You're mad," he says.

"Ya think?" My voice is shrill. "How about this? What if you walk into Number Ten and find me sitting on the couch, drinking beer with a hot guy you've never seen before?" Actually this is a really dumb question because I don't have a couch.

He flushes. "It's not what you think, Minnie. I'm trying to help her. She's…"

"Help? Is that what you call it?"

The woman in question is now standing in the doorway. Her mouth is agape. Not an attractive look, especially for a woman about to become a friend with benefits, more or less a certainty after I cut him off. Good luck with that, Haley.

Billy leans closer. "You probably don't believe me but Haley's just a friend who's having problems adjusting to life after Afghanistan, like I did."

"A friend you've never mentioned," I say. "A

friend who seems quite comfortable in your home." I crank up the engine. "Back off. I want to leave."

But Billy doesn't back off. He grips my shoulder again and lowers his voice. "Do you have any idea how relaxing it is to talk to a woman who isn't staring into my eyes to see if I'm lying?"

Okay, there it is. Even though I've been expecting this conversation, I grip the steering wheel until my knuckles turn the color of wallpaper paste. I refuse to look at him. "Is that what you think I do?"

"It is what you do."

I shake my head in denial. "You're wrong, Billy. It's what I try very hard not to do. Whatever is going on inside your head is of your own making."

I lift my head, and we lock gazes for a long moment. I don't want to look into his soul. Otherwise, I'm a liar...right? Unfortunately, the contents of his soul jump right out at me, and I see the conflict he's going through. I hesitate to apply a label, but if I had to swear in a court of law, I'd say, "Guilty."

I avert my gaze. "I need to go. Maybe we can talk later."

He place his big hand on top of my head and whispers, "I can't lose you, Minnie."

I take one last look in his eyes and see his soul is swamped with sadness. Unable to speak, I put the car in gear and creep forward.

He closes the door and steps away. When I look into the rearview mirror, he's watching me drive away, one hand lifted in farewell.

Chapter Nine

For the next few days, I sob into my pillow at night and work double shifts at Nick's in an effort to put Billy the Kid out of my mind during my waking hours. Formerly a regular at Nick's, Billy becomes a no-show. When my exhausted mind has no resistance, I see mental images of Billy, my Billy, making love to Haley McFadden.

The third day after the break-up, I'm waiting on Bert and Thelma, the old couple who arrive every day at precisely four p.m. for the early bird special. They always sit side by side in a four-person booth and leave me a one-dollar tip. It's okay because I know they are on a fixed income. To make their money stretch until the end of the month, they order dessert every other day even, though it's Thelma's favorite part of the meal. Sometimes she leaves half her dinner uneaten and dives into the pie until the last crumb is gone. Today is a non-dessert day.

I force a smile. "How are you two?"

Bert is holding Thelma's hand. His eyes are red-rimmed. "Not so hot, today, girlie."

He always calls me girlie, even though I've told him my name a dozen times.

I rouse out of my self- induced misery and lean close to Bert. "What's wrong?"

He jerks his head toward Thelma and whispers,

"The doc says my sweet lady has Alzheimer's."

And you think you have problems, Mel?

I pat Bert's arm. "Doctors aren't always right. She seems pretty sharp to me."

Thelma gives me a dazzling smile. "Hi, sweetie, how are you tonight?'

Thelma always calls me sweetie. She points at the empty bench seat across the table. "Are you okay? You look tired."

I assure Thelma I'm fine and take their order. On my way to the kitchen, I scurry over to Nick who's standing behind the bar, scowling at the newspaper.

"Hey, Nick, I have a favor to ask."

He lifts his irritated gaze from the newspaper. "Yeah?"

I tell him what I want to do and he says, "Go for it, kid."

Back in the kitchen, Nick's new cook, Frannie, is chopping up something green. Not sure what, since I'm so not into vegetables.

"Bert and Thelma want the special."

She stops chopping and smiles. "Big surprise, eh?"

Frannie is a transported Canadian and says *eh* a lot.

"Any of that chocolate cake left from yesterday?"

She gestures toward the industrial size fridge "Quite a lot. You hungry? Help yourself. Looks like you could use a bit of sweetening up. Nick says you're having boyfriend problems, eh?"

Halfway to the fridge, I stop and think about her words. I haven't talked to Nick about my break-up with Billy. If Nick, normally obtuse about all things romantic, has it figured out, I need to crawl out of my dark place and get back into the game.

I turn and smile at Frannie. "I'm okay." Strangely, saying the words makes them true. Is it possible my fractured heart has started to knit itself back together?

I slice off four big pieces of chocolate cake, put them in a to-go box and deliver it to Bert and Thelma's table. "I know you haven't had your dinner yet, but did you know today is National Chocolate Cake Day? Since you're loyal customers, we'd like you to have this token of our appreciation."

Thelma's eyes sparkle with excitement. She claps her hands and declares, "Oh, goodie!"

I hand her the box.

Bert looks suspicious. I might have known he would question a freebie. He's from a proud generation who believes in working hard for what you get. No handouts for Bert.

He says, "Are all your customers getting free chocolate cake?"

I chirp, "Oh, no sir, only our very special customers like you and Thelma."

He gives in gracefully and thanks me before turning his attention to Thelma who's ready to dig into the cake. In a gentle voice, Bert convinces her to wait after they've eaten today's special, chicken and dumplings.

After I deliver Bert and Thelma's order, Nick waves me over to the bar. He shoves the newspaper across the bar and points at a letter to the editor from a guy named Rick Rathjen. "Can you believe this shit?"

Before I can see what got him so riled up, he says, "By the way, Kendra will be here soon. Things are slow tonight, so take off. Time for a little girl talk. Trust me, you'll feel better."

"Wait. What? First you're pissed off about something in the paper and now you're yakking about Kendra?"

Nick leans across the bar and shakes a finger in my face. "You've been moping around here for three days. I'm guessing it has something to do the Kid. If you don't have sense enough to talk to your best friend about it, then you obviously need help."

Hands on hips, I glare at him. "How do you know I haven't?"

He smirks. "I asked her."

Well, damn. "Not your problem. I'm working it out."

"Oh yeah, you're in great shape. Have you talked to your mom? Or, Uncle Hulk?"

I refuse to look at him.

"Ha, that's what I thought."

"Busy body," I mutter. "And, his name is Paco, not Hulk."

"So," he continues. "When Kendra gets here, you're off the clock. Got it?"

I pinch my lips together and nod.

"While we're waiting, take a look at what this asshole wrote."

I scan the letter quickly. It seems Mr. Rathjen believes our country is in grave danger from evil foreigners, specifically Muslims, who are taking over small businesses in an effort to overthrow the American way of life. Rathjen uses a lot of big words to get his point across, but one thing is crystal clear: brown-skinned foreigners are not welcome in Central Oregon.

Nick, despite his gruffness, has little tolerance for bigotry in any form. He slams a fist on the bar. "The guy has a blog called 'Americans First' where he spews more of his hatred."

A sentence in the last paragraph jumps out at me. It says, "Here at the Rockin' R Ranch, we make sure all our employees are Americans."

I look up at Nick. "Does this guy own the Rockin' R Ranch?"

"Yeah, why?"

I think back to my last fill-up at the Gas and Grub and the star-crossed lovers, Yasmin and Riley. The guy in the cowboy hat behind the wheel of the pick-up checking me out as I walked by.

"What about his family—know anything about them?"

With an exasperated snort, Nick says, "Yeah, a friend of mine pastures his horse at the Rockin' R. He says the guy's in love with the letter R. The wife's name is Roxanne, his daughter's called Rachel and the boy is, um, Rick…no, that doesn't sound right."

"Riley?" I say.

"Yes, Riley. How do you know the kid's name?"

I tell him about our brief encounter at the Gas 'N Grub.

Nick's eyes narrow ominously. "So you think Rathjen's kid and this Muslim girl are an item?"

"I think they'd like to be an item. Yasmin's father watches her like a hawk. He probably wants her to marry a nice Muslim boy. And, after reading Rathjen's letter, I'm sure she wouldn't be welcomed into the family with open arms, even if her name was Rosie or Rhonda."

Our conversation ceases when Kendra bursts through the door. Even though she's across the room, it's easy to read her mood. She strides to the bar, fists clenched, eyes sparking with anger. When Kendra's on a mission, she's a little scary. At least she's not mad at me. I hope.

Nick grabs his newspaper, backs away from the bar and gets busy rearranging liquor bottles.

Kendra enfolds me into a crushing hug, murmuring, "That damn Billy. If he wasn't family, I swear I'd have him castrated. I'm so sorry, Mel."

I acknowledge her outrage, but don't allow it to take up residence in my heart. "I knew it was coming. He's been acting weird around me for a while. In a way, it was almost a relief. Like waiting for the other shoe to drop."

She grips my shoulders, presses me back, and stares into my eyes as if seeking the truth of my statement. "Well, I hope you know it's him. Not you."

"But it is me. Didn't he tell you?"

Her eyes widen in surprise. "Tell me what?"

"He can't handle the soul reading thing. He thinks I'm trying to catch him in a lie."

She sighs and shakes her head. "Idiot!"

Nick approaches cautiously. "Can I get you something to drink, Kendra?"

"No thanks." She grabs my hand. "Can I steal Mel for a while?"

Nick grins. "Hell, yes, take her away. She's scaring off my customers. She looks like she belongs in a painting of those creepy little kids with the big, blue eyes, brimming with tears, and…"

I wave a hand to stop him. "Don't listen to Nick, Kendra. He likes to exaggerate."

Speaking of eyes, before we leave, I remind him

about my eye exam coming up soon. "It's not until three thirty so I'll be late."

"Take the day off. You've been working your tail off."

"Perfect," Kendra says. "I've got plans for her."

This is news to me. "Like what?"

She grabs my hand and tows me through the door. "I'll tell you in the car."

We pull away from the curb before she'll say another word. Like she's in a spy movie mode and we're being tailed. She's so convincing, I turn and look behind us. All I see is a slow-moving cement mixer.

Finally, she says, "Here's the deal. Before Billy said the two of you were having, um, issues, he told me Eddie Morgan is hanging out at the Ponderosa. So, I have a plan."

Part of me is curious. The other part is filled with dread, triggered by the word plan. Past history tells me Kendra's plans may involve disguises, makeovers, lies, and intrigue.

The curious part wins. "Tell me more about your plan."

She looks over at me and winks. "After your eye exam, we're going to the Ponderosa."

When she tells me the rest, my worst fears are confirmed. It does involve all of the above. But, she's right. Time is of the essence. If we're going to prove Eddie's complicity in Dani's death, it has to be now.

Chapter Ten

My appointment with Rebecca Porter's eye doctor proves to be inconclusive. I go through a series of his office minions, starting with a young woman behind the counter who hands me a two-page form to fill out. When I return it to her, she peruses it quickly and rakes me with a sharp-eyed glance. "No insurance?"

I confess I do not and point out the section where I've written: Send the bill to CyberSecure Plus and it will be paid.

Her brow knits with concern. "In that case, we will need a $50 deposit to continue."

Well, crap. I dig through my purse and pull out twenty-five dollars, tip money I planned to save for my night out with Kendra. I slap the money down, lean across the counter and hiss, "This is all I have. If it's not enough, feel free to limit the exam to one eye."

She blinks rapidly, rises from her chair and holds a whispered conference with two of her colleagues. They take turns glancing over at me. I'm about ready to retrieve my money and skedaddle. The hell with Louise Goodhart.

Before I can act on the impulse, the woman returns. With a cheesy smile, she says, "So sorry about the misunderstanding. Chelsea will take you back now."

Why the change in attitude? I soon find out.

Chelsea, a rail-thin blonde dressed in blue scrubs

and sensible shoes, ushers me into an examination room. She plops down on a wheeled stool and says, "I know who you are."

Puzzled, I say, "Okay, good."

"You're her, aren't you?"

"Her who?"

"The woman who can read souls."

She scoots her stool up next to me and gazes into my eyes. "What do you see? It's okay, you can tell me."

This is what I was afraid would happen when Mick suggested Steve and I launch our soul-reading business. Complete strangers staring into my eyes.

I wrap my fingers around Steve's gift, the linked open-heart pendant and silently ask Hope to forgive me. "I'd like to help you but I can't. My twin sister, Hope, is the one with the soul-reading ability. Not me"

Thankfully, she believes me and backs away, fingers poised over the keyboard of her computer.

"Alrighty then, what type of exam do you want?"

"An eye exam," I say. For one panicky moment, I'm afraid I've wandered into the wrong office. What's next? Mammography? A pelvic exam? A colonoscopy?

She smirks at me. "Yes, of course you do. But, do you want a medical exam, a contact lens fitting exam, an exam for corrective glasses or some other type?"

Whew. I say, "Oh, just the regular old exam. You choose."

This satisfies her, and she leads me to a space-age looking machine and flips the on switch. I startle in surprise when it emits a series of squeaks and groans before launching into sound not unlike a jet engine warming up.

After Chelsea does her thing, I'm escorted into the

presence of Dr. Porter. He's a big, good-looking dude with wavy black hair and a brilliant smile. I'm wondering what would motivate him to invade the personal space of his female patients. Obviously, he'd have no problem attracting women. Then, I remember what I learned in Psych 101. It's not about sex, it's about power.

After scrubbing his hands with soap and water, he shakes mine and says, "Call me Dr. Dirk."

He shines a light into my eyes and mumbles something unintelligible to Chelsea who says, "Yes, Dr. Dirk. Right away."

I soon find out she's been ordered to dilate my eyes. After she administers the drops, she coos, "Alrighty then, you just relax a while and Dr. Dirk will be in soon."

I'm not sure how to interpret what happens after the dilation. My vision is blurry, so I have to depend on my other senses.

Like, when Dr. Dirk wheels his little stool up, presses against my clenched knees until I open wide and is suddenly smack dab between my legs and, I assume, peering into my retinas. Is that normal? And, when he brushes a hand against my boob while he's gazing into one of his space age doohickeys, is it an accident or is he copping a feel? At one point, I feel his hands on my thighs and feel his hot breath against my cheek. It feels like an invasion, but am I willing to destroy a man's career without solid proof?

Kendra is waiting in the parking lot when I'm finished. Not that I can see her. I stagger through the door, ramming my left shoulder into the doorjamb in the process. I stumble off the curb, rubbing my shoulder and muttering, "Ow, damn it. Ow!"

Kendra grips my right arm. "Didn't they put drops in your eyes to reverse the dilation? Or give you dark glasses?"

I shake my head. "Nope, I had the budget exam. No freebies."

"What's wrong with those people? You're blind as a bat. And they just turned you loose to drive?"

I know Kendra and sense she's snorting and pawing the ground. I reach out and grab her arm before she marches into Dr. Porter's office, on a mission to avenge my ill treatment. "Let it go," I say. "Remember Eddie? We got things to do."

She gives in reluctantly and leads me to her car, muttering, "Damn officious assholes. They need to learn how to treat people."

It's a twenty-minute drive to the Ponderosa, located south of 3 Peaks in a little town called Pine Village, a favorite hangout for bikers and peckerwoods who, by all accounts, have learned to tolerate each other. We work out the details of our plan.

Kendra warns, "Remember to be nice to Eddie. I know it's hard, but we have to make him believe we're sincere, get him to relax. Maybe then he'll revert to his stupid self and you can peek inside his nasty little mind and see what's going on."

"Then what? Remember, the original plan included Billy. We hoped Eddie would get sloppy drunk and say something incriminating, giving 3 Peaks P.D. a reason to question him."

Kendra says, "That ship has sailed."

"Along with a new crew member named Haley McFadden," I mutter.

"What?" Kendra shrieks.

"You mean he didn't mention the new girl in his life? Big surprise."

She pounds a fist against the steering wheel. "Wait until I get ahold of him."

"Kendra, promise me you won't interfere. I'm asking as your friend."

She reaches over and takes my hand. "I promise, but it won't be easy."

By the time we pull into Ponderosa's expansive gravel parking lot, my vision has cleared a little, and I spot Eddie's ride, a deluxe model Toyota Tundra with all the bells and whistles.

Kendra drives slowly by the Tundra and then parks the minivan at the back of the lot, away from the other cars. She reaches behind the seat and extracts a plastic bag, which she thrusts into my hands. "Your jeans are fine, but the baggy T-shirt has to go."

"I'm fine."

"No, you're not. Remember, you're playing a role. Change. Now."

I know it's pointless to argue, so I slink down in the seat and remove the offensive garment.

"Bra as well."

"Why?"

"You'll see. It's what I wore a couple of sizes ago, before I married Craig and had babies to nurse. Glad I saved it."

I stuff myself into the push-up bra and slip on the low-cut black fitted tee. When I look down, my boobs are so perky, they're practically screaming, "Hey, look at us. What a pair!"

"Oh, good Lord save me," I whisper.

Kendra whips open her jeans jacket. "What do you think? Too much?"

She's wearing a pink sweater, tight jeans and high-heeled boots. The sweater's neckline dips low in front, revealing a voluptuous bosom.

"Very impressive," I say. "Did Craig like it?"

"Oh, yeah. He says he'll wait up for me."

Kendra's not finished with me. She's reaches into a cosmetic bag and, despite my protests, begins dabbing at my face like she's painting the Mona Lisa. Hair next. Using a round brush and mousse, she spritzes and sprays, whipping my unruly black hair into an unfamiliar style. When she's done, I check out my reflection in the rearview mirror and gasp. A spikey-haired, blue-eyed vamp with pouty red lips and long, lustrous lashes gazes back at me. "Oh, my God," I murmur.

Kendra holds out a fist to bump. "You're welcome. Now, let's go get him."

We head for the rustic tavern fashioned to look like a frontier saloon with weathered siding, rough shingled roof and a wide front porch with rickety Ozark rockers. Loud blasts of country music leak through the closed door.

Kendra stops me before we enter. "Now, remember, this is like a big game hunt. If we want to get the bull moose, we have to be stealthy. If he spots us and thinks we're after blood, he'll spook and run. So, we go in, look for Eddie and ambush him before he can get away. Sound good?"

The hunting analogies make my head swim with confusion. Are we trying to trap Eddie in a lie or shoot him with a high-powered rifle? Also, my vision isn't what it should be and my stomach is growling. Not a good combination. Guess I'll have to trust Kendra and see how it plays out.

We slip through the front door, pause and take in our surroundings. Actually, in our present incarnation—sexy sluts—slip is not an accurate description of our entrance into the Ponderosa. The predominately male crowd stops in mid-sip, their gazes fixed on the two minxes who've entered their territory. I can almost feel the testosterone wafting across the room, propelled by beer-driven dreams of sexual conquest.

We spot Eddie and he spots us.

Chapter Eleven

He rises to a half-crouch. Even with impaired vision, I can see the look of panic on his face. Deer in the headlights.

"Red alert," Kendra says. "Must take action to keep subject within range. Stat."

I assume we've gone from big game hunting to spy mode. I trail behind as Kendra sashays across the Ponderosa, hips swaying seductively, thanks to her pointy boots. The path she's chosen blocks Eddie' escape route, unless he opts to clamor over tables occupied by rough-looking dudes and topped with multiple pitchers of beer.

In typical Eddie fashion, he chooses the easiest course of action. He lifts his hands in surrender and whines, "Jesus, you girls never quit. I can't even drink in peace anymore."

Kendra springs into action. She leans forward, giving him an up-close and personal view of her cleavage. "Oh, sweetie, you couldn't be more wrong. Haven't you heard? It's ladies night out, and we're just two girls looking for a good time."

She grabs my arm and yanks me in front of her like a peace offering. I force a smile and go with the storyline concocted earlier. "She's right, Eddie. Billy and I just broke up and Kendra had a fight with the hubster. We got together and realized we've treated you like shit. You can't be all bad since you married our best friend. This is probably our last chance to apologize before you leave 3 Peaks."

Eddie's face is a classic picture of conflicting emotions. His initial panic is followed by a look of suspicion. But the words ladies night out and looking for a good time definitely triggered lust-filled fantasies in Eddie's primitive brain. He licks his lips and invites us to sit at his table. The other occupant is his long-time pal and my old nemesis from Nick's. Darrell. He's in his usual pose; chair tipped back, legs spread. Ick.

Now we have two idiots to ply with liquor, tantalize, pretend to seduce, eventually rebuff, and make our getaway unscathed. Piece of cake.

We settle into our chairs. Darrell returns his chair to the upright position and studies my face before dropping his gaze to points south. "I know you. You're the barmaid from Nick's."

He jabs an elbow into Eddie's ribs. "I told you about her. She's the one who spilled a shitload of beer and then fell into it face first. Talk about a wet T-shirt. I swear she gave every guy in the place a massive woodie, and…"

I stiffen in my chair, barely able to check the rising tide of my anger. Kendra, sensing I'm in attack mode, kicks me under the table and coos, "What are you boys drinking? We want to buy you a pitcher."

I take a couple of deep, calming breaths while the server is summoned and the pitcher of MGD delivered. Eddie fills all four glasses, waggles his eyebrows and offers the following toast. "To ladies night. May all your dreams come true."

We all raise our glasses. Kendra takes a tiny sip

and smacks her lips appreciatively. "Yum."

She's really getting into her role. I need to try harder. I tip the glass up and chug it. It hits my empty stomach like a bolt of lightning. When my head stops spinning, I realize Eddie is speaking directly to me. "Whoa, you're pupils are huge. You're higher than a kite. What did you take? Is that why you're here? You think we're dealing drugs?"

"No, no," I protest. "I had an eye exam."

Eddie looks over at Darrell and winks. "Yeah, right."

Darrell scoots his chair closer to mine. "So you and the Kid broke up? When you guys were together, we all knew better than to even look at you. The Kid is one tough dude. Does this mean you're up for grabs, so to speak? You're not his woman anymore?'

I'm offended on so many levels, I find it impossible to pick one to defend. My mouth falls open, but no words come out. Once again, Kendra comes through.

"I think Mel's taking a little time off. Actually, the real reason for our visit is to tell Eddie we have no hard feelings. We know he loved Dani as much as we did. She was such a sweetheart. Right, Mel?"

I nod my head, still unable to verbalize. Probably a good idea since Darrell expression now resembles a hungry wolf stalking a sheep who's wandered away from the flock. I'm sure he won't be deterred, no matter what I say.

Kendra refills Eddie's glass, leans across the table and pats his hand. "Here's the thing, Eddie. We didn't get to tell Dani goodbye."

Eddie snatches his hand away. "But you've got

Destiny. Right? My daughter?"

This throws Kendra off her game. She didn't think the baby would be an issue since Eddie had basically given her to the Rockwells, and had made no attempt at visitation when custody of Destiny went to Kendra and Craig. Time for Mel to jump in.

"Eddie," I say. "Look at me. We know you loved Dani and there's no doubt you love Destiny, too. We also know how difficult it is for a guy to take care of a baby without help. It's true, Destiny is now with Kendra's family. She's doing very well, and I'm sure you would be welcome if you'd like to visit her. Right, Kendra?"

Kendra looks dubious, but manages a nod.

Eddie's eyes widen in surprise. It's not what he expected to hear. "Well, um, maybe I'll drop by before I leave town."

He's lying. I know because I'm peering into his pale gray eyes with black pupils like exclamation points. I see the lie flash across his muddy brown soul. It's then I realize I'm in over my head. It's true, I can detect a lie, but under the present circumstances, it would be awkward to say, "Did you kill Dani?"

Does the soul of a murderer have certain characteristics? I kick myself for not checking this out earlier. There's only one person in the entire world (as far I as know) capable of answering my question. I excuse myself and head for the bathroom. I hope Kendra has recovered her mojo and will fill the void with enough flirtation to keep the boys interested.

Thankfully, Steve picks up after three rings and, in typical Steve fashion, delivers the goods without undue questioning. Before we click off, he adds, "You okay?"

In all likelihood, I'm slurring my words after chugging down a full mug of beer on an empty tummy. "Yep, I'm fine."

"Take care," he says. "Call if you need anything more."

I thank him and re-join the group. Eddie's face brightens when he sees me. He picks up the pitcher. "Ready for another?'

I force a giggle. "Sure, why not?"

He fills my mug to the brim. "Damn, Billy's an idiot to fool around on you. Is that what happened?"

I take a sip and lean across the table, staring directly into Eddie's grimy gaze. "Wow, you must be psychic. How did you know?"

He ducks his head modestly before returning my gaze. "Well, if you don't mind me saying so, Mel, you're hot."

I play the simpering fool. "Thank you, sir. You're not so bad yourself."

While this idiocy is going on, I take a good, long look into Eddie's soul. Steve gave me a couple of markers to look for when dealing with a killer. The most obvious is a blood-red stain with ragged edges. Another is a series of black slash marks barely visible, usually found in the lower right quadrant. I might also see a deep purple cloud-like blob whisk across the soul as if the devil himself is after it. After a few seconds, I see it. The purple jagged shape dips down from the upper left section of Eddie's soul before it streaks down and vanishes. But, I saw it and now I know. Eddie is a murderer and the victim is most likely my closest friend. Dani.

What's next? First, I have to hold it together

because I so want to reach across the table and strangle the son of a bitch. Next, we need to boogie on out of here.

I look over at Kendra and say, "What time are you supposed to be home?"

This is the phrase we'd agreed upon earlier. When it's uttered, Kendra knows I've found what I'm looking for.

She pulls out her cell phone, checks her messages and gasps, "Oh my God, Craig just texted me. One of the kids has a fever. Gotta go."

Before the two idiots can figure out they've been punked, we dash out of the Ponderosa, hop in the minivan, and head north.

Finally, Kendra says, "So?"

"Totally guilty. One hundred per cent positive."

Her hands tighten on the steering wheel. "I knew it. Now, we have to figure out what to do about it. I guess we start with Billy."

"You start with Billy," I say. "He's never been keen about me using my soul reading ability to figure out if Eddie is guilty or innocent. He'll say there's no evidence to warrant questioning Eddie, and he's right. But maybe you can guilt him into taking action. Let me know what he says. In the meantime, I'll keep bugging Mick at Homeland Security. It's low priority for him but at least he believes in what I do."

Kendra reaches over and grabs my hand. "Eddie really did it? You're positive?"

"Yes, he killed her but I don't know how. When she went to the hospital, she was still alive. I've got a feeling he sneaked into her room in the middle of the night and put a pillow over her face."

Kendra looks over at me. Her eyes brim with tears. "We gotta get him, Mel."

I lift my right hand and offer it to her. We link our pinky fingers and say together. "Pinky promise."

Chapter Twelve

Kendra delivers me to Buttercup, still parked at Dr. Dirk's office. She shines a flashlight in my eyes to make sure I can see properly and then follows me to Nick's before taking off for home. If she had followed me into the parking lot, she'd have seen Billy's bike parked outside Number Ten, alongside a generic gray sedan with government plates.

I'm so not in the mood for Billy and briefly consider heading for the nearest McDonald's for a cheeseburger deluxe. Before I can act on the impulse, the door to Number Ten flies open. The doorway is filled with Billy the Kid who looks grim. His eyes are bloodshot with dark circles beneath them. It's how he looks when nightmares plague his sleep.

Since he's seen me, I might as well face the music. I park Buttercup and walk to the door. "What's up, Billy?"

He steps back and waves me through the door. Mick, Homeland Security Mick, is stretched out on my bed, his arms folded behind his head. He's wearing faded jeans, a form-fitting black tee and leather boots. His pale blond hair is now light brown and considerably shorter than when he was undercover. The TV is on and his gaze is fixated on Jeopardy.

"What the hell?" I say to Billy. He remains silent.

I point at Mick. "And you? Get off my bed!"

Mick gives me a half grin and scoots up to the end of the bed. "So," he says, "Let's test your knowledge. If a Oxfordian and Stratfordian are engaged in a debate, what famous person would they be talking about?"

Hands on hips, I say, "Who is—I don't give a shit. Why are you here?"

"Wrong. The correct answer is, 'Who is William Shakespeare?'"

Billy says, "We need to talk."

He extends his right hand, a plastic baggie pinched between his thumb and forefinger. Inside the baggie is a slip of paper. "This was in Yasmin Ayoob's pocket when we found her body."

It takes a moment for my tired brain to collate the information. When I finally connect the dots, I say, "Are we talking about Yasmin from the Gas 'N Grub? She's dead?"

"Yes," Billy says. "Her family reported her missing a couple of days ago. This morning, her body was found by a couple of kids riding horseback in a remote area of Red Ridge." He waves the baggie. "She had a gas receipt in her jeans pocket with your cell phone number on it."

I clap a hand over my mouth, not wanting to believe what I'm hearing.

Mick stands. "You're looking a little pale. Maybe you should sit down."

Without waiting for an answer, he takes my arm and guides me to a chair. I look up at him. "Why are you here?"

"It's a possible hate crime. Yasmin's father mentioned a guy named Rick Rathjen who owns a ranch out in Red Ridge, not far from where Yasmin's body was found. Apparently Rathjen has a big hate-on for foreigners, particularly those of the Muslim persuasion."

"Did you talk to his son, Riley?"

"We talked to his dad. Is there a reason we should talk to Riley?"

"I stopped at the Gas and Grub for gas a while back. Riley and his dad were there. I was inside talking to Yasmin. She and Riley were looking at each other through the window like lovesick puppies, at least until Yasmin's dad showed up."

Mick says, "You think Yasmin and Riley were seeing each other?"

"Probably on the sly," I say. "Her dad would never allow it. Actually, I'm sure Rick Rathjen wouldn't be happy about his son dating a Muslim girl." I shake my head. "Damn, this sucks. Poor Yasmin."

With a heavy sigh, Billy plops down in the other chair. "Why did she have your cell number?"

I took a moment to think back on my conversation with Yasmin. "I noticed her looking at Riley and said something like, 'He's pretty cute. Do you know him?' At the time, I didn't realize her dad was stocking shelves and heard me. He marched up to the counter and said he'd take care of the sale. I felt bad because Yasmin looked scared. So, I followed her to another part of the store and gave her my phone number in case she wanted to talk."

"And did she," Mick asks, "Call you?"

I shake my head. "No, I never heard from her. How did she die?"

"Broken neck," Billy says. "Looks like she was choked first."

I shudder and try to fight back tears. Sweet, beautiful Yasmin. Dead.

I glance over at Mick. "Have you read Rathjen's blog?"

Mick's eyes take on a steely quality. He nods. "Americans First."

"You said you talked to Rick Rathjen. Did he mention anything about Yasmin and Riley?"

Billy says, "Not a word. We didn't know there was a connection until now."

"Was Riley there when you talked to his dad?"

"No, just his wife and daughter."

Mick says, "We'll do it first thing tomorrow. Thanks for the info."

I think about all the moving parts. "It doesn't make sense. If Rick Rathjen killed Yasmin, why would he dump her body so close to his property?'

Mick says. "We did question Rathjen. He has solid alibis for the last seventy-two hours. We're waiting for the coroner to give us the exact time of death, and we'll know more. It's possible she was killed in another location and dumped in Red Ridge."

I look from Mick to Billy and suddenly, the light bulb clicks on. "Surely you don't think I had something to do with her death."

"Of course not," Mick says. "We just needed some answers. Billy recognized your cell number right off the bat. We had to follow up. Otherwise, we wouldn't be doing our job."

Billy says, "So, you haven't seen Yasmin since the day you filled up your car?"

"No. I don't exactly remember the day, but it's probably on the receipt. It was the day I left early to meet with my dad. He had a job for me and…"

My voice fades away as I remember what happened earlier that day. Billy faking sleep. Music suddenly blasting as Billy grabbed me and whirled me around until I was dizzy and laughing hysterically. Billy touching me. Billy loving me. When he meets my gaze, I know he remembers too. He nods and presses his lips together.

I stand. "Are we done? I'm tired and you guys have a job to do. Let me know if I can help."

Silly me. I thought my words, couched in civility, were a nice version of, "Get the hell out and leave me alone."

I forgot. Guys are clueless when it comes to subtlety. Billy springs up but doesn't move toward the door. Mick, once again, perches on the end of the bed and looks me over. Thoroughly. From my mascara-enhanced lashes, down to my pushed-up boobs and back again. Billy is checking me out as well.

I say, "Are we done?"

He says, "Wow, what have you done to yourself. You look different. Hot. I like it."

Does his statement mean I don't normally look hot? But, then again, why do I care? I try to come up with a plausible explanation for my new look and opt for the truth. "Kendra decided I needed to look sexy since we were going after Eddie."

Billy perks up. "You and Kendra went to the Ponderosa?"

"Yes, and guess what? Eddie did it. He killed Dani. Not that either one of you want to hear it."

"I assume you know this because you read it in his soul." There's a hint of disapproval in Billy's voice.

"Yes." I narrow my eyes at him. "I know this because I read his soul."

Billy slams his mouth shut and gazes at the floor.

Mick says, "You're absolutely sure?"

"Yes."

"Let me think about it. I'll get back to you."

"Thanks, Mick. I know it's not the concrete proof needed to arrest Eddie for murder, but it's nice to be believed."

Yes, this is my snarky way of getting back at Billy. In my opinion, he deserves it.

Billy heads for the door. "I'll be in touch."

I'm thinking, Oh, really? Why?

Billy opens the door, pauses and looks back at Mick. "You coming?"

Mick makes no move to leave. "Quick question." He waggles his pointer finger back and forth between Billy and me. "Are you two a done deal? For sure?"

I can't believe what I'm hearing. Is Mick hitting on me? Now?

Billy flushes. A muscle twitches in his jaw. He takes care not to look at me. "We're taking some time off."

Suddenly furious, I say, "Is that what you call it? Time off? So after a month or two, or when you get tired of Haley McFadden, it will be time in?"

I'm aware my voice has taken on an unpleasant, screechy tone, but in for a dollar, in for a dime. The words continue to pour out. "Guess again, Billy. This isn't time off, like you're on sabbatical before you go back to the hard work of being my boyfriend. So, let's call it what it is. Over."

Mick fights a grin but continues to ignore me and

directs his comment to Billy. "Guess it's no secret I'd like to spend time with Mel. Just wanted to make sure it's okay with you."

I can't believe this. Twice in one night. First, Darrell wants to know if I'm up for grabs. Now, Mick is asking Billy if I'm on the auction block.

Billy also acts like I'm invisible. "Are you saying you want to date Mel? I'm not sure how I feel about that. She might not be ready to…"

"Stop!" I yell. "Do you see me? I'm right here. In this room. And the two of you are acting like mongrels fighting over a steak bone. Let's get one thing crystal clear. I'm nobody's steak bone. All I want is for both of you to leave so I can heat up a bowl of noodles in the microwave, take a shower, and go to bed in a man-free environment. Got it?"

Since they're both obtuse, I look around the room for something to throw. Finding no missiles, I settle for the broom propped in the corner of the room. I grab it like a baseball bat and begin swinging it at both men. "Out, get out!"

They both run for the door. Mick is laughing his butt off. Billy keeps looking over his shoulder, saying, "Wait, wait, we need to talk."

I slam the door and lock it, thankful I'm alone.

Chapter Thirteen

The next morning, I sit at my little round table and make a list, prioritizing my options. (1) Get key back from Billy so I don't have any more surprise visitors. (2) Talk to Louise Goodhart about my appointment with Dr. Dirk. (3) Fill Kendra in on last night's drama. (4) Take care to avoid Mick unless he has a viable plan for locking up Eddie. (5) Go to the Ayoob's house to offer my condolences to Yasmin's family (even though I dread it).

First things first. I call Billy's cell, hoping it will go to voicemail. It doesn't. He answers, "Mel?"

When I confess it is indeed me, he says, "Sorry about last night. Actually, I'm sorry about everything. Can we talk?"

"I need some time, Billy. I was wondering if you would mind returning the key to my room."

He doesn't answer right away. "I was hoping we could talk first."

"Guess I don't feel much like talking."

"If this is about Haley," he says. "She's just a kid, ya know, and she's been going through a rough patch after seeing her friends getting their legs blown off by IED's. She needed somebody to talk to, somebody who's been through it."

I so want to believe him but my pride and hurt feelings won't let me.

"So, she's what? A little time-out from your for real girlfriend, the one you don't want looking into your soul?"

I hear him breathing, but he doesn't answer.

Finally, I say, "I am what I am, Billy. If you can't deal with it, it's best to end it now."

"I love you, Mel."

"I know you do. I love you, too." My voice is choked with tears. "But, maybe we're not right for each other."

After that conversation killer, he tells me he'll bring my key back, even though he doesn't want to. I thank him, and we say goodbye like we're polite strangers. Maybe we are or will be.

Time for number two on my list. I call Goodhart and ask to see her later this morning. We make an appointment for 11:30, which will give me time to talk to my father first.

Kendra answers on the second ring. I hear kid noises and a baby crying in the background. "Too busy to talk?"

"Aida's here," she says.

After Aida had her baby, Kendra hired her as a mother's helper. God knows she needs one. Her oldest boy, Aaron, is three. Her youngest son is nine months, and she also has Dani's daughter, Destiny, whose first birthday is next month.

I fill her in on last night's visit from Billy and Mick. I hear her call to Aida, "Be right back," and footsteps as she moves to a quieter place.

"How awful! I knew Yasmin. We get our gas there. What do you think happened?"

I confess I don't know and then update her on the

Eddie Morgan thing.

She says, "Sounds like Billy blew you off. Do you think Mick will come through?"

"Fingers crossed," I say and get ready to click off.

"Wait," she says. "How did Billy act? Does he want the two of you to get back together?"

"It's not going to happen, Kendra. I know he loves me and I love him. But, he can't handle who I am. What I am. It's over. He just doesn't know it yet."

I didn't tell her about the whole Mick asking permission from Billy to date me thing. No sense in giving her further ammunition when she's already furious with her brother.

I skip over number four (avoid Mick), which leaves the last, and most difficult item. I need to pay my respects to Yasmin's family who must be devastated by their loss. I hop in Buttercup and stop by McDonalds to gird my loins with an Egg McMuffin before facing Bibi and his family who live in a two story older home located behind their business.

When I arrive at the Gas 'N Grub, I'm surprised to see it's open. A pimply-faced youth is parked behind the counter. His nametag says Pierce. He's gazing at his smart phone and muttering under his breath.

When he doesn't bother to acknowledge my presence, I say, "Excuse me. I want to pay my respects to the Ayoob's. Is it okay if I go to their house?"

Pierce looks at me and I can see it's a struggle for him to focus on an actual human being rather than the video game he's been playing. "So, you're not buying gas?"

I sigh and try not to roll my eyes. "No, Pierce, I'm not buying gas." I pause and enunciate slowly. "I want to visit Yasmin's family and tell them how sorry I am."

"Oh, yeah," Pierce says. "Yasmin. Sure, go ahead. You know where they live?"

I don't bother to answer. I simply point toward the Ayoob's living quarters.

Once outside, I walk down the gravel path toward the house. Five vehicles are parked in front of the door. I recognize the immaculate red pick-up truck. It belongs to Yasmin's brother, Darrak, who often helps out in the store. I remember Yasmin telling me how much she adored her big brother. Of all her siblings, Darrak was her hands down favorite. As I lift my hand to knock, I hear a keening sound, so filled with pain, it lifts the hair on the back of my neck. Unbidden, sympathetic tears spring to my eyes.

I rap on the door and hear the crunch of tires on gravel behind me. A long, black hearse pulls in slowly and parks next to Darrak's truck. I see two men in the front seat, but they make no move to exit the car.

The door flies open. Darrak and Bibi stand in the dimly lit hall. Bibi nods and brushes by me. Darrak greets me with a grimace of a smile. His face is pale. His black eyes burn with anger. "Please come in, Mel. I'm afraid I must go and talk to the men who have come to collect the body of my sweet sister."

He waves at a basket containing headscarves. "Please cover your hair and remove your shoes."

I'm relieved to know I'm not the only clueless, non-Muslim person to stop by and offer condolences. Darrak joins his father outside. I pull off my sneakers, check my socks for holes and snag a pale blue scarf from the pile.

Not sure what to do next, I cover my hair, turn

84

right and take two steps down into a cavernous living room. I walk toward the grieving sounds. Two steps up and left turn lead me to a long, narrow room running the length of the house. I stop at the threshold to take in the scene before me. Yasmin's body is on a long table and completely swathed in white. I focus on her face, the only visible part of her body. Her eyes are closed and it is obvious, the beautiful essence of her life has been extinguished. The table is surrounded by members of her extended family, all clothed in black. The contrast between black and white is startling, and brings to mind the image of a beautiful swan encircled by black crows of death.

The loudest wails emanate from a tiny woman with a wrinkled brown face. Grandmother? She stands at the head of the table. Yasmin's mother, Saarah, is next to her. The rest of the family seems to have appointed places to stand.

Saarah steps away from the table and walks to me, both hands extended in greeting. "Our family is honored by your presence. Welcome."

Her hands are like ice. I want to hug her, but not sure if it's proper protocol. She senses my dilemma and opens her arms wide. I step into her embrace, shocked by the frailness of her body.

Saarah takes my hand and leads me into the living room. We sit on the couch side by side, Saarah still gripping my hand. She says, "It is kind of you to come. Many of our non-Muslim friends and customers stay away for fear of offending us. I know you and Yasmin were not close, but she always smiled when she spoke of you. In another time and place, I think the two of you would be kindred souls."

Hot tears sting my eyes. Kindred souls. Her words are spoken with such sincerity I feel them resonate in my heart. I take a shaky breath and try to hold it together, although part of me wants to join the mournful chorus coming from the next room.

The front door opens. Bibi and Darrak enter followed by the men from the funeral home pushing a wheeled gurney.

Saarah rises. "These men are taking my daughter away. I must go."

I give her one last hug, adding, "Let me know if I can help in any way."

Distracted, she nods and joins the men. I want to remember Yasmin as I saw her, a beautiful angel dressed in white. I have no desire to see her body loaded into the hearse. Therefore, I hurry to Buttercup and drive away without looking back.

****

"No, like I told you, my eyes were dilated. I couldn't see diddlysquat," I tell Rebecca Porter. "Yes, his hand brushed against my breast, and he got a little up close and personal while he was looking into my eyes, but there's no way I'll put it in writing and sign it."

I'm in Goodhart's office, seated at a table with Louise and Porter who's glaring at me, a look of outraged indignation on her thin features.

She leans back in her chair and smirks. "You probably enjoyed it. After all, he is a good-looking man."

Her statement is so patently ridiculous, I can't even work up a good head of steam. Fortunately, I'm able to dredge up an appropriate word from the word of the day calendar my mother gives me every year. "You're wrong. I did not find it a titillating experience. I'm simply saying I won't ruin a man's career with so little proof."

In a soothing tone, Louise says, "I don't believe you would want that either, Rebecca. I know you feel you've been violated, but unless others come forward, there's very little I can do. Surely you understand."

Rebecca clamps her mouth shut and refuses to answer. Her anger is palpable and hangs in the air like a black cloud filled with static electricity. Actually, the fierceness of her rage seems off the charts considering the situation we're in. Louise hasn't given her the boot. Yet.

I really want another look into her soul, so I say, "Rebecca, I understand you're upset, but what course of action do you want Louise to take? Send somebody else for an exam? And, if the results are the same as mine, send another person?"

She grips the edge of the table and stares directly into my eyes. "Whatever it takes to nail the son of a bitch."

Louise blinks rapidly. I'm not sure what she's thinking. It's possible Rebecca could become her cash cow. Or would Louise's code of ethics allow her to take advantage of the woman? I decide to test the waters. "It might cost you a small fortune. "

I soon get my answer.

Louise says, "I'm sorry, but I can't proceed with your case. I know you gave me a five-hundred dollar retainer. I think it's only fair I use part of the money to pay for Mel's eye exam. I'll return the rest to you. I do have one suggestion. If you hear of other women who've had the same experience as you, get together and go to the police."

Rebecca's body stiffens. She springs up. Her chair crashes to the floor. "I told you, law enforcement will blow me off after what happened before. You said you'd help me, and now you're saying you won't."

Louise's eyes turn steely. She rises slowly. "Rebecca, if the doctor is doing what you say, there must be other women who've had the same experience as you."

"Which is exactly why I wanted to hire you. To find them."

Louise says, "Have you heard of the privacy act? What you're asking me to do would require me getting into the doctor's records. Sorry, but I'm not willing to lose my license."

Rebecca rakes me with a hateful look. "So your solution was to send her? How do you know she's not lying?"

I've had enough. I stand and lean across the table. "What would I possibly gain from lying? If Louise doesn't want to take your case, maybe you can find somebody else who will."

Rebecca looks away, slings her handbag across her shoulder, and stomps toward the door. She places her hand on the doorknob, turns and stares at us. Her words are clipped and icy with hatred. "Okey dokey, then. You two take care now. Watch your backs. You never know who might be out to get you."

She exits and slams the door.

We both sink into our chairs. Louise shakes her head. "She's bat shit crazy."

"You better believe it. Be glad you didn't take her

case. I saw something in her soul, and it scares the hell out of me."

Louise's gaze darts to the door and back. "What did you see?"

"Like you said, she's deranged. It's hard to explain, but her soul has no balance. Generally, the basic design of a person's soul remains fairly consistent once he or she reaches adulthood."

Louise gives me her undivided attention. "I'm listening."

I take a deep breath and try my best. "Reading a soul is like looking at your backyard. Let's say your backyard has a fence around it, a tree in the middle and you can see mountains in the distance. In the spring, brand new leaves are forming on the tree. The grass is turning green. Tulips are blooming. There's still snow on the mountaintops. Now, fast forward to late summer. The tulips are gone. The grass has brown spots where the sprinkler doesn't quite reach. The mountaintops are bare. But basically, your back yard is still your back yard. The fence and tree are still there. You can still see the mountains in the distance."

This is a long speech for me. I pause to gather my thoughts.

Louise prompts, "And the soul?"

"Most souls have a predominant color and, in my experience, it stays the same. In the process of living one's life, markers appear, like stains, blotches, slash marks and even ragged edges. But the overall appearance of the soul is unique to the individual and does not change."

"Is Rebecca's soul different?"

"Yes. The first time I met with her, it was

predominantly pink with streaks of gray. Two pulsating spots of red indicated she had pent-up aggression. I saw a black cloud flitting across her soul, which gave me reason to believe she was hiding something. Now, the pink is entirely gone. Her soul is muddy brown and the red spots have increased in size. Before they were barely visible. Now they're front and center, still pulsating and have a black border."

An involuntary shiver creeps down my spine. "I don't know how else to say it. Her soul looks evil."

"Maybe she's not hiding the evil anymore," Louise says.

"You might be right."

"Do you think we're in danger?"

"It's possible. She was pretty pissed off when she stormed out of here. Do you know what kind of car she has?"

Louise gives me a quick smile. "No, but that particular task is definitely in my wheelhouse."

Later, when I drive off in Buttercup, I obsessively check the rearview mirror for Porter's silver BMW, unable to shake my feeling of impending doom. Maybe it's because my day started with death (Yasmin's) and ended with Rebecca's anger-fueled threats of bodily harm.

There's only one person in my world who makes me feel absolutely, one hundred per cent safe. It's time to call Uncle Paco.

Chapter Fourteen

I know Aida's helping Kendra today. This means Paco may be wandering around at loose ends. When I get to Number Ten, I call his cell. He answers on the first ring.

"Where are you?" I ask, and for good reason. Paco, and his fellow Los Habañeros run a lucrative business. In the immediate family, we call it Paco's don't ask, don't tell employment path to success. Therefore, Paco sometimes vanishes for several days with no forwarding address. Selfishly, I want to make sure he's here in 3 Peaks.

"Where am I?" he booms. "I'm at Nick's drinking a brewski. The question is, girl, where are you?"

I tell him I'm home and have a couple of days off. "Do you have time to stop by?"

"Be right there, little girl."

To Uncle Paco, I'll always be his little girl, maybe even when my hair turns gray.

Minutes later, he's standing in my doorway. His Harley is parked next to my window. He stomps over to the table and takes a chair. It creaks under his bulk.

I sit across from him. "Where's the muscle car?"

"Aida drove it to Kendra's 'cause it's got the baby seat."

"You let her drive?"

Aida has a learner's permit, not a valid license.

Paco's been giving her driving lessons in Buttercup for a couple of months, but says she's not ready to take her test because she drives too slow and can't parallel park.

"I followed her over on the bike," he says. "At fifteen mile an hour. I keep telling the woman she'll get pulled over for driving too slow. But, you know what?"

He doesn't wait for me to answer. "I finally figured it out. She enjoys driving slow."

"Does she like the ring?"

"I guess so. She bawled her head off. Kendra told me crying is a good thing. Do you agree?"

I nod.

After a brief silence, Paco says, "So, what's the problem?"

"Who said anything about a problem?"

He reaches across the table, takes hold of my chin and tilts it back until I'm looking into his eyes and his tranquil, forest green soul. I've always loved looking into Paco's soul. It makes me feel peaceful which is counterintuitive, since Paco is, almost assuredly, involved in some sort of criminal activity. Go figure.

"Look at me, little girl. Tell me what's wrong. I'm guessing, Billy. Kendra told me the two of you are splitsville. Would have been nice if I'd heard it from you. Remember what I told you about these guys with PTSD. Takes a long time for them to get over the heebie jeebies."

Paco knows about my ability to read souls. Hell, the entire city of 3 Peaks knows about it after the big bust went down in June. "Not sure it's the heebie jeebies, Unc. The soul-reading thing really bugs him. He thinks I'm trying to catch him in a lie. I guess it boils down to the fact we can't trust each other anymore."

The words, spoken off the top of my head, cause the dim light bulb inside my skull to brighten. Unwittingly, I'd hit upon the answer I'd been seeking. Trust. It all comes down to trust. Billy doesn't appreciate or trust my God-given gift, a gift I can't return even if I want to. He thinks I use it as a form of entrapment. This affects his behavior. He avoids looking into my eyes, which, in turn, leads me to believe he's hiding something, and therefore, I don't trust him. In other words, it's a vicious cycle with no apparent solution. The conclusion hits me like a sledgehammer to the heart and, once again, here I am, wallowing in the abyss of self-pity. I so don't want to be one of those girls, weeping over my lost love, plotting how to get him back. No way.

Paco warm brown eyes soften. He pats my cheek. "The damn fool needs to get his butt back into counseling. I'll tell him so the next time I see him."

"Don't you dare! I mean it, Paco. I'll know if you do."

He lifts his hands in surrender. "Whatever you say, little girl."

"Besides," I say. "Billy's not the reason I needed to talk to you."

He brightens. "Got a job for me?"

I fill him in on my work for Louise Goodhart.

At first, he's sidetracked by the description of my appointment with Dr. Dirk. He says, "The asshole calls himself Dr. Dirk? And, you say he touched your boob and wheeled up close to your private parts? What's wrong with you? He's a perv. No doubt about it."

"Like I told you, I couldn't see squat. So, yes, there

is doubt in my mind. Focus, Unc, the real danger here is Rebecca Porter. She's not only crazy, I think she wants to kill me and maybe Louise, too."

This gets Paco's attention, and now he's all business. After jotting down a description of Porter's car and her license number, he says, "What does she look like?"

"Tall. Thin. Frizzy brown hair."

Paco thinks for a moment, stroking his Fu Manchu 'stache. "Think she's up for seduction by a mucho macho, Harley-riding Mexican man?"

I'm horrified at the suggestion, but try not to show it. "There has to be another way. Correct me if I'm wrong, but are you not engaged to be married?"

Apparently, I'm not too good at hiding my emotions. Paco howls with laughter and slaps a ham-sized palm on the table, which squeaks in protest. "Gotcha good, girlie. Just kidding. No worries, I'm on it."

When Paco leaves, I toy with the idea of going for a run. It's a beautiful late autumn day in 3 Peaks, Oregon. There's a bite to the wind, promising snow in the near future. Aspen groves in the distance are burnished with gold and the maple trees lining our street have turned a brilliant shade of red. The sun is shining, and I know I need the endorphins I will gain from a five-mile run.

I'm tying the laces of my running shoes when I hear a car pull up and stop outside my door. I go to the window and see Homeland Security Mick, exiting his car. My to-do list is still on the table. The words avoid Mick jump out at me. Looks like my run will be put on hold.

I throw the door open before he can knock. "You again? Where's your buddy, my former boyfriend, Billy?"

Mick grins and charges through the door like he owns the place. "Don't know. Don't care. The operative words are former boyfriend. I'm here. You're here. Does anything else matter?"

I roll my eyes. "Oh, please. What do you want?"

He glances at the bed, and I think he's about to flop down on it like the other night. I shake my head. "Don't even think about it." I point at a chair. "Sit there. Tell me what you want and get out."

His bright blue eyes crinkle with amusement. "My, but you're hostile. And here I am about to deliver good news."

He sits. I sit across the table from him and scoot my chair back, well out of his reach. "Okay, so what are the glad tidings you're about to deliver?"

He folds his arms, places them on the table and fixes me with his laser beam stare. "I'll tell you in a minute."

I scowl at him. "Why the delay?"

"Because we need to get something settled first. Between the two of us."

I flap a hand at him. "There is no two of us."

He cocks his head to one side. "I have a challenge for you. Look into my soul and ask me anything."

"Why?"

"Because," he says, "I have nothing to hide, other than I want to get closer to you."

"Not going to happen. Remember what happened a few months ago? I thought you were a hired killer. You threw me in the trunk of a car. I believed I was about to die. Even when I found out you were one of the so-called good guys, you tied me up in your apartment, and I had to go through agony to get away. The memory of that experience does not make me all fuzzy and warm, eager to get it on with you."

"Doesn't the fact I saved your life count for anything?"

A flush of shame warms my cheeks. I look at the floor. "Yes, of course it does."

Mick is not to be deterred. "I know you like my soul because you've told me so. Here's a sincere offer. Peek into my soul. Take a good, long look if you like. See if I have any secrets. Then, make up your mind."

He steps to my side of the table and places his hands on my shoulders. He looms over me, but I feel no threat. I look into his eyes. Into his soul. I have to admit he's right. When I first met Mick, he was undercover and hanging around with some very bad people. Mick's soul was a crystal clear shade of blue without the telltale muddy splotches associated with his shady sidekicks. In an effort to save my life, I'd shared this bit of information with him. I now wish I'd kept it to myself.

I figure the only way to get rid of him is to play along. "I can ask anything I want?"

This amuses him. He smiles and his eyes light up. "Sure. Go for it."

His hands remain on my shoulders. Touch often increases my ability to read a soul. I gaze into his eyes. His soul is still a clear shade of blue, but it's picked up a few dings and scratches since last June. Noticeably absent, are the signs of anger and frustration, almost always presented as flaring spots of red. I'd seen them recently in Rebecca's soul and in a lesser degree, Billy's.

Mick apparently harbors no rage. But something new has been added. The upper right edge of his soul is slightly ragged and streaked with black. The black is in stark contrast to the sky-blue background. I suspect I know why it's there, but have to ask. "Have you ever killed anyone?"

He doesn't hesitate. "Yes."

"Recently?"

He holds my gaze. "July. In Portland. A bust went south. I had to take a guy out before he got to me."

I ask a couple more generic questions and see no trace of a lie flash across his soul. Finally I say, "Do you have a girlfriend? Or, perhaps a wife back in Russia?"

He chuckles. "No to both. Anything else, Madame Interrogator?"

"I'm done."

He gives my shoulders a squeeze and bumps his forehead against mine, still gazing down at me. "Since you asked the girlfriend/wife question, may I assume you don't find me as scary as you claim?"

"I'm not scared of you."

He shakes his head. "Now you're lying. You think I can't tell?"

I gnaw on my lower lip, trying to figure out exactly what I'm feeling. "When I think about how you were back then, yeah, it's a little scary. I know what you're capable of doing. On the plus side, I know you don't have anger in your soul and you did save my life. I have to factor in all those things before I decide how I feel about you."

"Good enough."

He turns a chair around and straddles it. "And now the real reason I'm here. Do you ride?"

"Excuse me?"

"Horses. Do you know how to ride horses?"

"Never been on one in my life."

"Perfect," he says. "I've got a job for you."

Chapter Fifteen

It's three days later and Rebecca Porter still looms large in my mind although Paco is keeping an eye on her. However, I am a bit concerned for my safety right now. I'm standing in the barn at the Rockin' R Ranch next to an extremely large brown horse named Sneaky Pete. He's gazing down at me over his Roman nose with a superior expression as if to say, "I'll show you who's boss."

Thanks to my friend, Mick, I am now taking riding lessons. Mick assures me I will earn the undying gratitude of the Department of Homeland Security and be paid handsomely in the process. Probably won't do me any good if I'm stomped to death by Sneaky Pete.

Various and sundry law enforcement agencies tried their best, but bumped up against a dead end with the Rathjen family who closed ranks and appear to have ironclad alibis. Therefore, I'm it, law enforcement's last, best hope for ferreting out the truth. Added bonus: I don't have to fake inexperience with all things equine.

Mick hoped my riding instructor would be Rathjen's son, Riley. He suggested Riley would feel comfortable talking to me because we're close to the same age. He also told me not to be afraid to flirt a bit.

"Hold it," I told him. "He's just a kid."

"He's nineteen," Mick said.

"I'll take your stupid riding lessons but I'm not

seducing a kid. Otherwise, forget it."

Now, it's a non-issue since I'm firmly in the clutches of Rick Rathjen, the patriarch of the family. Literally in his clutches. After giving me a snoozer of a lesson on how to saddle Sneaky Pete—a lesson I don't plan to use—he seizes me around the waist, hoists me up and orders, "Put your left foot in the stirrup grab the saddle horn, throw your right leg over the saddle, and you'll be mounted."

I try my best. Left foot in the stirrup, I reach up for the saddle horn, clinging to it with both hands. I fling my right leg upward. My toe barely touches the saddle since the stirrups are set for a much taller person. I try again and hook a heel over the edge of the saddle. Now, I'm hanging on for dear life, spread-eagled with my face smushed against Sneaky Pete's neck. Irritated, he dances in place and snorts his disapproval. This scares me so bad, I give a little shriek and fall backward into Rathjen's arms.

He chuckles and tosses me up on the saddle like I'm a rag doll. "Sit tight, I'll shorten those stirrups for you."

I'm sitting on top of a giant horse. It's a long way to the ground. I could fall off, hit my head, and end up in a vegetative state for the rest of my life. Why did I let Mick talk me into this foolish venture? My mission is to delve into the secrets of the Rathjen family, and I'm too scared to utter a word.

I feel a little better when my feet are firmly in the stirrups, but then Rathjen frowns at my sneakers. "Those won't do. You should have worn boots."

"All I have are dress boots with skinny high heels."

"I'll find you a pair. Hang on."

Ohmigod, he's walking away. Still not feeling secure, I grip the saddle horn with my left hand and grab a handful of Sneaky Pete's mane with the right. He shifts slightly, turns his head and gives me an evil stare. This horse hates me.

Rathjen returns with a pair of battered boots. "Dismount and put these on."

I know this is a test, since he offers no help and is smirking at me like I'm today's featured entertainment. No problem.

Still clinging to Pete's mane and the saddle horn, get my right leg over the saddle, slip my left foot from the stirrup and drop to the wooden floor, happy to be on solid ground.

"These'll be too big so here's some wool socks," Rathjen says.

I sit on a bale of straw and remove my sneakers. The socks smell like horse, but beggars can't be choosers.

"Now," Rathjen says, "Let's see if you can mount by yourself."

I'm up for the challenge and find it much easier with the shortened stirrups. Why do I have the feeling Rathjen is enjoyed my rear view way too much?

I look down at him. "Now what?"

"Now, we ride."

"We? Where's your horse?"

He grabs Sneaky Pete's reins and leads him out of the barn. "We'll start in the corral, so if you fall off, it will be nice and soft."

I'm getting a little miffed. I snap, "I don't plan on falling off."

He chuckles again. "Hold that thought."

He hands me the reins and opens the gate to the corral. I'm all alone on top of Sneaky Pete, and the horse knows it. He makes a one hundred and eighty degree turn and trots toward the barn. I flop forward and wrap my arms around his neck, determined not to fall. Once inside the barn, Pete walks into his stall and begins munching hay.

Rathjen appears, shaking his head sadly. "You gotta show him you're in charge. Otherwise, you'll end up back in the barn every time."

I draw myself up and glare down at him. "You act like I'm supposed to know all this stuff. I told you I've never been on a horse before."

He grins at me. "Feisty little gal, huh?"

I open my mouth to retort when the Rockin' R pick-up truck pulls in. Riley Rathjen exits the truck and walks into the barn. His shoulders are slumped. Dark shadows under his eyes tell me he's not sleeping. When he glances at me, I think I see a glimmer of recognition in his expression.

Rathjen says, "This my son, Riley."

I release the saddle horn and give him a little wave. "Hi, I'm Melanie Sullivan. You can call me Mel."

Riley gives me a nod and asks his dad, "Why do you have a little bitty thing like her on Pete? Bella would be better."

Rathjen says, "Your mom's riding Bella."

Seems like Riley has more horse sense than his dad.

"He's right," I say. "This friggin' horse is too tall. Don't you have any short ones?"

Riley looks at his dad, "What about Sugar?"

Rathjen's jaw drops. "Are you kidding?"

Riley says, "No."

His father emits a disgusted snort and flaps a dismissive hand. "She's all yours." He wheels and stomps out of the barn.

I'm not sure who Sugar is, but I really don't give a damn, because now I'm alone with Riley.

"Can I get down now?" I say.

"Sure," Riley says. Unlike his father, he holds onto the reins and places a hand on my back to steady me when I climb down. I'm embarrassed to see my legs are trembling. I've never considered myself a coward. The total lack of control I felt atop Sneaky Pete surprises me.

Riley checks me out and sees my trepidation. He points at a straw bale. "Have a seat. I'll unsaddle Pete, and we'll start over. Sound okay?"

"Is Sugar a short horse?"

"Much shorter. My sister learned to ride on Sugar. She's kind of elderly now." He looks over at me, and his lips quirk upward in a poor facsimile of the charming smile I'd seen at the mini mart. "Sugar, not my sister."

With an economy of motion, he unsaddles Sneaky Pete, slaps the horse's rump, and shuts the door to the stall. Pete looks over his shoulder at me, lifts his upper lip revealing huge, yellow teeth, and emits a loud whinny, his version of a gotcha horselaugh.

"Yeah, yeah," I mutter. "I don't like you either."

Riley says, "Pete's a hard head, but he has a good gait for beginners."

I nod my head, like I know exactly what he's talking about.

"You stay here. I'll get your new ride."

He walks to the back of the barn and reappears leading a squat little four-legged creature with a bushy, blond mane. Riley says, "Meet Sugar Lips. She's a Shetland pony. I'll get her saddled up for you."

I'm pleasantly surprised. "I didn't know horses came this small."

I walk toward Sugar Lips and extend a hand to pet her.

"Careful," Riley says, "Make sure you don't walk behind her. She kicks. She bites too, so try to stay out of range."

"Hence, the name Sugar Lips," I reply, a trace of bitterness in my tone.

"Like I said, she's a senior citizen horse and little crabby. She'd rather just stay in her stall and sleep."

I cross my arms. "Don't you guys have any nice horses? Seems like you should since your ad in the yellow pages says, 'Riding Lessons'."

He gives me a genuine smile this time. He looks so exhausted, my heart goes out to him, and here I am giving him a bad time. I lift a hand in apology. "Forget I asked, Riley. I know you're trying your best."

"No, it's okay. My mom was really into giving riding lessons. Big time. But, now, well, I guess she has other interests, so she sold off some of her horses. We never got around to changing the ad."

When Sugar Lips is prepped, we go to the corral, and I climb aboard. My feet don't quite touch the ground, but they're close. Just the way I like it.

Riley spins around, covers his mouth with his forearm and lapses into a coughing fit. It's a poorly designed effort to hide his amusement.

I feign anger. "Hey, are you laughing at me?"

He turns around. Grinning broadly, he looks like the carefree kid I'd seen flirting with Yasmin. Chalk one up for Mel.

"Sorry," he says, wiping his eyes. "If you could just see yourself."

I smile back. "I don't mind looking ridiculous. Now, teach me to ride."

I spend the next hour learning how to neck rein, stop and start. I try desperately not to jounce out of the saddle when Sugar Lips, encouraged by Riley, breaks into a jerky trot. When this happens, the amount of air between my butt and the saddle is truly embarrassing.

"It's just a matter of relaxing into the rhythm," Riley says. "Next time, I'll saddle up Pete and show you how it works." He gazes directly into my eyes for the first time. They're blue, luminous, and red-rimmed. "You are coming back, aren't you?"

The sadness in his soul breaks my heart. Presented as a storm cloud heavy with rain, it free-floats across his soul, dimming its brightness as it touches down. Suddenly, my new mission in life is to lift the unhappiness from this kid's soul.

"Sure, I'll be back, even though I probably don't need any more lessons since I'm such a natural."

This earns me another genuine smile. It lasts until his mother joins us.

Chapter Sixteen

I'm still astride my new friend, Sugar Lips, when Riley's mother trots up on a beautiful Palomino. Watching her, I instantly understand what Riley means about relaxing into the rhythm. She's bracing her feet in the stirrups and effortlessly rolling with the horse's gait. She looks like part of the horse, natural and graceful. I also notice the horse perfectly matches her blond hair. Just for a moment, I want to be her. Not for long, though.

She pulls the horse to a stop next to the corral, dismounts, and walks to her son. The horse trails behind her like an oversized dog. She rakes me with a curious look. "Well, what have we here, Riley? And why is she on Rachel's pony?"

Her words and facial expression make me feel dehumanized, as if I'm a homeless bum who stumbled onto her property uninvited.

Riley flushes. "She's here for riding lessons, Mom. And since you were riding Bella, Dad had her on Pete. She's never ridden before. She needs a smaller horse."

"Horse, not pony," she corrects.

An awkward silence, I decide to take the bull by the horns. I dismount—not a difficult task—and walk over to Mrs. Rathjen. I hold out my right hand. "Hi, I'm Melanie."

She extends a gloved hand and, using only her

fingers, gives mine a teensy shake. "I'm Riley's mother."

I notice she doesn't tell me her given name. Nope, apparently I'm not worthy of a first name, which I happen to know is Roxanne. Part of me is sorry I didn't introduce myself as Riley's Lame Riding Lesson. Nevertheless, I buck up and say, "Nice to meet you, Riley's mother."

Riley is obviously embarrassed by his mother's lack of warmth. He shuffles his feet in the dirt and, when he speaks to her, makes a point of looking over her head. "We're just finishing up here, Mom. You want me to take care of Bella for you?"

She pinches her lips together and looks me over again. "Are you done with your lesson?"

Riley nods.

Without a word, she picks up Bella's reins, places them in Riley's hand and walks away.

When she's well out of range, I say, "Is there a problem? Should I go?"

Riley clenches his jaw and takes a big breath. "Sorry. It's not you. We have some stuff going on."

Leading Belle, he heads for the barn. "Bring Sugar, okay?"

"Who me?"

He looks over his shoulder and grins. "Yeah, you. Pretend she's a German Shepherd. You can handle it."

The way he says it makes me feel like such a slacker, I march over to the pony and say, "Hey, Sugar Lips, you're coming with me whether you like it or not."

She tosses her head and gives me the evil eye. I grab her reins and follow Riley to the barn, glancing over my shoulder in case she decides to bite my butt.

After we take care of the horses, Riley pulls a couple of soft drinks from a cooler. He places them in an empty metal bucket like it's a silver-serving tray and walks to the straw bale. "Got a minute?"

"Sure."

We sit side by side on the straw, guzzling our drinks. Finally, he says, "I saw you talking to Yasmin at the Gas "N Grub."

"Yeah," I say. "What happened to her is awful. She was a sweet girl."

He glances over at me. His eyes are brimming with tears. "Did you know we were a couple?" He gulps back his tears. "I should say, we wanted to be a couple."

I pat his hand. "Tough situation. I could see she was crazy about you. But, I know there was the situation with Bibi."

"Not just Bibi," Riley says. "My dad, well he's not too fond of Muslims, if you get my drift."

I try to think how to say it without dissing Riley's father and decide to go with, "I'm familiar with his opinions."

Riley totally gets it. With a faint smile, he says, "Conservative redneck who hates foreigners, right?"

I don't want to be too obvious, so I tread carefully. "How did you meet Yasmin?"

Riley's eyes take on a dreamy quality. "Her dad let her go to school until she turned sixteen. Then, he made her drop out and work at the store. We had a geometry class together. She was super smart and I, um, let's just say math isn't exactly my strong suit. We used to sit together at lunch, and she'd help me with my homework."

"I hear you. I hated math. If you know how to add, subtract, multiply and divide, who needs geometry?"

We bump fists in a moment of anti-mathematics solidarity.

He says, "It's weird, but the first time I saw her..." he looks away in an attempt to control his emotions. When he speaks, his voice is choked with tears. "I loved her."

We sit in silence for a while. Finally, I say, "Any idea what happened to her? Who might have killed her?"

He stares at the ground. "The cops think my dad had something to do with it."

"What do you think?"

His face tightens. "He has strong opinions, but basically, my dad's a good guy. He wouldn't kill anybody."

I want so badly to say, what about your mom, but bite my lip instead.

Riley swipes at his eyes and gulps loudly. "The cops have been out here a bunch of times asking all of us questions. The way my mom was right now? It's nothing against you. She just wants it all to go away."

I'd taken a little peek into Roxanne Rathjen's soul and know Riley's assessment of his mother's behavior is not correct. She doesn't just want it all to go away. She didn't kill Yasmin, but she's definitely hiding something. It could be related to Yasmin's death or it might be something entirely different. Not my place to point it out to her son, though.

Speaking of souls, I know Riley is guilty of nothing more than falling in love with the wrong girl.

And then, we have Rick Rathjen. He was too busy looking at my body to make eye contact. Therefore, I'll need another opportunity to engage him in conversation. This means more riding lessons.

"Hey, Riley," I say. "If I come back for more riding lessons, who will be my instructor? You or your dad?"

"Depends on the time and day. I'm taking some classes at the community college. I'll write down the schedule for you. If I'm not here, my dad will do it."

Now, I'm torn. I really need to talk to Rathjen alone but I have another concern. "If it's your dad, will I have to ride Sneaky Pete?"

Riley chuckles. "I'll tell him to put you on Sugar or Bella."

I smile at him. "Promise?"

He uses his index finger to cross his heart. The kid is so sweet, he's breaking my heart.

I want to question him further, questions like: When did you see Yasmin last? Did you argue with your father about Yasmin? Did your mom or sister know Yasmin? I don't say any of these things though. I want Riley to trust me, and I need to look into his father's soul, even though I'm not looking forward to it.

Before I leave, we schedule the next few riding lessons. Riley suggests I wait a couple of days before I come back. He blushes as he says, "Your, um, fanny might be a little sore after riding today. Just saying."

I give him my cell number. "See you soon, Riley. I know you're hurting. If you need to talk, call me."

He walks me to Buttercup and with the vast superiority of youth says, "Jesus, is this your primary ride? Whaddaya call it, the Mustard Mobile?"

"Actually, I call her Buttercup. She likes it and runs like a champ. Maybe even better than your macho pickup truck. So there."

He lifts his hand in farewell, and I see him in the rearview mirror, watching me as I drive Buttercup down the long, dusty lane leading away from the ranch.

Mick will be coming around soon, wanting answers, wanting something for the money DHS is paying me. I hope he'll be happy with what I believe to be a good start. Hopefully, more answers will follow.

Chapter Seventeen

Two nights later, I'm carrying a heavily-laden tray of brimming beer mugs to the Corral where the heavy hitters (beer guzzlers) hang out and play pool. I set it down at a table for six and switch my hips to the left when a grinning young guy in a University of Oregon baseball cap tries to grab my butt.

I step up nice and close and make eye contact. Don't see anything dangerous. Just a kid having a little fun. I dial it down a notch. "Not a good idea, my friend. Not if you want to keep on drinking at Nick's. Got it?"

He nods vigorously and mumbles, "Sorry. The guys here, they…"

"I know. The boys said they'd pay for the beer if you grabbed my ass. Right?"

"Yeah."

I force a friendly grin and shake my fingers at the rest of the crew. "No more, unless you want Nick to ask you to drink somewhere else."

They all agree and I walk away, trying not to limp. Normally, I don't take issue with the grab-ass guys who camp out in the Corral, other than to stay out of reach. But since my riding lesson, I'm feeling pain in muscles I didn't know I had. I've always prided myself on being in good shape. I do Brazilian Jujitsu. I stretch. I run at least three times a week.

Damn you, Sugar Lips! Bouncing up and down on

your back has given new meaning to the term saddle sore. It's not just my butt. The inside of my thighs are screaming, What the hell? Thus, my hypersensitivity to the aforementioned incident.

Mick comes in an hour later and, for the first time since June, I give him a thorough visual inspection. He's leaner and more muscular than he was a few months ago. Back then, he had to cultivate a slob-like appearance because he was under cover. He needed to fit in with his beer-drinking criminal cohorts. He takes a seat in my section and peruses the menu.

Nursing my sore muscles, I hobble to his table. "May I help you, sir? I'm guessing wodka. Grey Goose. Am I right?"

I'm teasing him a little. When he was undercover, he pretended to speak English with a Russian accent and always asked for wodka. Mick's eyes are a unique shade of blue and slightly slanted upward, thanks to his Russian heritage. Because he's lost weight, his cheekbones are more prominent. His light brown hair— I assume it's his natural color—is cut fairly short and sort of does its own thing, like he rakes his fingers through it and it's good to go. Unfortunately (for me) that particular combination lights my fire. Add to the total picture, his nicely formed pectorals and six-pack abs are prominently displayed when he removes his denim jacket. Damn, Mel, remember, Mick is a scary guy. He's Homeland Security, for God's sake. They have no rules.

The corner of his mouth turns up in a brief smile. "You got it, girl. Grey Goose. Vodka."

He pronounces the word with pride, like it may have taken him some time to master the intricacies of the English language. Maybe it did. I don't know him well enough to guess.

"Coming right up. You want the chicken and dumpling special?"

He nods and clamps a hand around my wrist. "Break soon? We need to talk."

"Things should slow down about the time you're done eating."

"I'll be at your place."

"Oh, really?" I narrow my eyes at him. "How do you propose getting in?"

He shrugs. "Shouldn't be a problem."

I really want to argue, but I have a room full of thirsty and hungry people to serve. I pull free of his grip and settle for, "Fine. Stay off the bed."

An hour later the hungry hordes have been fed and Nick tells me to take a break. I head for Number Ten. The aspirin bottle in the medicine cabinet is my main goal. True to his promise, Mick is inside, but not on the bed. He's sprawled on a chair, legs extended, studying his cell phone.

I don't bother with a greeting. Instead, I head straight for the aspirin. I wash down two with a big slurp of water and then flop down on the bed.

Mick walks to the bed and stares down at me. "You sick or what?"

"Or what."

He folds his arms across his chest and smirks. "Ah, I get it. It's the horse thing. Your ass hurts...right?"

"Yes, Sherlock, it's my ass, along with a bunch of other parts."

Quick as a big cat, he reaches down, flips me onto my stomach and grips my buns with powerful hands and begins kneading them like bread dough. "A little massage will fix you right up."

"Hey!" I offer a token objection before lapsing into a groan of pleasure overlaid with pain. Damn, but it feels good. In fact it hurts so good I can't muster up enough strength, muscle-wise or character-wise, to stop him.

"Relax and enjoy it," he murmurs, kneeling on the foot of the bed. He gets his thumbs into the action, massaging my inner thighs and zeroing in on the sore spots.

"Oh, oh," I moan. "Should tell you to stop. Feels so damn good."

I'm so totally in the moment, I fail to hear the sound of the key card in the door. The next thing I hear is Billy saying, "What the hell? Didn't take much time for you to move on, Minnie Mouse."

A couple of things happen simultaneously. I roll onto my back. Mick leaps to a standing position and curses in Russian. It sounds like *chodit*!

He takes a step toward Billy. "You knew she was at the Rathjen's taking riding lessons. Her ass hurts. I was giving her a massage. Just a massage. Nothing else."

Oh, great.

I scoot to the end of the bed. "Don't bother explaining, Mick. He's in no position to judge."

Billy won't look at me. He tosses the key card on the bedside table. "Here you go."

He spins around and heads out the door. Mick follows him out. I drop my head into my hands, wondering how my life has become a daytime drama.

I hear the men outside my room, conversing in low

tones. Curiosity gets the best of me and I tiptoe to the door. I peer through the crack. Billy is bristled up as only Billy can be. He's not making eye contact with Mick. Apparently I'm not the only one he can't look at. Mick has a hand on Billy's shoulder and is talking a blue streak. I catch only a few words. Words like "you want me to back off?" and "thought you two were a done deal," as well as, "she's doing her best to..." Hmm, not sure what that means. Bottom line, they're still talking about me instead of to me.

I step through the door. "If you two have something to say to me, about me, or know of a situation which might affect me, say it now. I have to get back to work."

Billy's rigid posture relaxes. He steps away from Mick, reaches out and places his hands on my shoulders. "Sorry, Minnie. I was out of line. What you said is true. I have no right to judge you. At some point, I hope we can get together and have an honest discussion about our situation. I know the fault is mine. Haley was a convenient accident. She means nothing to me. In the meantime, you could do a lot worse than Mick. He's a good guy."

Tears spring to my eyes. Billy being reasonable is almost more than I can bear. Anger I can deal with.

I don't trust my voice, so, still snuffling, I pull back and nod. I watch him walk away, climb on his bike and tool away. The way he described his fling with Haley resonates in my mind. A convenient accident, he called it. Maybe he's breaking her heart, too. Do I really want to be with someone who can glibly explain away cheating as a convenient accident?

I close and lock the door to Number Ten and tell

Mick, "I need to get back to work."

"I'll walk with you. Fill me in on the riding lesson."

I don't speak for a few moments and try to get a handle on my emotions.

Finally, I say, "About the Rathjen family. Riley was crazy about the girl. He's hurting a lot. I'm one hundred percent sure he didn't kill her. We made a connection, so maybe I can find out more about their last days together the next time I see him. I met Mama Rathjen. She's a bitch, but probably didn't kill Yasmin. She is definitely hiding something. Could be about Yasmin, or maybe she's having a fling with another guy. No way I can tell. I didn't meet the sister, and was only with the dad for a little while. I'll try to get more info from him next time."

"When is next time?"

"Soon. When my butt feels better."

He flexes his fingers and grins. "Give Dr. Feel-Good a call. I'm available twenty-four hours a day."

He's so damn cocky, I have to laugh. "I'll keep it in mind."

Before I go through the back door of the restaurant, Mick catches hold of my arm. "So, what about you and me?"

His blue eyes are so honest and appealing, I don't blow him off like I know I should. "I'll take it under advisement."

"Good enough," he says. He gives me a mock salute and heads for his car.

The rest of the evening, Billy is in my thoughts. Is he back at his place with Haley? Is he looking for comfort in the arms of the convenient accident? I so want to drive by his place and see if her car is there. With my luck, Buttercup would blow a gasket in front of his house, and I'd be busted. Instead, I settle for a hot shower and a late night phone call to my mother. I need to tell her about my break-up with Billy before Uncle Paco spills the beans. And, he will spill the beans. It's only a matter of time.

I wake her from a sound sleep. Trust me, it's better than catching her wide awake. I hear her murmur to my stepdad, Abel. "Go back to sleep. It's Mel. I'll talk to her in the living room."

I hear her fumbling for her glasses. For some reason, she can't talk on the phone without her glasses. The sound of footsteps follows.

"So," she says. "What's wrong? Something must be wrong or you wouldn't be calling me in the middle of the night."

I give her the abbreviated version of the break-up and hold my breath. I know what's coming.

"I can be there tomorrow. Actually, today. Abel has a truck leaving at 7:00 a.m. which means…"

"I'm fine. We're taking a break. I knew it was coming. It was just a matter of time."

"Had to be another woman," she mutters. "The bastard."

Her statement makes me smile. I hadn't said a word about Haley. My mother simply made the leap, unable to understand why Billy has the unmitigated gall to break off a romance with her precious daughter. Clearly, it couldn't be my fault. It's nice to have Sandra in my corner. I feel better already.

"You sure you don't want me to come up?"

"And do what? Beat Billy to a pulp?"

"Maybe you need someone to talk to."

"That's why phones were invented. I'm not suicidal or anything."

To distract her, I tell her about Paco and Aida's engagement. "Maybe Abel can come up with the Godmobile and perform the ceremony. What do you think?"

Sandra is giddy with excitement. "I'll talk to Abel right away. Call if you need me."

Whew! Disaster averted.

Chapter Eighteen

I purposely scheduled my next riding lesson with Rick Rathjen, even though I would rather spend time with Riley. However, I need to get a good long look into Papa Rathjen's soul.

I arrive at the appointed hour, tired from working until two in the morning and still a bit saddle sore. As such, I'm not willing to dick around. When I meet Rathjen in the barn, I point at Sneaky Pete's stall. "No way I'm riding him."

He suppresses a grin and gestures toward the back of the barn. "Fine. But, no way you're riding Sugar Lips either. True, you're kind of a shrimp, but you are a fully-grown woman. Right?"

I'm offended, but pinch my lips together to hold back a smart-ass retort.

"So," he continues. "I'm putting you on Bella. She's my wife's horse. Okay with you, Queen Elizabeth?"

A quick peek at his expression tells me he's kidding. "If I'm the queen, does that make you Master of the Horse?"

He guffaws. "I guess it does, Queenie."

I sit on a straw bale while he fetches Bella from her stall. "You want to saddle her up?"

"Isn't that your job?"

I don't fool him for a second. He frowns down at

me, but there's a twinkle in his hazel eyes. "You don't remember how, do you?"

"Nope."

"Thought so."

Our eye contact had been fleeting. I need to get a better look. Which means I'll have to saddle the damn horse. "I'll give it a try. With your help, of course."

I pick up Bella's saddle and start to fling it over her back.

"No," he says, "Blanket first."

I set the saddle down. He hands me the blanket. Since we're now face to face, I pepper him with questions about the saddling procedure. He seems shocked I'm so interested in something I'd previously blown off. I remember Mick's suggestion about flirting with Riley to get information. Would it work with Riley's dad? Even though it's against my nature, I lapse into a spasm of girlish giggles and flutter my eyelashes. Embarrassing, but it totally works.

Rathjen moves closer to me than necessary, gazes into my eyes, and patiently explains the intricacies involved in saddling a horse.

Then, comes the hard part. I actually have to do it. Because I'm busy reading Rathjen's soul instead of listening to the instructions, this takes longer than it should. By the time Bella is saddled up, I'm sure Rathjen believes I'm the ditsiest female ever born.

Despite my sore bum, the riding lesson goes smoother this time. I mount Bella who seems to know I'm a novice. At least I think I see a glimmer of empathy in her big, brown eyes. Rathjen leads me to the corral and makes me demonstrate my ability to start, stop, neck rein, etc. He even tests me by leaving me alone in the corral with the gate open while he saddles up Pete. I fight off a panic attack and speak soothingly to Bella who twitches her ears in annoyance, but doesn't bolt for the barn.

Our first trail ride goes swimmingly until we're on our way back. Bella, whose patience has run out, decides enough is enough. We crest the hill leading to the ranch. The horse is keenly aware she will soon be rid of the lump of humanity on her back and breaks into a trot. It goes okay. I attempt to roll with the rhythm, even though I'm muttering, "Ow. Ow. Ow," as my aching buns take a battering. When Bella breaks into a full-out gallop, I try not to panic as the landscape whizzes by at warp speed. By the time we reach the barn, I'm still astride the horse, clinging to handfuls of horsehair and cussing a blue streak.

Rathjen is right behind me, laughing his ass off. He lifts me off the horse and sets me on the floor. My knees buckle and my butt hits the floor. He picks me up and sets me on my favorite straw bale. "Damn, girl, I'd never have guessed you knew all those words."

I gulp in some air. "Yeah, well, I thought I was going to die."

He grudgingly admits I've done well. "We'll make a horsewoman outta you yet."

After peering into his soul—and I've never seen one like it—I need more information. I ask, "Is Riley okay? He looks exhausted."

Rathjen's eyes narrow in suspicion. He folds his arms across his chest and gazes down at me as he ponders the question.

Just when I figure I've really screwed up, he answers. "Riley said you knew the girl from the gas station."

I tread carefully, not sure where this is heading. "Yes, I was acquainted with Yasmin."

Rathjen drops his gaze to the floor. Damn. "Riley thinks he was in love with the girl." He shakes his head sadly. "A Muslim girl. How crazy is that?"

I assume it's a rhetorical question and don't answer.

He lifts his head and looks into my eyes. "It's tearing him up, her body being dumped out here and all. But, he's just a kid. A teenage crush. He'll get over it."

"Did Riley ever bring her out here to, you know, meet the family?"

A muscle twitches in Rathjen's jaw. "Are you kidding me? Her family's Muslim. Riley knows how I feel about foreigners flooding into this country, popping out a bunch of kids, taking jobs away from white people. Hell, her family could be terrorists for all we know."

I see a streak of yellow flash across his soul and know his strongly held beliefs are fear based. Even though I'm certain the Ayoobs are not terrorists, I don't argue with him.

"Any idea who might have killed her?"

A blotch of fiery anger bounces through his soul. "You think I haven't answered that question a million times? Just because her body was found in Red Ridge doesn't mean my family had anything to do with her death."

"I suppose they have to ask since she and Riley wanted to be together."

"Well, they weren't together. No way. And it's not about Riley and her. It's all about my blog. Americans

First. Just because I'm exercising my right to free speech, the cops—even the feds—think I had something to do with her death."

I see he's getting riled up and, besides, I have the info I need, soul-wise.

I rise from the straw bale. "Hope things get settled soon."

He blinks rapidly and switches gears. "You need a few more lessons, so come back soon."

I assure him I will and head out to Buttercup. Before I climb in, Riley pulls in behind me.

He waves at his dad and asks me, "Got time for a cold drink?"

"Sure."

We walk together to the barn.

"How did it go today," he says.

"Better." I'll let his father fill him in on the hilarious details. "How was school?"

"Okay," he says.

He fetches the soft drinks serving them, once again, in the metal bucket. We sit side by side on the straw bale. It's rapidly becoming my favorite easy chair. Maybe I should buy one from the Rathjens and put it in Number10.

Riley still looks exhausted. I take a sip and ask, "Just okay? School, I mean."

He leans forward, braces one elbow on his knee and rubs his temples. "Can't concentrate. All I can think about is her. Yasmin. I miss her so damn much."

My heart is breaking for Riley. In spite of what his dad said, his relationship with Yasmin was not a teenage crush. He truly loved her.

"Tell me about her."

He gulps and swipes at his eyes. "She was beautiful and smart. So smart. She made me want to be a better person and..." his voice cracks with emotion. He buries his face in the crook of his arm, trying hard not to cry.

I slip an arm around his shoulder. "Believe me, I know how hard it is. My twin sister died when I was six. We were inseparable."

He lifts his head and gazes into my eyes. The pain in his soul is almost more than I can bear. "When your sister died, how did you deal with it?"

"Not well. I thought I caused it. I threw a ball over her head. She ran out into the street, and a car hit her. I was really screwed up for a long time. Maybe I still am."

As I say the words, I realize the burden of guilt I've been carrying around for years has lightened. Maybe Steve's little therapy session did me some good. "It's true what they say, though. The pain eases with time and you survive."

I know the words are trite, but it's what he needs to hear right now. "Yasmin will always be in your heart. Your job right now is to become the person she wanted you to be."

"I'm trying."

His body stiffens. I see a spark of anger flash through his soul. "I'll tell you what's screwed up. If we wanted to spend time together, she had to lie to her family and sneak out. I did too."

"Sounds hard," I murmur.

"Hard? Try impossible." He springs up and gives the empty bucket a vicious kick. It flies across the barn and bounces off Sneaky Pete's stall. The horse emits an irritated snort.

Face flushed with anger, he folds his arms across his chest. Exactly the same pose I'd seen from his father earlier. "It's the God damn, friggin' twenty-first century! What's wrong with people? We just wanted to be together."

I lift my hands helplessly. I can't think of a single thing I can say to comfort him. He simply fell in love with the wrong girl, a fact of which he's painfully aware.

His rage fades away and he plops down next to me. He turns his head and gives me an assessing look, as if deciding whether or not to trust me.

I grab his hand and give it a squeeze. I have about a bajillion questions I want to ask, but bite my lip to keep them from spilling out.

He takes a deep breath, lets it out. He glances over his shoulder at the open barn door and lowers his voice. "We were going to take off. Yasmin and me. It was all planned out. We figured if we spent a couple of nights, um, you know, together, her dad would make us get married."

"Married?" I repeat. "Really? You're kind of young to get married."

"It was the only way we could be together."

I don't say the obvious, like "Where would you live?" "How would you live?" "What about money?" Instead, I ask, "When?"

His face tightens. "The night she got killed."

Before I can say a word, Riley's father stomps into the barn, and Riley leaps to his feet. Rathjen says, "Riley. Your mom wants you inside."

Riley's expression turns defiant. He gives his dad a

126

curt nod. "I'll be there in a minute."

Rathjen walks into the tack room. He leaves the door open, making sure he's well within earshot.

Riley blows out a disgusted breath, grips my hand and pulls me off the straw bale. "Come on. I'll walk you to the Mustard Mobile."

In my best ditsy female voice, I chirp, "Bye, Mr. Rathjen. Thanks for the lesson."

Riley looks puzzled, but Rathjen gives me a lustful grin. "Yeah, see ya next time, Queenie."

I'm feeling slightly schizophrenic. When I deal with Rick Rathjen, I'm a foxy little airhead. My role with Riley is that of a supportive, sympathetic sister. And, those two are only half of the family. I haven't met sister Rachel or had the opportunity for a good, long look into Mama Rathjen's soul yet. When this gig is over, I'll be the one who needs therapy.

Chapter Nineteen

I zip back to Number Ten, take a shower to wash off the horsey smell, and call Paco. When he answers, I hear the distinctive sound of idling motorcycles in the background.

"Can you talk now?"

"Hold on," he says. His voice is muffled, but I hear him say, "So you're all set, guys? Need anything, give me a call."

The throaty purr accelerates to a roar and then fades into the distance.

"What can I do for you, kiddo?"

"What's the scoop on Rebecca Porter. Am I in danger?"

"If you were in danger, I'd have called you," he says. "I tailed her at different times of the day. In the morning, she goes to her fitness club and meets her friend for coffee."

"Every day? The same friend?"

"Same friend, every day. A muscular chick with coal-black hair. Every time they say goodbye, they hug. It's weird."

"Weird, how? Lots of women hug each other."

"Not like they do."

"Spit it out, Unc. Do you think they're lesbian lovers or what?"

"It's crossed my mind."

I ponder the information. Paco is a pretty good judge of character. I remember Louise telling me Rebecca had been previously married. Maybe she decided to switch teams after her experience with the male gender "Could be a good thing," I say. "If she has a relationship going, maybe she won't try to kill my ass. What does she do in the afternoon?"

"Not much. I followed her to Trader Joe's a couple of times."

"Okay, I guess you don't need to waste anymore of your time. Thanks."

"Anytime, little girl," he says. "By the way, your mother called me. She's all psyched about the wedding. She told me to put Aida on the phone, and they talked for an hour." He heaves a martyred sigh and curses in Spanish. "Now we have *LA LISTA*, the list. In case you couldn't tell, it's in capital letters. Dress. Flowers. Bridesmaids, of which you're one. The works."

"Sorry, Paco. I was trying to distract her. I told her about Billy and I breaking up."

Paco chuckles. "And she was ready to come up here and rip him a new one."

"Yep."

"Not a bad idea. Gotta go. Come see us."

I assure him I will. Before we click off, he says, "Hold on a sec. One more thing. Your Homeland Security buddy, Mick, has the hots for you."

"Yeah, yeah, I know."

"Hey, he's a good guy. Give him a chance. Bye."

He hangs up before my rebuttal can begin.

I breathe a little easier knowing Rebecca Porter is not a threat. I'll start jogging again. Tomorrow.

Next on my list. Mick.

I punch in his number and expect it to go to voicemail, as it usually does.

He picks up on the third ring. His voice has a sexy rumble. "Hi. How are you, *kotik*?"

"This is Mel. Whoever this kotik person is, it is definitely not me."

"Oh, I knew it was you. Your number shows on my phone."

"So, why didn't you say, 'How are you, Mel?'"

"*Kotik* is a Russian term of endearment."

"I'm not your dear. What does it mean?"

"Pussycat."

I give a little shriek of horror. "I am definitely not your pussycat."

When he speaks, I hear the amusement in his voice. "Fine. How about *kotyonok*? It means kitten. Better?"

I don't dignify this with an answer. Time to change the subject. "Are you still in 3 Peaks?"

"Coming your way. I've been in southern Oregon."

The Homeland Security office is located in Portland and undermanned. The agents are stretched thin with the entire state of Oregon to cover.

"I had a look into Rick Rathjen's soul today. I also connected with Riley."

I'm ready to launch into my story when he says, "Save it for later. I have news for you too. I'll tell you about it over dinner. It's a nice place. Wear a dress."

"I don't have a dress, and I'm working tonight."

"No, you're not. I talked to your boss."

"You what?" I snap. "Since when do you get to micro manage my schedule?"

"You're also working for us. Homeland Security takes precedence over your job at the pub."

I'm at a rare loss for words but manage to sputter, "Well, maybe I'll quit working for Homeland Security."

"Oh, really" He feigns surprise. "Guess you're not interested in hearing what I have to say about Eddie Morgan."

I grit my teeth in frustration. Mick knows how to push my buttons. Still, I have to object to save my pride. "I'm pretty sure your statement constitutes emotional blackmail. It's unethical and probably against the rules."

"Remember, I'm Homeland Security. We have no rules."

"I really, really hate you."

With a bark of laughter, he says, "But you really, really love my soul."

****

Mick and I are in the Riverfront Steakhouse, the ritziest restaurant in 3 Peaks. We're seated next to a window overlooking the Deschutes River. The trees bordering the river are backlit by the setting sun, their brilliantly colored leaves glow in multi-faceted shades of red and gold. A sudden gust of wind blows a smattering of dry leaves against our window. We watch a few hardy souls paddling their kayaks downstream, hanging on to the last bit of decent weather before the coming of winter.

Mick lifts his glass of Grey Goose in salute and gives me a thorough visual inspection. His blue-eyed gaze is laser sharp. "You look nice."

I nod my thanks and sip the glass of white wine the snobby server presented like it was nectar of the gods. He'd poured a couple of drips into the glass and encouraged me to sniff and swirl before I was allowed to imbibe.

"Pretty dress," he adds.

"Seven ninety-nine at the thrift store."

After Mick tempted me with the Eddie Morgan morsel, I caved. Even though it's against my principles to give in to bribery, adding a dress to my wardrobe isn't a huge deal. Every girl needs a little black dress. Right? And this one fits me like a glove. The only dress available in my size, the front dips down a bit lower than I like. Mick seems to be enjoying it a lot. Men are such simple creatures.

"Did Billy ever bring you here?"

"No."

Although I'm not sharing the info with Mick, Billy and I spent most of our time in Number Ten having sex. I'm beginning to realize our relationship was one dimensional, not to mention, doomed.

I wait until the server delivers our salads before I speak. "Okay, I'm here and I'm wearing a dress. Tell me about Eddie."

Even though we're seated away from other diners, Mick looks around the room and lowers his voice. "You first. No negotiations."

I have two choices. I can refuse to spill the beans until Mick tells me about Eddie. Or, I can get it over with. From the set of his jaw, I know Mick is willing to wait me out, until dawn arrives if necessary. The only reason I hesitate is because he always gets the upper hand. Just once, I'd like to be on top, so to speak.

I hold up a finger and shovel in some salad, making him wait until I chew and swallow. He watches me eat. The corner of his mouth curls upward in a victorious smirk.

I set my fork down. "Rick Rathjen's soul is unlike any I've ever seen. It has all three primary colors, red, blue, and yellow. His particular shade of red indicates an aggressive masculine nature. It's streaked with yellow, which tells me he's fearful and anxious. As I've said before, markers on the soul indicate history and intent. Rathjen's soul has a dark blue border. At one point, it is intersected with a jagged line, so I know he's experienced a severe trauma in the past. Naturally, I couldn't ask about it. Whatever it was casts a long shadow and affects his present actions, and it will likely continue to influence the future."

I pause and take a breath. "Maybe you can check into his background."

Mick nods. "Did the Ayoob girl come up in the conversation?"

"Riley told his dad I knew Yasmin. When I asked if he had any idea who might have killed her, he launched into a rant about law enforcement bugging him. His soul was on fire with anger, but I saw no indication of a lie."

Mick leans forward. His gaze is so intense, I almost wonder if he can see inside my soul. "Is it possible the flashes of anger you saw in his soul masked the lies?"

"I know what his lies look like. He lied to me earlier about something totally unrelated to Yasmin."

I feel my face heat up as I think about Rathjen's not-so-subtle lustful ogling of my body. Not to mention his habit of feeling me up under the guise of teaching me horsemanship.

Mick immediately picks up on my discomfort. Looking amused, he leans back in his chair and takes a sip of vodka. "So now we have another person trying to get in your panties."

It's a statement, not a question. He's absolutely right and it ticks me off. "Another person? You mean, besides you?"

He smiles. "Melanie, I have made no attempt to hide my feelings for you. Naturally, I want to know if there's another player in the game."

"You think this is a game?" My voice has an edge. Not the gravitas I intended my words to convey. Still, I soldier on and hold up my pointer finger. "First of all, there is no game."

My middle finger joins the first, even though I'd like it to be the only digit pointing skyward. "Number two. Rick Rathjen is a husband and father, therefore off limits, not to mention he's a man who holds radically conservative views, far different from my own." My ring finger rises. "Number three. If you think I am in any way attracted to him, you are seriously mistaken."

The instant the words leave my mouth, I realize they may be interpreted incorrectly. I hasten to add, "I'm not saying this to encourage you. It's simply a point of clarification."

His grin widens. "Got it."

Further discussion is squelched by the server, who delivers our entrees with a flourish. Before we can dig in, an underling appears wielding an enormous pepper mill.

Alone again, all conversation ceases as we dig into our food, which, by the way, is awesomely delicious. When we come up for air, Mick asks, "So. Rick Rathjen. Bottom line."

I dab steak juice from my lips. "He's an angry

man, but I don't see murder in his soul. When I asked him if he had any idea who killed Yasmin, he didn't give me a direct answer. It's possible he went on a rant because he's protecting someone." I shake my head. "Sorry, his soul confuses me. I'll talk to Steve. He may have some insights."

"You're sure it's not the kid?"

"Riley didn't kill her, but he has more to tell me. I'm sure of it."

Mick reaches across the table and pats my hand. "Good job, my *kotyonok*. We at Homeland Security appreciate your patriotism. Is your ass up to a few more riding lessons?"

I can't help it. I laugh at his ridiculous statement. He's thanking me on behalf of my country, yet calling me his kitten and inquiring about my sore ass. I wonder what his boss would say.

"Actually," I say, "I'm becoming quite an accomplished equestrian, but a few more lessons probably wouldn't hurt."

He looks skeptical. "You are now an accomplished equestrian? Perhaps we should go on a trail ride for our second date."

"This is not a date. We're two colleagues discussing a case."

"Dream on."

A long silence ensues. Finally, I say, "Tell me about Eddie."

Before he can say a word, his cell phone buzzes. He looks at the display. "Sorry, gotta take this."

He stands and walks to the window, looking out at the darkening sky. I hear a few monosyllabic responses. Grim-faced, he returns to the table. When he looks at me, I see dark blue streaks of sadness in his soul. It scares me.

He says quietly, "Yasmin was three months pregnant."

Chapter Twenty

We ride back to Number Ten in silence. My heart is breaking for Riley and Yasmin. It's obvious they were able to sneak away from their parents for at least one rendezvous. Maybe more. I'm wondering if Riley knew she was pregnant. Even though Mick likes to pretend he's impervious to feelings, I can tell by looking into his soul, he's also affected by the information.

Finally, I break the silence. "Riley said he and Yasmin were planning to run away together the night she was killed."

Mick gives me a sharp look. "What else haven't you told me?"

Okay, he's now morphed into Mr. Homeland Security with trust issues. "I was going to tell you once I heard the whole story. Riley clammed up when his dad came into the barn."

Mick parks in front of Number Ten and turns the engine off. He tells me, "When I questioned the kid, he said he and his dad were on a camping trip. His family backed him up. I wonder what else they're lying about."

I place a hand on his arm. "Please don't blow my cover until I have a chance to talk to Riley again."

Mick turns his head to look at me. His face, cast in shadow, is all hard angles. The intensity of his gaze awakens the memory of another night. Mick and I are alone in a car. I'm trussed up like a Thanksgiving turkey, certain I'm in the hands of a stone killer. I'm wondering if anyone will find my body after he dumps me like yesterday's garbage.

An involuntary shiver runs down my spine. I remove my hand.

When he speaks, Mick's voice is flat and devoid of emotion. "How do I know you're telling me what I need to know? You and Riley have obviously bonded. Are you protecting him?"

I reach for the car door. "I have no reason to lie to you."

He grabs my arm. "Even if you find out the kid's a killer?"

I jerk free. "Yes, even if I find out Riley's a killer." *But he's not.*

Boiling with anger, I slip out of the car. Before I shut the door, Mick says, "Don't you want to know about Eddie Morgan?"

I stop in mid-slam, muttering curses under my breath. I may have even thrown in his favorite, *chodit.* Wasn't Eddie Morgan the reason I agreed to spend time with this guy?

I point at Number Ten. "Guess you'd better come in."

He follows me through the door, and we sit at the table. He says, "You're probably not going to like what I have to say."

I've experienced the entire gamut of emotions throughout this strange evening. I'm all out of patience.

"Tell me," I snap.

Mick reaches across the table and takes my hand.

"Please, just listen. Let me start by saying, it's the best I can do. I'm sure you remember Myron."

The mere mention of the name causes me to snatch my hand away. Myron, who tied me to an examination table in a medical clinic and threatened to do unspeakable things to my helpless body. I try very hard not to think about him. Ever. But sometimes Myron appears in my nightmares, waving his razor sharp hunting knife. When that happens, I awake in a sweat until I remember he's safely behind bars.

"There's no way I'll ever forget Myron. What about him?"

Mick says, "He says he knows Eddie's secrets."

"And?"

"He's willing to trade prison time for information."

My blood stops boiling as an icy fist of fear grips my heart. I wrap my fingers around the edge of the table to keep them from shaking. "How much prison time?"

"If we make the deal, Myron won't die in prison. He'll still be locked up for a good, long time. One of the murder charges will be dropped to a lesser degree. We've already got him on several kidnappings, including yours. He'll be in prison for at least twenty-five years, providing he has good conduct which I very much doubt."

The panic Myron's name triggered is clouding my judgment. I take a couple of deep breaths. Mick's right. I don't like making a deal with the devil. In order to nail Eddie for Dani's death, Myron, who's rotten to the core, gets his prison sentence reduced.

"Did Myron say Eddie killed Dani?"

Mick says, "When I went over the transcript of his

questioning, I noticed somebody dropped the ball. Eddie Morgan's name never came up. I talked to Myron yesterday and asked about Eddie. He may be a cold-blooded killer, but he's no fool. He'd finger his own mother if he thought it would shorten his jail time. He claims he has solid proof implicating Eddie in his wife's death."

"Do you believe him?"

"Yes, but it's not my call. It's yours."

I gnaw on my lower lip a while. "I'll think about it."

"Since Eddie's moving away, you'd better decide soon."

I stand and stare down at Mick. "I'll sleep on it."

He walks around the table and folds me into his arms. Gently stroking my back, he says, "I know you're afraid of me. Please believe me when I say I will never hurt you, physically or in any other way."

Hot tears spring into my eyes. I blubber into his neck. "Then why do you always say, 'We have no rules?' What am I supposed to think?"

I feel laughter rumble deep in his chest. His hands drop lower, dipping beneath my skirt. Now, he's massaging my buns and they're still sore, so, damn, it feels good. "*Malysh*, it's just what we in Homeland Security say. Do not concern yourself with the semantics."

Against all my principles, I relax against his muscular body. I don't bother to ask what *malysh* means. After pussycat and kitten, I know it can't be good. Unbidden, my arms encircle his neck. After a long, blissful moment, he picks me up and crosses to the bed. He whips the covers back and lays me down.

After dropping a chaste kiss on my forehead, he says, "I'll call you tomorrow."

He reaches for the door, turns and gives me a brief salute, grinning when he sees the look of disappointment on my face.

"Nighty night," he says. "Sleep well."

****

After a fitful sleep (thank you, Mick) I'm up early, attending to chores I've neglected. Two hours later, the laundry is done, the bed has fresh sheets, my itty-bitty rug is vacuumed and my bathroom fixtures sparkle like diamonds.

Feeling righteous, I head out for a jog. Because Nick's Sports Bar and Motel is on the corner of a busy intersection, I run through the parking lot and head for the next side street, the one that leads to a residential, less traffic-intensive area. My mind is a million miles away, free-floating as I decide what to do about the Myron/Eddie Morgan issue.

Who am I kidding? My whole reason for moving to 3 Peaks was to be with Dani. Didn't Kendra and I make a pinkie promise? Didn't we ambush Eddie at the Ponderosa in Pine Village, so we could nail him to the proverbial cross? Even though Myron will get a lighter sentence, Dani's death will be vindicated.

I decide not to wait until Mick calls me. I pull the phone from my pocket and punch in his number. Since I'm the mistress of multi-tasking, I keep on jogging.

"Yeah?" he answers, sounding distracted.

"Can you talk?"

"Make it fast. I'm on a stake-out and my guy is getting ready to run."

"About Eddie Morgan and Myron," I begin. I'm

puffing now, trying to keep up my pace and talk on the phone simultaneously. Maybe I'm not the mistress of multi-tasking after all. I stop and lean against a light pole, gasping for air. "Go for it. Nail the big bastard. While you're at it, go talk to his neighbor, an old guy named Hank Peterson. He keeps a journal every day and he's no fan of Eddie."

Mick growls, "What the hell are you doing? All I hear is heavy breathing. You back with Billy?"

I make a disgusted sound. "I'm jogging, you idiot. Did you hear what I said?"

"Got it."

I hear another voice in the background. Mick says, "I'll call you back."

I click off and push away from the light post, resuming my run. I'm trying to decide if I've made the right decision about Eddie when I hear the sound of a big engine coming closer. I glance over my shoulder. A black SUV with tinted windows is creeping along behind me. Glittering shafts of sunlight bounce off the windshield, obscuring my view of the driver. I run a little faster. The SUV keeps pace.

I'm getting a little freaked out, so I stop and turn around, fixing my gaze on the car. Sadly, my wish for no traffic has been granted. The street's utterly deserted except for the two of us. Me and the SUV. Even the houses seem shuttered. It seems everyone in the neighborhood is at work or school.

I'm toying with the idea of approaching the vehicle when the engine revs and the driver hits the gas. The big car leaps forward and swerves toward me, its front wheels gaining purchase on the sidewalk. Screaming in terror, I break into a sprint, stepping off the sidewalk onto the closest front lawn. I feel the heat of the engine and do a tuck and roll to the left. The front bumper missed me by inches. I'm still screaming for help when the car backs up and takes another run at me. I scramble to my feet, but this time I'm not as lucky. It's a glancing blow, but the impact lifts me from my feet, and I sail through the air toward a concrete retaining wall. My left hand reaches out to cushion the coming blow. My right hand curls around the open-heart necklace, and I hear a child's voice cry, "No!"

My world turns black.

Chapter Twenty-One

My mouth, so dry it feels lined with cracked leather…my previously injured elbow throbs in time with the ache in my head. Something circling my left arm, squeezes and hisses like a poisonous snake. Hushed male voices murmur in the background.

Do I want to open my eyes? Much easier to stay submerged, wrapped in a billowy cloud of blissful oblivion. I opt for the former and struggle through thick, gray fog to consciousness. Lifting my heavy eyelids is so difficult, I almost change my mind.

Then, I hear, "I think she's waking up."

It's Uncle Paco's voice. I open my eyes. His face is inches from mine. He grips my hand in his giant paw. His voice booms, "Are you okay? Can you hear me?"

I wince at the volume of his tone. "Dammit, Paco, I'm not deaf."

He grins, turns his head and says, "Yeah, she's okay."

Paco vanishes. I try to lift my head but it hurts. I hear somebody say, "Crank up the head of her bed."

Another male voice says, "No, she's supposed to lie flat."

An argument in hushed tones follows.

Paco's face re-appears, accompanied by a crabby looking nurse who pushes him to one side, bends close, and peers into my eyes. "So, waking up, are we?"

I mutter, "Not sure about you, but yes, I'm waking up. Can I sit up now?"

"No, you had a head injury."

"When can I get out of this place?"

She frowns down at me. "I'll page the doctor."

She says the word doctor like it starts with a capital D. She swishes out of the room.

Paco's back, along with Billy and Mick. They all stare down at me like I'm the eighth wonder of the world.

I focus on Paco. "Please tell me you didn't call Sandra."

He lifts his cell phone in front of my face. The display shows my mother's number. "If you hadn't come around in the next five minutes, it was my next call. I did call Steve, though. He's on his way."

I make eye contact with Billy and Mick. "Why are you two here? Don't you have work to do?"

The two exchange a glance. Mick gives me his steely blue-eyed gaze. "Stop asking questions. We're here because we care about you."

Paco chuckles. "I'd say she's acting pretty normal for someone who just got hit by a car."

Hit by a car? The brain fog begins to lift as my fractured mind tries to connect the dots. Why am I lying in a hospital bed? The memory comes back in a flood of disturbing images. I hear the big engine rev. Smell the burning fuel. I see the grill of the car bearing down on me, certain I'm about to die. Terror. Unadulterated terror.

As the memories return, I gasp. I feel my heart pounding against my ribcage like a frightened bird trapped in a closet.

Paco leans close and whispers, "You're safe now, little girl. Don't worry, Uncle Paco's on the job. Whoever did this to you will soon be sorry."

Paco's words calm my troubled mind. I take a couple of shaky breaths and will my racing heart to settle down.

Paco steps back. Billy leans over me. I look in his eyes. His soul is streaked with sadness. He says, "Kendra said to tell to tell you she'd be here but she doesn't have a sitter. She'll call later." He blinks hard and continues, "I know you're still mad at me, but I'm here for you. Okay?"

Billy being nice. I can't handle it, especially in my weakened condition. Tears fill my eyes. I nod, even though it hurts my head.

I hear footsteps approaching the bed. Paco, Mick, and Billy step back. Doctor? No, it's bio dad, Steve. He's carrying a ceramic pot of colorful flowers, anchoring a red and blue balloon.

He sets the flowers on the bedside table and leans over the bed. Takes my hand. *"Mi hija,* you gave us such a scare. What happened?"

"Big car," I say. "SUV. Chased me down the sidewalk like a wolf stalking a lamb."

As I gaze into eyes so much like my own, another memory surfaces. I whisper, "I have something to tell you I don't want the others to hear."

Steve leans closer.

"I heard her," I say. "It was Hope. She spoke to me."

Steve's eyes widen in surprise.

"Just before the car hit me, I grabbed on to the open heart locket. It was then I heard her scream, "No!""

Steve lifts his head. His eyes now swim with tears. "Remember what I told you on your birthday. If you open your heart and mind to the possibility, Hope will reach out to you. Who knows, she may have kept you from being killed."

"Maybe," I agree. "I wonder why the driver didn't finish me off after I hit the wall."

"Good question," Steve says.

He turns to Mick. "Anybody know what happened after the car hit her?"

Mick says, "Apparently, the driver was going to take another run at her. The neighbor across the street looked out and saw a little girl come out of the house where Mel was lying on the front lawn. The driver of the SUV must have noticed the child and took off."

Steve said, "I assume you went to the scene. What did you find out."

"The neighbor wasn't able to get the tag number of the car. She said the house where Mel was hit is for sale. Unoccupied."

Steve and I make eye contact. He whispers, "Hope."

I feel for the locket. It's not around my neck.

Steve opens the drawer of my bedside table and pulls out a plastic bag containing my personal items. He extricates the locket and places it in my hand. As my fingers close around it, I feel a warm breeze sweep over me. The red balloon bumps gently against the blue one before rising in the air, settling against the ceiling directly over my bed.

Steve gives me a wink. "Knot must have come loose."

I gaze up at the red balloon bobbing overhead and

feel Hope's presence. The sensation is much like being swaddled in a warm, fluffy blanket. My eyelids droop. It's impossible to keep them open.

Steve brushes a kiss across my forehead and whispers, "You're safe now, beautiful girl. Your sister is watching over you."

Barely awake, I hear Steve's footsteps as he exits the room.

I really, really want everybody to leave so I can sleep, but it is not to be. I hear Mick, Paco and Billy conversing in low tones and catch a few words. Words like Eddie, Myron, Dani. I vaguely remember talking to Mick before the massive SUV bore down on me. Struggling to patch together the jagged holes in my memory serves as a wake-up call.

My eyes spring open, and I prop myself up on one elbow. "Mick, did I tell you to go forward with the Myron/Eddie thing or did I dream it?"

All three men crowd around my bed. Mick presses me back to a prone position. "You're supposed to lie flat. And, yes, you called me. Don't worry about it. I'm on it."

Billy's face appears in my line of vision. "Mick just filled me in on Eddie's neighbor. I'll go have a chat with him."

"He keeps a daily journal, and he despises Eddie. Win-win situation," I say, adding, "Thanks, Billy."

Paco pushes his way through Mick and Billy and stares down at me, his eyebrows drawn together in a fierce frown. He leans close. "I've gotta go—business to take care of. Call when you get kicked out of here, and I'll pick you up. Not on the Harley, of course. I'll bring the car."

He lumbers away, clearly a man on a mission. Before he reaches the door, he halts. "Almost forgot. Chuy's right here, outside your door. He'll be sticking to you like glue for the duration."

"Chuy?" I repeat.

"Yeah," Paco says. "If somebody's out to get you, you need protection." He tilts his head toward Mick and Billy. "I doubt these guys have the manpower. No problem. I do."

Billy's jaw drops in surprise. Mick's eyes narrow in suspicion.

"Hey, Chuy," Paco says. "I'm leaving now. Come on in and keep an eye on my girl. I'll be back soon."

He makes a beckoning motion, and Chuy steps through the door. He's a good eight inches shorter than Paco, but built like a fireplug. A blue doo rag covers his head. A chain dangles from one pocket of his baggy jeans. Motorcycle boots and a black leather vest over a white Los Habañeros T-shirt complete the outfit. He flashes me a smile enhanced by a shiny gold incisor. His dark gaze flicks to the two law enforcement men. He mumbles something in Spanish to Paco who nods and leaves.

Chuy saunters across the room and settles into the chair in the corner. He slumps down, crosses his arms across his chest, his hooded gaze fixed on me.

Billy and Mick have apparently lost their ability to speak, so I take the bull by the horns. "Looks like you two can go back to work. Paco will come get me when I get discharged."

A deep male voice says, "Nobody's getting discharged today."

The voice belongs to a tall, slender man in a blue

dress shirt and tan khakis. He crosses to the bed followed by a nurse who casts nervous glances at Chuy.

"I'm Dr. Pritchard," he says. His gaze drifts from Mick, to Billy, and lastly, to Chuy. "Would you gentleman please leave the room so I can examine Ms. Sullivan."

Billy says, "I'll let you know what I find out from the neighbor."

I nod my thanks.

Mick leans close, his lips next to my ear. "I'll be back tonight."

Billy and Mick head for the door followed by Chuy who keeps an eagle eye on Pritchard in case the good doctor has plans to snuff me in my hospital bed. When I see the last of the men, I breathe a sigh of relief. I'm grateful they care, but the testosterone overload was making the oxygen thin.

The doc pulls the curtain around the bed and tells the nurse, "Let's take a look."

She pulls the sheet back and peels back my hospital gown under which I'm buck-naked. The doctor's touch is gentle as he probes my innards and runs his fingers over my ribs. "Bruised but not broken," he murmurs. "Painful, but you'll live."

"Good to know," I answer.

He pulls a penlight from his pocket and shines it into my eyes. "Guess you know you had a gash in your head. They sewed it up in the ER."

News to me. I lift a hand and pat my hair, surprised when my fingers locate a bald patch bisected by rough stitches.

I whisper, "Will my hair grow back?" Vanity, thy name is Melanie.

The nurse says, "Oh, honey, not to worry. As thick as your hair is, it will cover the scar."

Pritchard nods, his eyes crinkling in amusement. "Don't worry. You won't be the bald lady in the circus."

He completes his exam. "We're keeping you overnight. You're pretty beat up, but it's the head injury we need to keep an eye on. I'll check on you in the morning. Then, we'll see."

"If I can go home?" I urge.

He won't commit. "We'll see," he repeats.

The nurse covers me up. They leave, and Chuy slinks back into the room.

I drift off to sleep but wake up screaming in terror as my troubled dreams conjure up a vision of the black SUV bearing down on me. I swear I hear the roar of the engine, smell the tires burning rubber, see death staring me in the face.

Chuy pulls his chair over to the bed, murmurs to me in Spanish, and hums a soothing melody in a sweet baritone voice.

I take a shaky breath, place a hand over my pounding heart, willing it to slow down. I lift my eyes to the ceiling where the red balloon hovers directly above me. I feel Hope's presence, and a sense of calm steals over me. Even so, I don't sleep for a long, long time.

Chapter Twenty-Two

At 10:00 the next morning, Dr. Pritchard gives me the green light, but not without dire warnings. "If you get frequent headaches or double vision, call me."

I assure him I will and reach for my phone to call Paco. Chuy is still glued to the visitor chair, but tells me in convoluted Spanglish he has only his Harley which Paco does not consider an appropriate form of transportation for an individual with a head injury.

Before I can punch in Paco's number, Mick strides into the room. "Sorry I didn't make it last night. I'm here to take you home."

"Not necessary. I was about to call Paco."

Chuy nods. "*Si*, Paco come."

Mick rattles off some Spanish, too fast for me to understand. But Chuy gets the message. He shrugs and tells me, "I wait in hall. Follow you home."

I see Mick is about to object, but I glare him into silence.

Being discharged from a hospital is a lesson in patience. However, when the billing department discovers Steve had arranged to pay all charges, things move along faster. Also, Mick flashes his homeland security creds. Shortly after, a nurse's aide arrives with a wheelchair, loads me in, and guides me to the front door with my entourage, Mick and Chuy, trailing behind.

Mick's car is in the loading zone, passenger door open. I spring from the wheelchair and climb in as Chuy sprints off to claim his bike.

Mick says, "Hold on," and punches the accelerator.

My head snaps back. "What the hell? Are you trying to lose Chuy? He knows where I live."

"You don't need him. I'll make sure you're safe."

I sigh. How did my life get so complicated? I know the answer. Too damn many men trying to take care of me.

"Mick," I say. "You don't understand. Paco is my uncle. As such, he feels it is his responsibility to watch out for me. It's never going to change. Chuy is part of Paco's crew. All of Paco's guys have great respect for him and most likely, a healthy dash of fear. If he gives an order, they will carry it out even if it puts them in danger. Therefore, Chuy is now in my life whether I like it or not. That's how it is. So, if you can't handle it, feel free to say, 'adios.'"

Mick looks over at me with a scowl and mutters something in Russian. I bite my lip to keep from laughing. Fifteen minutes later, we pull up in front of Number Ten with Chuy riding our back bumper.

I open the door. "Thanks, Mick. See you around."

"I have to get back to work, but I want to clear up a couple of things first. Can I come in?"

Actually, I'm longing for a hot shower to wash off the hospital smell, followed by a butt load of greasy food at Nick's. But, it would be pretty crass to turn him down after he helped get me out of the hospital. "Sure."

He points at Chuy. "What about him?"

"Don't worry about Chuy. He'll hang out until Paco calls him off."

Mick follows me through the door and grabs a chair, resting his arms on the table top. Thanks to the acute cleaning attack I had before the accident, my tiny home looks spiffy and inviting.

"About Myron," Mick says.

I slide my bruised and battered body onto the other chair, trying not to grimace in pain. "What about him?"

"You probably know he's incarcerated at the federal prison in Sheridan, Oregon."

I stiffen in my chair. "I know he's locked up. Don't care where. I try not to think about him at all."

"Here's the deal," Mick says. "He says he has solid proof of Eddie's involvement in the wife's death, but he's only willing to talk to one person. You."

My heart kicks up a beat. I clasp my hands together to keep them from shaking. There's a scared little girl quality to my voice when I speak. "Me. All by myself. At the federal prison in Sheridan."

Mick's eyes narrow. "Yeah, I know. But, you'll be safe. Myron will be shackled and chained to a table. There will be guards watching."

It's then I realize what Mick is not saying, and I'm ashamed of myself. I've nagged him unmercifully for months, trying to get him to look into Dani's death. Now, he has. The ball's in my court, and I'm acting like a wimp, wallowing in my victim role. I've been a coward. The mere mention of Myron's name sent me scurrying away to hide in my dark place, quivering in fear like a child caught in a nightmare. Even worse, I'd stuffed the fear away, scared to death to face it.

No more.

Mick says, "You don't have to do this, *myska*. You can let him rot in prison for the rest of his life. Probably best for the rest of the world."

I so want to know what *myska* means, but will save my inquiry for later.

I lean across the table and stare into Mick's eyes. "Dani. Her name was Dani, not the wife. And, yes, I'll go to Sheridan. I'll face the bastard, and he better damn well give me the proof. Because, I know Eddie killed her, and I won't give up until he's behind bars."

The corners of Mick's mouth quirk up in a smile. "That's my girl."

He lifts a hand. I slap it and smile back at him. "Are we done?"

Mick's intense gaze is locked on me like a heat-seeking missile. "Not quite," he says.

"What?"

"I guess it's no secret I'm attracted to you."

Hmmm, so it's going to be one of those talks. "I'm aware."

"Is it over with Billy?"

"Yes, why do you ask?"

"I don't want to be the bounce guy."

"The what?" English is Mick's second language. Sometimes a translation is necessary.

"You know," he says, "The guy you turn to because you miss the first one."

The light bulb in my brain flicks on. "You mean, like on the rebound?"

"Yeah, that."

I feel a headache coming on. I really don't want to have this conversation right now. Maybe if I keep my mouth shut, he'll get the hint.

He doesn't. Instead he bumbles on, "Plus, I don't like to share."

Anger sparks to life, fueled by pain and his unfortunate choice of words. I feel my face heat up and smack the tabletop with the flat of my hand, which makes the pain in my head worse.

Mick looks amused. It puts me over the edge.

"Share?" I repeat. "As in now you own me and want to make sure I'm not sleeping with Billy or some other guy who leaves a nice fat tip after I serve him dinner?"

"Why are you so prickly?"

"Why are you such a damn chauvinistic pig?"

He's struck dumb for a moment and then lifts a hand in supplication. "No, no, wait. Calm down."

I stand and stare down at him, enunciating carefully. "Do-Not-Tell-Me-To-Calm-Down."

His smirk vanishes. His hands grip the back of the chair. "I'm making a mess of this. I'm just trying to say, I care about you, Honor Melanie Sullivan, and I want you to care about me."

He looks so miserable, my heart softens. "Okay, I get it. I'll talk to Billy."

His grin returns.

"Now," I say. "Please leave so I can take a shower."

He lifts a finger. "One more thing. You won't be taking riding lessons for a while, but we're still in the dark about the Yasmin Ayoob case. We backed off because you were getting close to Riley. We need to know what happened the night they planned to run off. Did he know Yasmin was pregnant? If so, maybe he wasn't ready to be a daddy and..."

The unfinished sentence hangs in the air between us. In my heart, I know Riley didn't kill Yasmin. Mick, as law enforcement, is required to look at facts, not emotions.

"I've also been wondering the same thing," I said. "But there's a problem. I can't let on I know Yasmin was pregnant without him wondering how I found out."

Mick thinks it over. "Maybe tell him your boyfriend is a cop and he told you about the autopsy."

I shake my head. "No way. If he thinks I have a pipeline into the police department, he won't trust me."

Mick's gaze sweeps over my body. He winks. "I'm sure you'll think of something. Use your charms. Works for me."

I scowl at him. "I have never knowingly used my charms on you."

"Will I know when you do?"

I flap a hand at him. "Forget about it."

Back to business, he continues, "I've got an idea how you can follow up at the ranch without actually getting on a horse. And, maybe get a look into the souls of his mother and sister as well."

"I'm all ears."

He stands, grips my chin and rotates my head, examining the organs in question.

"Actually," he concludes. "Your ears are quite small. I'm surprised you can hear."

I burst into laughter. "It's just a figure of speech, Mick. It means you have my full attention."

With a snort of irritation, he huffs, "Well, it's a very odd way of expressing it."

He fills me in on the plan, pulls out his wallet and places folded bills on the table. "That should cover it."

After he leaves I stand in a steaming hot shower for ten minutes, willing myself to do what I promised. I opt for a text, afraid I'll lose my nerve if I hear Billy's voice. Wrapped in a towel, I pick up my phone, key in, —*Wanna talk? Name time and place.*—and hit send.

I'm barely dressed when he calls. I take a deep breath before I answer. "Hi, Billy. Thought you were working and couldn't talk." No mention of my cowardice.

"Lunch break," he says. "Your place?"

I glance at the bed. Not a good idea. "We can meet at the restaurant. Come to the back door. I'll let you in."

"See ya in ten."

I run a brush through my hair, taking care not to rake it across the stitches. Chuy falls in behind me as I walk across the parking lot. When I reach the back door, I see a fat orange cat sitting on the steps, a dead mouse beneath one oversized front paw. I know Nick sometimes gives scraps to the neighborhood cats. Apparently this one has brought him a gift.

"Nice kitty," I murmur, hoping he'll move. He doesn't, so I step over him and tap on the back door. Nick opens it and glares down at me. "No way are you working today. Go rest."

I glare back at him. "I'm fine."

"No you're not. You got hit by a car, for Christ's sake. What's the matter with you, girl?"

Despite his gruffness, I know Nick means well, so I dial it down a notch. "Actually, after eating hospital food, I was hoping to grab a bite."

Nick steps back. "Why the hell didn't you say so? Get your butt in here."

Before he closes the door, he gestures at Chuy. "Is he with you?"

"Paco thinks I need a bodyguard."

"Smart man," Nick says. "Does he want to come in?"

Chuy flashes his gold tooth in a grin and shakes his head. "Chuy wait here."

I point at the cat. "He brought you a present."

"Dammit, Thunder Paws." He picks the dead rodent up by its tail and flings it into the dumpster.

"Thunder Paws, huh?" I say. "Once you feed it and name it, it's yours forever."

"Yeah, yeah," he grumbles.

As Nick and I walk through the kitchen, I fill him in on my upcoming rendezvous with Billy the Kid. He flicks on the overhead light in the dining room and points at a booth. "Sit. I'll bring you guys some food, and I'll be close by if things get out of hand."

I smile at him. "Don't worry, boss. Chances are slim to none we'll be screwing on top of the table."

He flaps a hand at me. "Not what I meant, and you know it."

Billy arrives five minutes later. Nick ushers him into the dining room before busying himself behind the bar, out of earshot, but keeping an eye on yours truly.

Billy is looking fine in his detective clothes. Leather jacket over a blue dress shirt. Pressed jeans. He slips off his jacket revealing his department issued gun in a shoulder holster. He looks semi content.. Suddenly, I feel like a slob in my jeans, Nick's Place pink tee, and spiky, uneven hair.

He sits across from me, reaches over and takes my hand. "I'm glad you texted me. I don't like ending it like we did."

Ending it. Somehow, the phrase takes me by surprise. I open my mouth, but no words come out.

What did you expect, Mel? An apology? Billy begging me to forgive him so I could play the injured party card and haughtily refuse? Do I look into his eyes...or not? Oh, man, I should have thought this through.

He gives my hand a little squeeze and releases it. "It's okay, Mel. You can look at me. I was pretty messed up for a while, but I'm working on it. I'm back in counseling."

I gaze into his clear, hazel eyes and know he's telling the truth. I force a smile. "I'm glad you're feeling better." I can't think of a single thing to say.

Fortunately, he fills the gap. "I should have paid more attention to my counselor early on. He told me I wasn't ready for a serious relationship because of the PTSD, but I didn't listen."

"And, now you are? Ready?" Oh, God, what am I saying? Sounds like I'm trying to get him back.

Hastily, I add, "I mean Haley, not me."

"Haley and I are just buddies. Nothing serious. You know, workplace buds."

Something drifts across his soul. Not a lie. I know what a lie looks like. I'm not sure what I'm seeing. Confusion? Regret? I don't want to stare, so I avert my eyes.

"Good to know," I murmur.

Our conversation winds down. Nick brings us each a steaming bowl of beef stew and crusty French bread. Billy digs in. I take a bite and set my spoon down, unable to swallow.

You wanted closure, Mel. You got it.

Or, did I? Note to self: talk to Steve about what I saw in Billy's soul.

Chapter Twenty-Three

I take it easy for the next few days. Really, I have no choice. Nick won't let me work. Chuy is steadfast in his duties and has taken up residence in Number Nine, paid for by Paco who is still mysteriously absent. I'm sure Chuy's ear is pressed against the wall all night, waiting for me to scream, "Help!" I almost hate to disappoint him. Mick too, is among the missing. Fortunately, Kendra is not.

She shows up Saturday, the day after my conversation with Billy. She taps at the door. When I open it, she slips through and whispers, "Did you know there's a gangbanger parked outside your door? He's sitting on a Harley, and he winked at me when I got out of my car."

I flop on the bed and explain the Chuy situation. She listens, nods, and then flops down beside me and takes my hand.

"Are you okay? I was so scared for you. Plus, I'm worried about Billy. He told me the PTSD came back. Big time. At least he realizes he needs help. He's back in counseling. Please don't give up on him."

I point at the stitches in my head to get her off the subject. "Let's not go there. I'm not up to it."

"Oh, sorry." Her eyes brighten. "Anyway, Craig's home, plus I've got a sitter to help with the babies. Are you up for lunch?"

As a devoted mom with a three-year-old and two babies under a year old, a couple of kid-free hours and lunch with a friend would be a real treat for Kendra. Who am I to rain on her parade?

But first, I need to fill her in on the Myron situation. I tell what I have to do to get proof of Eddie's involvement in Dani's death. Her expression ranges from surprise, to horror, to questioning. "Are you okay with this?"

I squeeze her hand. "Yes. I need to face Myron, let him know he has no power over me. Think about it. I'm free. He's behind bars."

Kendra props herself up on one elbow and gazes down at me, fire in her eyes. "I'm so proud of you, girlfriend. Damn, we're going to nail Eddie!"

She jumps up and pulls me from the bed. "This calls for a celebration. Ready for a margarita?"

"So ready."

After lunch, Kendra hands Chuy a BLT wrapped in foil and drops me off at Number Ten. She gives me a parting hug. "Let me know when you're going to Sheridan. I'll get a sitter and ride down with you."

The cat, Thunder Paws, now has his big butt parked in front of my door. I reach across him with my key card, and he gets a whiff of the leftover fish and chips in my to-go box. In a move amazingly agile for such an obese animal, he springs up and bats the to-go box from my hand. The lid flies open. The cat pounces and warns me off with a feral growl. He gulps down the remainder of my lunch, including the chips, before strolling away

"Well, damn," I mutter.

I turn to Chuy. "Did you see that? Unbelievable."

Chuy pats the bulge in his leather vest. "You want Chuy to shoot?"

"No, no," I say. "No cat killing. Guess he was hungry."

"El Gordo," Chuy says. "Too fat."

I opt for an afternoon nap after which I'm desperate for something productive to do. I call the Rockin' R Ranch. A woman whose voice I recognize as belonging to Roxanne Rathjen, answers. I identify myself and ask to speak to Riley.

"He's not here right now. Can I help you?"

"I'd like to come out and pay for my riding lessons."

After a slight hesitation, she says, "I'll send you the bill."

I sense she's about to hang up. Quickly, I slip into the ditsy persona I'd perfected while working with her husband. "Like, I'm really bad with money. I need to pay you now, 'cause, well, I don't want to spend in on something else. When your bill comes, I might be broke," I say, adding a little self-conscious titter to sound more convincing.

She heaves a put-upon sigh. "Yeah, okay. Come on out. If I'm not here, you can pay my daughter, Rachel."

Chuy is astride his motorcycle parked next to my door. I step out and fill him in on my mission. Knowing he'll insist on following me, how in the world can I explain Chuy's presence to Roxanne Rathjen?

"Chuy," I say. "Is Paco around? I need to talk to him."

Chuy lifts his hands, pretending he doesn't understand what I'm saying. I know he does. I'd tried to call Paco yesterday and the phone went straight to voice mail. Maybe it's time for play-acting. Will Chuy believe me if I pretend to talk to Paco? Worth a try.

I pull out my cell and punch in Paco's number. To my great surprise, he answers on the first ring.

"Unc," I say. "Call off your watch dog, or I'll be contacting the humane society to come and net him."

Paco chuckles. "Sounds like you're feeling better."

"I'm fine. I need to go to the ranch where I take riding lessons, and there's no way to explain Chuy."

Paco howls with laughter. "You're taking riding lessons? On a horse?"

"Long story. Has to do with Homeland Security. I'll fill you in soon. Are you in town?"

"Yeah, trying to get to the bottom of something. Let me talk to Chuy."

I hand my phone to Chuy who listens attentively, murmurs *si*, and returns the phone. "Paco. More talk."

Paco says Chuy will follow me out to the ranch and wait out on the road until I'm done.

"Not necessary," I protest.

"Non-negotiable. Bye." He clicks off.

After pursing my lips in disgust, I turn to Chuy. "First, I need gas. Guess I don't have to tell you to follow."

A wave of sadness and deja vu sweeps over me as I park Buttercup next to the pump at the Gas and Grub, knowing I won't see Yasmin's beautiful face. This is where it all started, at least for me. Yasmin and Riley. Rick Rathjen. "Americans First."

Chuy follows me into the store and heads for the junk food shelf. Man after my own heart. Yasmin's brother Darrak is behind the counter, keeping an eye on Chuy. I see no sign of Bibi.

I point at Chuy. "No worries. He's with me. Sort of like a bodyguard. I had a little accident."

"Are you okay?"

"I'm fine. What about you?"

Darrak looks ten years older than he did at Yasmin's lying in. He's always been slim, but now looks emaciated. His face is all sharp edges and hard angles, giving him a hawk like appearance. I see a streak of gray in his dark hair. I know Darrak is older than Yasmin, but certainly not old enough for gray hair.

When he gazes into my eyes, I see his soul is burning like an out of control brush fire. It's aflame with anger, along with, something else. Something scary.

He says, "Thank you for asking, Mel. It is very hard without my sweet sister. My family still grieves."

I reach over the counter and pat his hand. "I miss her, too."

I pay my bill and start for the door. Before I exit, I turn back to Darrak. He is in anguish. I can't ignore it, and what I see in his soul frightens me. As I'd done with Yasmin, I scribble my cell number on the receipt and hand it to him. "Call me if you want to talk. I lost my sister, too."

His eyes widen in surprise. He takes the receipt and tucks it in his pocket. "Thank you."

Chuy sticks close behind me as I drive the ten miles to Rathjen's ranch. As promised, he pulls to a stop outside the long drive leading to the Rockin' R. He pulls a sleek cell phone from his pocket and notes the time.

"One hour. You be back, or I come in."

This was the longest speech in English I've ever

heard from Chuy. I nod in agreement, visions of Chuy, guns blazing, storming the Rockin' R Ranch dancing through my head.

I drive slowly toward the house and park next to the barn. No sign of Riley's pick-up. As I step out of Buttercup, I hear a loud whinny. Sneaky Pete is in the corral. He trots to the fence, throws his head back and bares his big, horsey teeth in a sneer. I know when I'm being dissed and mutter, "Screw you, Sneaky Pete."

I walk across the driveway to the expansive L-shaped ranch house with an attached three-car garage. The front of the house has a brick façade and burgundy decorative shutters. Two of the garage doors are open. A spiffy, midnight blue Mustang convertible is parked in one of the bays. The other is filled with (gulp) a big black SUV. I step closer, telling myself this could not possibly be the vehicle that chased me down the sidewalk and smacked me into unconsciousness. My self-talk continues as I walk close enough to see the SUV is a Land Rover. Don't be stupid, Mel, there are hundreds of black SUVs in Central Oregon. Besides, what possible reason would a member of the Rathjen family have to run you down? My poor horsemanship skills? Riding the daughter's favorite pony? Getting too close to Riley?

No, it doesn't make sense, but still, I want to get a look at the grill, the only part of the vehicle I actually remember. Unfortunately, the car is so big, it's practically pressed against the front wall of the garage. I'd have to drape my body across the hood, scoot forward, and peer through the tiny space between the car and the wall to get a look at it. Might be hard to explain if I get caught. Hmm, worth a try?

Before I can act on the impulse, I hear the sound of shrill female voices. I step away from the garage and skulk toward the front door where I pause to eavesdrop. After a few seconds, I realize I'm listening to a raging mother-daughter mini war. I recognize Roxanne's voice. Rachel's is similar but pitched higher.

Roxanne: "You think you know what's going on, but you don't. Therefore, you have no right to judge me."

Rachel's voice is quivering with emotion. "I know you're screwing around on Dad, and I feel sorry for him. He thinks you're acting all weird because of Riley's situation, but I know better. You think I won't tell him? Don't bet on it."

Roxanne's voice lowers, and I only catch a few words. Sounds like, "stuff you like costs money" and "could stop."

A silence follows. Maybe it's time for Mel to pop in as if she's just arrived and heard none of the above. Sounds like a plan.

Chapter Twenty-Four

I punch the doorbell and hear an answering gong. The door flies open filled with Roxanne, bundled up for the outdoors and clutching a purse. When she sees me, her look of fury changes to an expression of bland indifference.

I don't have time to peek in her soul because she looks over my head toward the road. "I'm late for an appointment. Just put the money on the hall table. I'll have your receipt the next time you come out for a riding lesson."

"Oh, gee," I say. "My dad says not to leave without a receipt. Is Mr. Rathjen here? Maybe he could give me one."

With a grimace of irritation, she says, "He's not here and, like I said, I'm late."

I'm blocking the doorway. She can't leave without knocking me over. Guess we'll see how badly she wants to get to her secret lover.

She turns her head and calls, "Rachel, this person needs a receipt. Will you please take care of it?"

I hear Rachel mutter, "Yeah, I guess."

I step aside, and Roxanne dashes to the garage. Moments later, the Land Rover springs to life, backs out of the garage and tears away, back tires spitting bits of gravel. Maybe she and her boyfriend are paying for a motel by the hour, and she wants to get her money's worth.

I wait for an invitation to enter. When it isn't delivered, I step into the entry hall and close the door behind me.

To the right, I see the kitchen, outfitted with lush, cherry wood cabinets and a matching island with a built-in cooktop. A corner sink flanked by granite countertops is positioned next to a large window for maximum viewing of the snow-capped mountains beyond while washing up. A stainless steel French door refrigerator dominates one wall next to two ovens, one up, one down. Every surface is polished and gleaming. Somehow I can't picture Roxanne in this setting, preparing a wholesome meal for her stressed out family.

"Come on in." The female voice comes from the living room to the left.

I step closer and see a white area rug centered over wide-plank walnut hardwood flooring. Far from the ranch style I expected to see, the décor is entirely modern with a white leather sectional, glass tables and offset lighting. No braided rugs. No gun rack, and certainly nothing as tacky as a mounted deer head.

Rachel is barefoot and curled up on the leather couch.

"Um, hi." I walk along the hardwood floor border, taking care to keep my dusty shoes off the white rug

No doubt about it. She's a pretty girl. Her shiny blond hair falls in a silken sheath across one cheek. A Brazilian blowout, if I'm not mistaken. Easily a four hundred dollar procedure. Factor in the diamond studs in her pierced ears, designer jeans, pricey tee, French manicure and spray tan...Ka-ching. She doesn't bother to look up as she keys a text into her cell phone.

I say, "Your mom said you would write me a receipt for the riding lessons."

Apparently satisfied with her text, she hits send, lifts her head, and gives me a brief glance. Her hair swings to one side. She has a red mark on her cheek. Surely a zit wouldn't dare take up residence on her perfect skin. Had Roxanne smacked her in the face?

She sets her phone down. Her gaze flicks over me, no doubt evaluating my thrift shop ensemble. When she finally makes eye contact, I see the misery in her soul and feel a wave of pity. And shame. Who am I to judge a person I don't know.

"You're Rachel…right? Riley mentioned you. I'm Mel."

She uncurls her legs and places her feet on the floor. With a ghost of a smile, she says, "Oh, yeah. You're Melanie Sullivan, the chick who takes riding lessons on Sugar Lips. Riley told me about you. He says it's hilarious."

I return the smile. "Works for me. I like being closer to the ground in case I fall off."

She flashes a real smile this time and pats the couch. "Wanna sit down? I'll get your receipt."

I glance at the pristine carpet and lean over to remove my shoes.

"No need to take off your shoes," she says. "The cleaning lady will be here soon."

Even so, I brush the dust of my running shoes and make a grand production of tiptoeing to the couch.

Rachel giggles. "You're funny."

"Glad to provide some comic relief. You look like you need it."

I perch on the arm of the couch, fighting the urge to ask about the mark on the face. I don't want to spook her, so I say, "Boyfriend problems?"

She purses her lips and shakes her head. "Not even close."

She slips the cell phone into her jeans pocket. "I'll get your receipt."

"Sorry," I say. "Didn't mean to pry. None of my business."

She strides away without answering.

You blew it, Mel.

She returns a few minutes later and hands me a neatly printed receipt.

I stand. "Thanks."

She plops down on the couch. "Riley really likes you."

I take a step toward the hardwood floor.

Rachel pats the couch again. "He'll be home soon if you want to hang out."

Maybe I didn't blow it. "Sure, I'll hang out for a while. Have to go to work later, though." (It's a lie, but I might need an escape plan in case Chuy gets restless.)

I sink onto the luxurious, but enormous couch. The leather surrounds me and molds to my body like it's a living, breathing organism. It scares me a little. Can't help but wonder if I'll be able to get free if the need arises. Though I'm dying for some girl talk, I will myself to stay silent, see where it goes.

Out of the blue, Rachel asks, "Do you like your mother?"

"Yes, but we live over nine hundred miles apart. Makes it much easier for us to get along. Why do you ask?"

She gazes into my eyes. Her soul is predominantly dark blue and gray with a streak of orange along the leading edge. Spotting the color orange makes me feel better. It means she hasn't given up entirely. She's not totally immersed in sadness. Because orange is a combination of red and yellow, it appears in a variety of shades. Though it's thin, Rachel's is the color of a glorious sunset. This tells me she values home and family and is hopeful for the future. It also indicates the fun-loving part of her nature hasn't been snuffed out.

"Because," she says, "my mother is really messed up, and my family is falling apart. I tried to talk to her about it, and we ended up screaming at each other."

"You have a mark on your face. Did she hit you?"

Rachel shrugs. "No biggie. She slapped me after I shoved her. I was just so damn mad. She tries to control me by threatening to take away my debit card and my car."

"What about your dad? Can you talk to him about it?"

Her eyes fill with tears. "I don't want to make it worse for him. He's already hurting because of the thing with Riley."

"Does Riley know about your mother's, um, situation?"

She shakes her head. "Riley's going through hell right now."

A flush rises in her cheeks. She stares at the floor. "This is crazy. What's wrong with me? I don't even know you, and I'm telling you all this personal shit."

"It's okay, Rachel," I say. "You need somebody to talk to, and your family's not available. How old are you? Sixteen?"

"Just turned seventeen."

"I'm twenty-three, but I remember being seventeen like it was yesterday. I was miserable too, but for different reasons."

"But, you could talk to your mom. Right?"

"Wrong," I say. "I was skipping school. Hanging with bad people. My mom and I were barely speaking."

She leans forward, searching my expression. "And, now you are. What happened?"

I stay quiet for a minute, debating whether or not to go into my sordid past. Will hearing my story help Rachel see past her misery? I decide to go for it. "When I was eighteen, I was defending my best friend. A guy was bullying her. I threw a punch, aimed for his nose, but I missed. I hit him in the throat. He fell backward and hit his head on a curb. He died."

Rachel's eyes widen. "Oh, my God. Did you get arrested?"

"The guy was a senator's son, and his dad wanted to throw the book at me. I narrowly escaped prison time. It was ruled an accident. I was on probation for four years and had to live with my mom. We learned to get along."

Rachel gnaws on her lower lip for a while. "You and your mom live a long ways apart. Why did you leave home?"

Dani. I left home because of Dani.

"I guess I needed to grow up."

When she doesn't respond, I say, "Don't give up on your family, Rachel. Things can change. I'm living proof. Hopefully, you guys can get counseling sometime soon."

She rolls her eyes. "Probably won't happen until

my mother gets her shit together. If she ever does."

She's right and I've run out of comforting words. I scoot to the edge of the couch and push to a standing position, not an easy task. I swear the damn couch tried to suck me back in. "Gotta go. Hang in there, girl. Maybe I'll see you around when I come out for more riding lessons."

Misery overtakes her, and she curls back into the fetal position. She pulls her phone from her pocket and examines the screen, her mask of indifference firmly in place. Exactly like Roxanne's. "Yeah, see you around."

I think about Rachel as I guide Buttercup down the driveway. Yes, she's a spoiled, privileged kid but, inside, she's a sad little girl who wants her mother to give her a hug and say, "It will be all right, honey."

I can relate. Damn, it makes me want to cry.

I meet Riley half way down the drive, and pull up until Buttercup and his pickup are side by side. We zip our windows down, and Riley points behind him. "There's a guy on a Harley parked out on the road. He looks dangerous. Says he's with you."

"He is. Long story."

His eyebrows shoot up. "Okay." He waits for a further explanation. When I don't respond, he says, "Hey, do you drink coffee?"

"Do I ever."

"There's a coffee place in Red Ridge. You can follow me there." He inclines his head back toward the road. "Your friend can come, too."

"Believe me, he will."

I briefly consider inviting Riley to Number Ten for a chat, but the perv factor looms large. Riley is nineteen. I'm twenty-three and live in a motel. Enough said.

Riley throws the truck in reverse and backs out to the road. I tell Chuy the plan, and we're off.

Chapter Twenty-Five

Riley orders hot cocoa with whipped topping. After my visit to the ranch, I require a heavy-duty infusion of caffeine and opt for an Americano with a couple shots of chocolate. I deliver Chuy's caramel Frappuccino to the parking lot where he sips it astride his bike.

Riley and I pick up our drinks and head for the outside seating area. It's devoid of customers and perfect for a private conversation. Just as we step through the door, the weather gods flip a switch. The sun is barely visible, occasionally peeking out from under dark, scudding clouds driven by an icy wind. The temperature has dropped at least twenty degrees. Chuy pulls a heavy jacket from his saddlebags. Riley and I step back inside and settle into a corner booth away from the other patrons. He tells me snow is predicted.

I protest. "No way. It's not November yet."

Riley forces a smile. "You're in the mountains now, California girl. You'd better get snow tires on the Mustard Mobile."

He leans across the table and points at the top of my head. "Are those stitches? What happened?"

I really don't want to go into the whole car chasing me down the sidewalk scenario, especially if it was his mother was behind the wheel. "Had a little accident."

He gestures toward the parking lot. "Hence, the bodyguard?"

"I have an extremely protective uncle who seems to think I need watching over."

"How bad were you hurt?"

"Bumps and bruises. Slight concussion."

"Well damn." His shoulders droop and he looks like a lost little boy. "No more riding lessons I guess."

"Are you kidding me? I'll be back in the saddle as soon as I heal up. I just paid your sister for the last two lessons, plus enough money for two more. You better wake Sugar Lips and get her prepped."

His eyes light up. "Good. I like talking to you."

"I like talking to you too. Is school going better?"

He shakes his head. "I dropped my classes last week. I was flunking out. Can't concentrate. Maybe I'll try again after the first of the year."

"What did your folks say?"

"I haven't told them. They paid for my tuition and books, so they'll be pissed."

"I talked to Rachel earlier." I try to steer the conversation in a new direction. "She seems really worried about your mom."

He flushes. "It's because of me. The whole family is screwed up because of me."

It seems he knows nothing about his mother's extracurricular activities. He won't hear about it from me. His whole demeanor reeks of hopelessness and scares the hell out of me. I need to do something to rattle his cage.

I reach across the table and take his hand. "So, I guess your family was perfect before Yasmin was killed. Everybody got along fine. No arguments. Just peace and love all around."

The color in his cheeks fades to pallor. It

emphasizes the dark circles under his eyes. He opens his mouth to speak and then clamps it shut. Finally, he nods. "Yeah, I get what you're trying to say. We weren't perfect, but at least we talked to each other. Now, it's like we all live on separate islands."

I release his hand. "What happened the night you and Yasmin were going to run off together? You started to tell me the other day before your dad walked in."

He leans across the table. I look into his sad-eyed gaze and see there's a storm brewing in his soul as well as outside.

"I shouldn't be talking to you. My dad made us all promise to stick to the same story."

He pauses and swallows hard. "The lies are killing me. I feel like I'm dishonoring her memory."

Now is the time for me to reassure him, say something like, "You can trust me. You're secret is safe with me."

I can't do it, knowing I'll have to report to Mick. Who knows what will happen then? I'm stuck between the proverbial rock and hard place. My only comfort is the possibility Riley's truth will help exonerate him.

"I'm not here to judge you, Riley."

He glances over his shoulder and lowers his voice. "I worked for my dad all summer and saved my money. Yasmin had some money too. Her dad hardly paid her anything, but she was smart. When Bibi wasn't in the store, she figured out how to slip a little cash from the drawer and hide it away. Maybe just a five or a ten, but, over time, she had a nice little nest egg."

He pauses and searches my face. "I don't want you to think badly of her."

I flap a dismissive hand. "I don't. Her dad should

have paid her a decent wage."

Riley continues, "She didn't have a car. We arranged to meet at the little park a block away from her house. You know the one?"

"Yes."

"The plan was to drive to Portland and get married and then call our parents and tell them, so they wouldn't report us missing. After a couple of days, we'd come home to face the music."

He pauses and takes a shuddering breath. "She never showed up. I waited and waited. Called her cell. No answer. Two hours went by. Right then, I knew something awful had happened."

Tears fill his eyes. "Yasmin was organized. When she made a promise, she kept it. She always showed up when she said she would. Always. Except for that night."

I think about how to phrase my next question so it doesn't sound like an accusation. "You two were so young. Did you ever consider waiting until you were a little older to get married."

His face tightens. "No." His soul is afire with anger and pain. "She was pregnant, and we wanted the baby."

I simply can't bear to look at the misery in his soul. I close my eyes and murmur, "I'm so sorry."

When he speaks, his voice is flat, devoid of emotion. "I suppose the cops will find out about the pregnancy when they get the autopsy report, and they'll have another reason to think one of us killed her."

"I assume your mom and dad don't know about the pregnancy."

He shakes his head.

"It might be best if you tell them before the cops

do. I'll go with you if you want."

This time, he takes my hand. "Whoever killed Yasmin, killed part of me, too. When I lost Yasmin, I lost everything I cared about. What's left over doesn't seem worth the effort."

"What do you mean?"

With a weary sigh, he says, "It's like I can't see colors anymore. Everything looks flat and gray. Lifeless. Dead. Like Yasmin."

I squeeze his hand. "Riley, is there anyone in your family you can talk to?"

"Rachel and I have always been close," he says. "She knew I was seeing Yasmin. She doesn't know about the baby."

"I talked to Rachel today. She needs somebody to talk to just as much as you do. I think you guys can help each other. Maybe you can double team your parents."

His eyes widen. "She's my little sis. I have to take care of her."

"I bet she feels the same way about you."

I point at the cell phone in his shirt pocket. "Call her. She's home alone. Now is a good time."

He hits speed dial. I cross my fingers. Please answer, Rachel.

"Rach? Mom and Dad still gone?"

He listens for a moment. "I've got something to tell you. I'll be home in a few."

He hits the off button and gazes into my eyes. The storm in his soul is still visible but subsiding. "She said, 'I love you, Big Bro,' and started to cry."

"Guess you'd better get on home," I say.

Before he leaves, he asks for my phone number. "In case, you know, I need to talk to you about something."

I scribble it on a napkin and give him a hug. "Any time."

He pauses at the door, turns and gives me a ghost of a smile. "Let me know when you're ready to ride. I'll get Sugar Lips saddled up."

"Looking forward to it," I lie.

As I drive toward 3 Peaks, followed by Chuy, I hope and pray I've made the right call. If Riley and Rachel support each other, it's possible their parents might get their act together and act like grown-ups for a change. Maybe then, the family will be able to handle the shit storm coming their way. Fingers crossed.

****

I'm back in 3 Peaks at a stoplight when my phone pings. I have a text from Paco. —*Where are you? Need to talk.*—

I key in. —*On my way home.*—

He doesn't bother to respond, which means he's already there or on his way. He's standing in front of my door when I arrive. Thunder Paws is rubbing his big orange body against Paco's leather chaps. Paco leans over and scratches the tomcat's head.

After greeting me with a grizzly bear hug, Paco steps over to have a word with Chuy. Does this mean I'm about to lose my faithful bodyguard?

Paco follows me inside and sits at the table. He pulls a folded paper and stub of a pencil from his jacket and points at the other chair.

"What's up, Unc?"

"How much do you remember about the SUV? Did you get a good look at the driver?"

"No. It was like the car was a living thing, a big,

black animal trying to kill me. All I could think about was getting away."

"What about the front end? Do you remember what it looked like?"

The image of the car bearing down on me appears in my mind. I suppress a shudder. "The grill looked like shark's teeth."

He pushes the paper and pencil across the table. "Sketch it for me."

I nod and close my eyes, attempting to conjure up the frightening image. "The grill was surrounded by a chrome frame. The chrome strip was wide across the top." I open my eyes and start drawing. "The sides curved down and under. There were individual vertical chrome strips inside the grill. It looked like an open mouth filled with big, shiny teeth."

I sketch the grill as I describe it.

Paco says, "Did you see any kind of a logo?"

I close my eyes again and try to remember the details panic had driven from my mind. It's safe now, Mel.

"Yeah, I think so. The top center of the grill has some kind of a logo, looked like a rectangle with a symbol inside it. Maybe a cross or a t."

I draw what I can remember.

"What about the tag number. Do you remember any of it?"

I shake my head. "I was too busy running for my life."

Paco's face is grim. He picks up the sketch, studies it and sets it down. "You just drew the front end of a black Lincoln Navigator, exactly like the one owned by Noelle Hoffman."

Puzzled, I stare at Paco, trying to connect the dots. "Who's she?"

"Noelle Hoffman, wife of Dr. Dirk Hoffman, your pervie optometrist."

Chapter Twenty-Six

My head is swimming with confusion. Answers. I need answers. Sadly, I can't even form a semi-intelligent question.

Paco walks me through it. He remembered the threats made by Rebecca Porter and tailed her to the fitness club again. When she emerged, she was with her black-haired friend. They hugged and the brunette walked to her car, a black Lincoln Navigator. Paco jotted down the tag number on her license plate, and Louise Goodhart traced it to Dirk and Noelle Hoffman.

"Seems like a reach," I say. "What possible reason would Dr. Dirk's wife have to run me down? Maybe it's just a coincidence. Maybe it wasn't her."

Paco shrugs. "I'm pretty sure it is, little girl."

He stays silent for a minute before saying, "What do you know about the Cypress Inn?"

"Other than it's named for a tree?"

He rolls his eyes. "Smart ass. Yeah, other than the name."

I shake my head. "Nada."

"Your dad knows about it."

Warning bells ring inside my head. "Okay. What about it?"

"It's where Rebecca and her gal pal were meeting."

Before I allow myself processing time, I blurt, "What does it have to do with Steve?"

184

Paco says, "Really? You need to ask?"

I close my eyes as unwelcome images flash through my mind.

"Aw, come on, he's my dad."

"Everybody has needs, Chica."

I'm tempted to put my fingers in my ears and loudly sing, "La, la, la," but resist.

Paco says, "The Cypress is an upscale inn east of town. It caters to gay people who want a nice setting with discreet personnel. Your dad knew what Rebecca Porter looked like. He'd seen her coming out of Goodhart's office. He spotted her at the Cypress along with a woman who matched Noelle Hoffman's description. Me and the guys started tracking them and, sure enough, it's where they do the deed. We greased a few palms and used a few other forms of persuasion and got the proof."

In my mind, I see folded bills slipped into willing hands as well as bloody noses. Remember don't ask, don't tell?

"What kind of proof?"

"All I'm gonna say is: Pinhole camera. Tissue box. Bedside table."

"Oh, geez, Unc, now what? Obviously you can't tell Mick or Billy."

He shakes his shaggy head. "No need. You're family." He thumps his chest. "I take care of my family."

"None of this makes sense. Porter hires Louise Goodhart to prove Dr. Dirk's a perv, but she's having a fling with his wife? And, why in the world did they pick me out for a target?""

"Exactly what we need to find out. I've been

talking to your buddy, Goodhart. She thinks we need to set up a sting, get some proof."

"Number one, she's not my buddy. Number two, I don't want to be anywhere near Rebecca and her girlfriend."

"Even if we can prove it was the Hoffman women who tried to kill you and maybe even get her arrested?"

I think about it for a moment and sigh. "What do you want me to do?"

"I'll set up a meet with Louise, and we'll work it out."

He rises and drops a kiss on my forehead. "I'm pulling Chuy off. We've got both the bitches covered 24/7. Call ya soon."

He starts for the door.

I lift a hand. "Hold it."

He pauses.

"Please don't tell me you're making your guys tail these women in this weather."

A sly expression slips across his face. "Ever heard of GPS tracking?"

I stare at him in stunned silence. I finally regain the power of speech. "You put tracking devices on their cars?"

He nods and raises a finger to his lips. "Shhh."

Before I can ask about the legality of the matter—maybe I don't really want to know—he's out the door.

I stand in the open doorway and watch Paco and Chuy tool away on their bikes. Riley's prediction is coming true. The sky is the color of lead, and it's snowing. A frigid, gusty wind drives a flurry of snowflakes across the parking lot. I open my mouth and catch one on my tongue. Hailing from Southern

California, this is my first up close and personal experience with snow.

Finally, the cold seeps into my bones. I step back into the room, close the door and crank up the heat.

First thing first. Before I jump into the Rebecca Porter thing, I need to report to Mick. I pick up my phone. Before I can punch in Mick's number, I hear a series of loud thumps, coming from outside my door. Bang. Bang.

What the hell? It's growing dark but my blinds are still open. I pull them to one side and peer out. Thunder Paws is on my front stoop performing a series of acrobatic moves designed to get my attention. He crouches, gathers himself, leaps into the air and slams his front paws against my door. Again and again.

I open the door a crack. A crack is all he needs. He squeezes through, trots to the bed, jumps on and proceeds to give himself a tongue bath.

"Well, damn," I say. "Guess I know why your name is Thunder Paws."

He glares at me through squinty yellow eyes. I see he has a raggedy left ear, no doubt a souvenir from a tangle with another tomcat. I don't want a cat. I don't need a cat. But, hell, it's cold out. I'll let him stay in my room. Just for tonight.

Bathing ritual over, the cat leaps off the bed and walks to the mini fridge. He bats at the door with one enormous paw, then looks over at me and emits a menacing growl.

"Okay, okay, don't get testy," I tell him. "Let's see what we can find. You can't be too hungry. You stole my fish and chips earlier today."

I open the fridge, pull out yesterday's leftover

macaroni and cheese, put it on a paper plate and set it on the floor. He gobbles it up, strolls into the bathroom and stares pointedly at the toilet.

"I get it, you're thirsty." I say. "Not out of the toilet. Gross."

I fill a coffee mug with water, bow from the waist and set it on the floor. "Your beverage, sir."

He ignores the sarcasm and daintily laps water from the mug.

Having eaten and drunk his fill, the cat curls up on my pillow and begins to purr, a sound not unlike a small engine.

I'm peering through the window, fascinated by the falling snow, when a Jeep Wrangler pulls up and parks. The driver side door flies open, and Mick emerges.

I pull the door open. He stomps the snow from his suede boots before he steps inside, shuts it, and throws the dead bolt.

Hmmm.

"Planning to stay a while."

He winks. "Might get snowed in."

"I doubt it. You're driving a Jeep Wrangler. New ride?"

"The government wheels don't cut it in a snow storm. The Jeep's mine."

He throws his coat on the bed and spots the cat. Thunder Paws rises. His ears flatten, he hunches his back and hisses.

Mick frowns. "What the hell is that?"

I smile sweetly. "Looks like a kotyonok to me."

He gives me a sideways glance. "Anybody ever tell you you're a smart ass?"

"Yeah, just a few minutes ago."

He extends a hand and approaches the cat.

"Careful," I say. "He's not exactly domesticated. Like some people I know."

"Animals love me." With a full-out grin, he adds, "They probably love my soul like you do."

I flap a hand at him. "Give it a rest. Why are you here?"

Mick doesn't answer because he's trying to charm the stupid cat. He takes a step closer, murmuring what I assume to be Russian feline endearments to Thunder Paws who crouches and cocks his head to one side. Unblinking, he's staring at Mick's face in fascination. Is he thinking about clawing out eyeballs or submitting to a belly rub? I hold my breath, wondering if I should fetch the first aid kit.

Still conversing softly in Russian, Mick eases onto the bed and sprawls on his back, arms outstretched, the traditional sign of surrender. Thunder Paws thinks it over for a moment before slinking across the bed. He places a tentative paw onto Mick's belly and waits a beat before hopping aboard. Accompanied by a throaty purr, he begins kneading his front claws in and out of Mick's muscular chest.

"Ow," Mick says. He lifts the cat from his body and places him back on my pillow. "Nice pussy cat. Nice *kotik*."

He sits up and with a smug smile, says, "Told ya."

"Yeah, yeah, you're amazing. Now, tell me why I am graced with your presence."

He shakes a finger at me. "You have a very bad attitude. I am here for several reasons. First, let's get business out of the way. You have talked to members of the Rathjen family…yes?"

"Yes, not Roxanne, but I did speak with both Rachel and Riley today."

I fill him in on what I've learned about Roxanne's infidelity and finish by telling him how concerned I am about both kids. "Their world is falling apart."

Mick is all business now. His blue-eyed gaze pins me to the wall. It feels like it is drilling deep into my brain, trying to determine if I'm telling the truth.

He says, "You are emotionally involved. Do you think you can be objective?"

Part of me is offended. Then, I take a moment to remember I'm a paid employee of the Department of Homeland Security and rein in my emotional retort.

"Yes, it's true I feel empathy for the Rathjen family, but I know Rick, Rachel, and Riley did not kill Yasmin. They might have other secrets, but they didn't commit murder. I'm pretty sure Roxanne didn't either, but I need another look."

He studies my face. "I believe you."

After a long silence, he says, "You asked me to look into Rick Rathjen's past after you wondered about something you saw in his soul."

"Signs of fear," I say. "I figured it was something in his past. What did you find?"

"When Rick was a lad of twelve, a man described as 'dark complexioned' broke into their house. The father was murdered before he could grab his gun and defend the family. The killer got away with some valuables and was never apprehended."

"Wow," I murmur. "Guess it explains why Rathjen is so paranoid of foreigners."

Mick doesn't answer. He just looks at me and nods.

"So, now what?"

"See if you can get up close and personal with Roxanne. If you don't come up with anything incriminating with her, the Rathjen family will be in the clear."

"Okay."

He stands and stares down at me. "Now, we move on to the other reason for my visit."

Chapter Twenty-Seven

His gaze is intense, and for a moment, I can't breathe.

He takes a step toward me and places his hands on my shoulders. With a gentle touch, his hands slide up to cup my face. He lowers his head and brushes his lips across mine, murmuring to me in a mixture of Russian and English.

My hands creep around his neck, and I lean into his body. Every cell in my physical being is responding to him. If only I could quiet the whispers flying through my mind at warp speed. Dammit, girl, are you ready for this? You still have trust issues. Is it safe? Is this a rebound relationship? Probably. Does the fact you want to jump into bed with Mick mean you're a slut? Have I lapsed into slutitude?

He must sense my hesitancy because he tilts my head back until we make eye contact. "Are you sure?"

I don't answer right away because I'm busy staring into his eyes, into his soul. Even though we make jokes about it, Mick's soul is uniquely beautiful. It pulls me in, mesmerizes me. A sense of calm steals into my busy mind. A sense of rightness.

I nod and allow my body to relax into his.

He leans down to kiss me again. It's then I realize I have coffee breath. This is our first time. I can't have coffee breath. I push him away.

His brows shoot up. "I thought you said…"

I hold up a finger. "One sec. Gotta brush my teeth."

With a bark of laughter, he says, "Whatever it takes, *maylsh*."

"Pussy cat or kitten?" I ask.

"Baby. Just baby."

"Better."

He comes into the bathroom as I finish up my vigorous oral hygiene ritual. He grips my shoulders and turns me to face him, pressing his body against mine.

His lips brush my ear. He takes my hand and places it over the erection straining against the front of his jeans. "See what you do to me? All I have to do is look at you."

His voice is husky, sending ripples of intense need to every sensitive nerve ending in my body. When I gaze into his eyes, I see a soul smoky with desire.

I try to catch my breath, to form a simple sentence, but fail. A little moan is all I can manage.

His hand slips between my legs and a brief smile of pride flashes across his face. He whispers, "Da, you're hot. And ready. Very good, *malysh*. No longer afraid of big, bad Homeland Security man?"

"No fear," I manage to whisper. As I speak the words, I'm pretty sure they are true. Still, some doubt remains.

He lifts me onto the bathroom counter. I open my legs and wrap them around his body, pressing my heated center against him. His lips are alternately soft and demanding as he trails kisses along my neck until he reaches my mouth. His tongue slides across my lower lip and I shiver. It's not enough. I pull him closer, inviting him in until our lips, our breaths and our bodies strain together, hungry for completion. His tongue sweeps across mine while his hands slip beneath my shirt. In a flash, my bra is undone and his fingers are caressing my breasts.

When he reaches for the fastener on my jeans, I manage to push him away and gasp, "Not in the bathroom."

He carries me to the bed, a bed still occupied by Thunder Paws who doesn't look willing to share.

"Well, shit," I mumble. "I can't do it if the cat's watching."

"I'll put him out." Mick sets me down and grabs the cat, who yowls in protest.

"It's too cold. Lock him in the bathroom."

Mick hastens to the task, tosses the offended cat into the bathroom, and closes the door. I hear throaty growls and wonder about our safety when the cat is released from his porcelain prison.

Vicious cat attacks disappear from my mind when Mick returns. He reaches in a pocket, pulls out a six-pack box of condoms and sets it on the bedside table.

"Six?"

He pulls off his shirt and unbuttons his jeans, staring down at me. "I find it best to be prepared."

This strikes me funny, and I lapse into a fit of giggles. Stop it, Mel! Why do you always do this when things get intense?

Mick sits on the edge of the bed and strokes my hair. "Beautiful girl. My *malysh*, do not be nervous. I will make you very happy. I promise."

I sober quickly and reach for him. Clothes tossed hastily to the floor, we come together, exploring each other's bodies, whispering our need. His tongue touches each of my breasts, igniting a path of fire before sliding to my belly and then, oh my God, even lower.

He lifts his head. "Did I mention, I will also make you scream?"

****

The next morning, I'm deep in dreamland. My mother is trying to teach me to use her sewing machine, and I'm a reluctant, not to mention, extremely disinterested student.

"Look," she cajoles, "It's fun.

She hits the foot pedal. The machine growls and whirs. I watch, fascinated as the needle bounces up and down at warp speed on a white dishtowel, my practice piece.

She vacates the chair and guides me into it. "Think of all the cute outfits we can make."

"Yeah, yeah," I mutter.

"Just depress the pedal gently, at first, until you get the hang of it."

Never one to heed my mother's advice, I stomp down on the pedal. My hands are on either side of the racing needle, holding down the dishtowel.

She screams, "Stop!"

I take a peek at her terrified face and the needle goes off course and pierces my thumb.

"Ouch, dammit, ouch!"

I lift my foot from the pedal, but the motor is still racing and my thumb is still impaled. Weird. So weird, it wakes me up. I open one eye and discover I'm sprawled on my back with my arms spread wide. I turn my head and see Thunder Paws on Mick's pillow. The cat is purring loudly and digging his claws into my outstretched hand.

I snatch my hand away and glare at Thunder Paws. "Why are you here?"

I get my answer when I hear the shower running in the bathroom. A glance at the bedside table tells me there are only three condoms left in the six-pack. With a satisfied smile, I yawn, stretchm and curl up on my side. The cat takes it as invitation to come closer. Still purring, he winds himself into a ball and snuggles into my abdomen. The purring and warmth of his body make my eyelids droop, and I doze off.

The aroma of fresh coffee and freshly-shaven man rouses me. I open my eyes and gaze into a soul as blue as the fiords in Norway.

Mick's lips brush across mine. "Good morning, *malysh*."

He slips a hand beneath the covers and manages to hit all the right places. "Wish I didn't have to go to work."

I catch my breath and gasp, "Me too."

He gives me a look of regret and straightens. "Unfortunately, I have to be in Portland by noon and the roads are icy. If you have someplace to go, don't drive. The tires on that thing you call an automobile are bald."

"Hey, don't dis Buttercup. She might get mad and refuse to run."

"No driving. Not unless it melts. Promise me."

"I promise."

He tucks the covers around me and drops a kiss on my forehead. "I'll set up your meeting with Myron and call you tonight."

"I'm back to work today."

He nods and heads for the door. With one hand on

the doorknob, he turns. "Do you still love my soul?"

I smile. "Yes, among other things."

After Mick leaves, the cat stalks to the door and thumps it with his front paws.

"Yeah, I get it. You want out."

I open the door a crack. He slides through and bounds through the snow to the back of the restaurant where he uses his paw pounding technique to make his presence known. Nick emerges and sets a plate of food next to the door. Thunder Paws has us well trained.

Minutes later, a pick-up truck equipped with a blade appears in the parking lot and begins scraping snow, depositing it in a pile next to the curb. Fascinated, I watch through the window.

I hear a familiar squeak and glance to the right. Consuela (Connie, Queen of the Motel Maids) is guiding her cart down the newly cleared parking lot. My first instinct is to duck and hide. Then, I remember I am no longer required to clean rooms to pay for my lodging and remain at the window.

Connie spots me and stops her cart in front of my door. I panic for a moment. Has Nick decided I'm not paying enough rent since I've been on medical leave? Surely, he'd have let me know.

Connie pounds on the door, screeching, "I know you there. I saw you peeking out of window."

Busted. I decide to face the music. Better now than later.

I open the door a crack. Connie peers in, her gaze gravitating toward the rumpled bed.

An avid gleam appears in her eyes. "Hah, what I thought. Melanie has a new, hot man. Connie is right. *Si?*"

"Um, well," I begin, feeling resentful. It's not like I sleep with a different guy every night.

"Billy the Keed is now available?"

I stifle a grin. "I believe Billy the Keed has a new girlfriend. Sorry."

She emits a little snort of disgust. "I guess Connie is too late for Billy. What about big Mexican man?"

"Paco?"

"*Si*, Paco." She flutters her lashes, heavy with mascara. "Tell Paco, Connie thinks about him when she is all alone at night."

I decide to withhold the information about Paco and Aida's upcoming nuptials. "Sure will, Connie. You have a good day."

I close and lock the door, wondering if the course of true love ever runs smoothly.

Before I step into the shower, the man himself calls. Before I can convey Connie's message, Paco says, "I'll pick you up in fifteen minutes. You, me, and Louise Goodhart are going to figure out how to nail Rebecca Porter and her girlfriend."

Chapter Twenty-Eight

It's two days later and time for the Big Sting. We have a plan. Yes, it's convoluted and quite possibly dangerous. There are a lot of moving parts, and it might not work, but what the heck? So many unanswered questions. Other than the obvious—Cypress Inn—what is the connection between Rebecca Porter and Noelle Hoffman? What do they hope to accomplish by ruining Dr. Dirk? Why did Hoffman try to kill me?

Figuring out the best way to make it work took several hours. We kept running into a brick wall. We wanted to confront the women together, but Rebecca doesn't know we know about Noelle Hoffman. Paco thought Louise should set up a time to meet Rebecca, after which he would kidnap Noelle and drag her sorry ass to Goodhart's office. Louise was horrified. Me, not so much.

Louise managed to dig up information about the Hoffman's finances, though she was reluctant to share her sources. Paco and I figured Louise had crossed the line into the shadowy world of bribery. All for the greater good, of course. She'd discovered Noelle, as the second wife of Dr. Dirk, signed a pre-nuptial agreement and would receive next to nothing if they divorced.

As Paco says, "It's always about the money."

After hashing it over, we decided the direct approach was the best course of action. When Louise set up the appointment with Rebecca, Paco and I listened in via speakerphone.

Louise skipped the pleasantries and went right for the jugular. I swear, a little smile of pleasure bloomed on her narrow face. "Hi Rebecca. We need to set up a time to meet. I think you'll be interested in an item I have in my possession. Bring Noelle Hoffman with you."

Rebecca gasped. After a long, stunned silence, she said, "That's crazy. Why would I bring Dr. Dirk's wife with me?"

"I think you know why. Does the name Cypress Inn mean anything to you?"

We heard the sound of ragged breathing and a choked sob. Then, Rebecca screamed into the phone. "What the hell is your deal?"

"Calm yourself, dear," Goodhart soothed. "I'm sure we can work together so we all end up satisfied. Don't you?"

Now it's Wednesday, and Louise and I are ready when the women show up five minutes early for the two o'clock appointment. Clad in pressed jeans, a striped blue and white boat-neck tee topped with a navy blazer, Louise is positioned behind her desk. She looks ready to commandeer a Navy ship and sail across the Pacific. I'm seated to her right. In front of the desk, two empty chairs await our clients.

Louise gives me a timely reminder. "Remember, you're still Marilyn, my colleague."

Rebecca Porter doesn't bother knocking. She pushes the door open and steps through. She's wearing a flowery, loose-fitting top over tapered black jeans and stilettos. My gaze is drawn to her red, dagger-like fingernails. Ready for a catfight?

Close on her heels is Noelle Hoffman. Her hair is black. She's clad, head to toe, in body-hugging spandex, a Nike jacket, and expensive running shoes. Her eyes burn with fury, and she looks ready to kick somebody into next week. Warning bells clang in my head. It's the first time I've seen the woman who tried to kill me with a six thousand pound automobile. Had it not been for the spirit of my twin sister, she probably would have succeeded.

Louise rises and waves them into the chairs in front of her desk. Before she sits, Rebecca turns toward me and stabs the air between us with her sharpened pointer finger. "What's she doing here?"

Louise reclaims her seat. "You'll find out soon enough."

The two women pointedly ignore me as they settle into their chairs. Because I can't look into their evil souls, I'm left with only their body language to analyze. It's obvious Rebecca is tense. She grips the chair arms so tightly her knuckles turn blue-white.

Noelle, on the other hand, looks a bit too chill. She's sprawled in the chair, legs outstretched, hands folded in her lap, a smirk on her artificially tanned face.

She speaks first. "Let's hear what you have to say, Goodhart. Just remember, you're as vulnerable as we are. Whatever you think you can do to us will come back on you, twice as hard."

Louise is the very image of the three C's. Calm. Cool. Collected. Wish I could say the same. Being in the same room with my would-be murderer has done a number on my nerves. My heart feels like it's trying to hammer its way out of my chest.

Louise leans across her desk and gives the women a frosty smile. "You're not exactly in a position of strength here, Noelle. It would behoove you to keep this in mind instead of making threats."

Hoffman lifts her shoulders in a shrug, as if she couldn't care less. She waves a hand. "Get on with it then. Show us what you've got. Obviously, you want money, which means you're crooked as a dog's hind leg. Like I said before, you hurt us, we hurt you."

Rebecca Porter turns her head and gazes into my eyes. The hatred in her soul burns with sooty smoke. "Are you listening, Marilyn, or whatever your name is? The hurt goes both ways."

I've had enough of their threats and bullshit. I rise from the chair. "The hurt has already come my way." I tip my head forward, parting the hair with my fingers. "Would you like to know how I got this scar, Rebecca? Ask your friend, Noelle. She chased me down a sidewalk and tried to kill me with her car. After she hit me, I flew through the air and hit a cement retaining wall. I barely escaped with my life, and spent time in the hospital."

I'm so angry, I have to stop and gulp in air before I continue. "All I want to know is why? What did I ever do to either of you?"

Rebecca and Noelle exchange a glance, but remain silent.

I take a step toward the women and wrap my fingers around the open-heart pendant. Help me, Hope. Since my near-death experience when I clearly heard her voice, I've come to believe Steve is right. My unwillingness to think about Hope has kept her spirit at bay. And, maybe she needs to know the story as much as I do.

Finally, Hoffman does what I'd been waiting for. Her gaze meets mine. Her dark eyes still burn with fury. "Don't be ridiculous. I've never laid eyes on you until today."

She looks away quickly, but not before I see the telltale sign, a flash streaking across her soul, surefire proof she's not telling the truth.

I glance over at Louise. "She's lying. No doubt in my mind."

Noelle sneers, "So, what are you? A human lie detector?"

I see no reason to hide my light under a bushel. "Actually, I am, and I know you're lying your ass off."

She springs from her chair. "We're done here. Let's go, Becky."

Louise smacks her desk with an open hand. "Sit. We're far from done. Walk away now, I'll call the cops and tell them to pick you up for attempted murder. Don't you get it, Noelle?" Louise points at me. "She saw you. If you stick around, and we finish our business, there's a chance there will be no repercussions."

Louise is totally bluffing. I was so busy running, I didn't get a look at the driver. We have no proof other than my description of the Lincoln Navigator's grill. Probably wouldn't hold up in court.

Noelle looks pouty, but grits her teeth and sits. So do I.

Louise lets the tension build before reaching into a desk drawer. She pulls out a pinhole camera the size of a cigarette pack and a thumb drive. She sets them on top of her desk.

"What we have here, ladies, is proof of your relationship, which, by the way, is totally your own business."

Rebecca says, "We know you want to shake us down. How much do you want?"

"Actually," Louise says, "I don't want money. I want the truth. The whole story. Then, I'll give you the camera and the thumb drive, no strings attached. Hopefully, we'll never cross paths again." She pauses and nods in my direction. "Bear in mind, my colleague can tell if you're lying."

"Oh, right." Noelle's voice is dripping with sarcasm.

"Careful," Louis warns. "I may withdraw my offer."

"Give us a minute," Noelle says.

The two women step to the back of the office and hold a whispered conference. Rebecca is agitated, hands on hips, chin jutting out. Noelle is nodding and staring at the floor.

Louise lowers her voice and tells me, "Sit where you can look into their eyes."

I plant one bun on the front of her desk and, once again, clutch the pendant and invoke the spirit of my sister.

The women return to their chairs. Rebecca rakes me with a malignant glare. Noelle perches on the edge of her chair, right hand in her pocket. Neither of them speaks.

Louise says, "Here's a wild guess. You two are planning to run away together and need money. Noelle, you signed a prenup; so if you leave the marriage, you're pretty much broke, and that's not how you like to live. How am I doing do far?"

Hoffman shrugs. Porter is motionless in her chair.

"So," Louise continues. "You figured you'd get proof of Dr. Hoffman's, um, sexual advances to patients, threaten him with the evidence, and force him to pay you off."

Hoffman scowls. "It's not like we made it up. He loves to get up close and personal with women patients. Oh, he pretends it's an accident when he touches a boob or wheels his chair up between a woman's legs. It's not. It's a power trip. He needs to be stopped."

"But, you weren't going to stop him," I chime in. "You were going to shake him down for money."

Rebecca reaches over and takes Hoffman's hand. "He can afford it. Noelle's put up with him long enough. Don't we deserve happiness?"

Louise says, "Not if it includes blackmail and attempted murder. If you really want to put him out of business, make a complaint to the AMA or law enforcement."

Noelle snaps, "You were going to blackmail us."

"I needed to hear the truth," Louise says. "And, I'm still waiting to hear why Noelle tried to kill Marilyn."

Me too.

Noelle stares at the floor.

Rebecca lifts her gaze to mine. Her soul is a kaleidoscope of pulsating colors, a soul lost in confusion and turmoil. She mutters, "Too bad she didn't succeed."

The viciousness of her words steals my breath away.

Louise pushes the camera and thumb drive to the

front edge of the desk. "If you want these items, Noelle, you'd better start talking."

I see evil flash through Noelle's soul. At the same time, something stirs to life in my subconscious. It feels like a tingle, a minor electric shock racing through my brain, and it's screaming, "Danger!" Gripping the edge of the desk, I slide forward until my feet touch the floor. My gaze is fixed on Noelle. Louise is talking, but I'm so focused on Noelle, it sounds like white noise.

Noelle says, "Screw you!" and lunges toward the desk and grabs the camera and thumb drive. I dive for her legs. Take out the knees first. I know this from my Brazilian Jui Jitsu training. My shoulder slams into the side of her left knee, and she's knocked off balance. I get my feet under me, wrap my arms around her ankles, and jerk. She lands on her back, with me still clinging to her ankles. Rebecca is screaming. Noelle is cussing. I hear the sound of heavy footsteps, and know Paco has joined the party from his hidey-hole in the bathroom.

Noelle slips a hand in her pocket and pulls out a large, black handgun. She aims it between my eyes. "Get off me, bitch."

I freeze.

Paco grabs me around the waist and sets me on my feet. Louise stands behind him, her face drained of color.

Paco looks down at Noelle. "Go ahead, sweetheart, pull the trigger."

The blood rushes from my brain, and I scream, "What are you doing? She's batshit crazy!"

He totally ignores me, leans over, and slips his finger through the trigger guard. "Need some help? Here we go."

I'm ready to pass out, gasping for air. I see shooting stars soaring across a night sky. My knees give out, and I plop down on the floor

Click.

I sit, speechless, trying to wrap my head around what I just witnessed.

Noelle rolls to her feet, tosses the gun over her shoulder, and grabs Rebecca's hand. "We're so outta here."

Paco says, "I don't think so, girls." He uses his favorite move, grabbing both women by the back of their necks and guiding them to their chairs. He tells them to sit and stay. They do.

"Now," he says. "We'll get down to business.

Chapter Twenty-Nine

Paco picks me up and places me on my chair. "You okay, little girl?"

"What just happened here?" I gasp.

He walks over, picks up the gun and drops it into the wastebasket. "It's a toy gun."

"Looks real to me."

"It's not."

He takes one big step and plants himself directly in front of the women. He stares down at them, arms crossed over his massive chest. "I gotta say you two are the dumbest criminals I've ever seen, and I've seen quite a few."

Rebecca is sniveling. Noelle's smirk has vanished. When she looks up, I see a trace of fear in her soul.

"Not so tough without your toy gun, are you, doll?" Paco says.

Noelle pulls herself together. "What the hell do you want from us?"

Paco says, "I believe Ms. Goodhart already told you what we want. But, in case you weren't listening…"

He inches closer to Noelle who shrinks back in her chair. He bellows, "See the girl over there?" He points at me. "She's family. You tried to kill her. You mess with my family, I mess you up. Got it?"

Noelle's eyes get huge. "Got it."

"Start talking," Paco says.

Noelle's surly expression returns, and her gaze swings over to me. "She upset Becky. I don't like it when Becky's upset."

I shake my head. Is this woman for real? "You tried to kill me because Becky was upset? Isn't that a bit of an overreaction?"

She's staring at the floor, mumbling now, "It was an impulse, really. We were in the car when Becky spotted you. She said, 'There she is, the bitch who screwed up our plan.' I guess I went a little crazy."

Louise and I exchange a look of disbelief. Really, there are no words.

With a ferocious scowl, Paco bends down until he's eye level with Noelle. She tries to make herself as small as possible.

He growls, "Even though I'd love to give you the ass kicking you deserve, I guess today's your lucky day. I'm gonna let you walk out of here with the goodies. But, if you ever come anywhere near my family or Ms. Goodhart again, you will be very, very sorry. Got it?"

Both women nod vigorously. Noelle repeats, "Got it."

Paco hands over the incriminating items, and the women beat feet to the exit.

Paco says, "Call Billy. Tell him to pick them up."

"But it's my word against Noelle's" I protest. "Remember, I didn't actually see past the grill."

Paco looks over at Louise. "Did you get it?"

She pulls a tiny recording device from her jacket pocket. "Sure did. True confession time."

"Wait a sec," I say. "Isn't that illegal entrapment or

something?"

Paco says, "We'll let the lawyer types figure it out. She tried to kill you, Chica, and she needs to pay for her crime. Call him."

Ten minutes later, Billy pushes through the door. "You okay, Minnie?"

"I'm fine."

Paco and Louise fill him in and give him the recorder. He promises to pass the information along.

"Pass it along?" Paco is outraged. "Go arrest the bitches!"

Billy shakes his head. "Sorry, Paco, wish I could. I don't have the authority. We have something called chain of command."

Paco's brows draw together in a ferocious glare. He points at me. "She was your girlfriend, man. You said you loved her. You gonna let some crazy bitch get away with attempted murder?"

Billy looks mortified and now, I'm embarrassed. I feel the heat rise in my cheeks and know my face is bright red.

I grab Paco's hand. "It's okay, Unc. He has to follow the rules. We'll figure it out."

Paco jerks free. "Good thing I don't have rules."

Without a "bye now," or "see ya later," Paco stomps to the door and slams it so hard I feel the reverberation under my feet.

Louise gives me a questioning look. "What's up with him?"

"Don't ask, don't tell," I say.

Billy says, "I'm sorry, Minnie. I'll run it by the lieutenant, see if I get the green light."

Quite honestly, I'm not sure how I feel at the

moment. Yes, I finally know the whole story, lame as it is. Yes, I think Noelle Hoffman should be punished for what she did. But, then I factor in the wild card. Paco.

I say, "Let me think about it first."

Billy says, "Guess I'll take off if you don't need anything else."

"Actually, I do," I say. "Paco was so upset, he forgot he was my ride. Could you give me a lift home?"

Before we leave, Louise hands me a check for five hundred dollars.

"No way. I didn't earn it."

"Don't argue," she says. "You did your job and nearly got killed in the process. Your dad told me you're saving for a down payment on an apartment. It's the least I can do, and I hope you'll consider helping me in the future."

I thank her profusely and head out with Billy who is driving a city-issued car. Strangely, the sun is out, and the snow is melting into grimy puddles along the side of the road.

Billy says, "October in 3 Peaks. Get ready for anything."

On the trip home, I keep my lips pinched tightly together. Really, all I want is a ride.

Billy pulls up in front of Number Ten. "Can I come in?"

I stare at him, trying to interpret the meaning behind the words. Does he want to talk? Billy's never been the gabby sort, so I sincerely doubt it. One last headboard-banging romp in Number Ten for old time's sake? No chance in hell. What else could it be?

Finally, I say, "Why?"

He shrugs. "I need to talk to you about something."

"We can talk in the car."

He taps a finger on the steering wheel and stares at the dumpster behind the restaurant like he's never seen anything so magnificent. I wonder if he's still afraid to look into my eyes. It's not like I don't know what cheating looks like.

"For a guy who wants to talk, you're pretty quiet," I observe.

He turns to face me and makes eye contact. I see something gleaming in his soul and know exactly what it means. Fiercely competitive, Billy played fullback for his high school football team. When a local sportswriter discovered his full name was William Henry McCarty, the same as the original outlaw, he wrote, "Billy the Kid flat mows his competitors down, not unlike his namesake." The nickname stuck.

Not long before our break-up, Billy was drinking with his buddies at Nick's. A group of guys wandered in, looking for trouble. One of them challenged Billy to an arm-wrestling contest. I was working that night and watched Billy mow 'em down, one by one, until they left the bar in disgrace. Each time he was challenged with a new competitor, his soul glittered with the same look of excitement.

Seeing the gleam of competitiveness in his soul seems so wrong for our present situation, I begin to doubt myself. Unless he's prepping for another arm wrestling match, there's no reason for it.

Before I can form a question, he wraps his big hand around mine, brings it to his lips and gives it a smooch. "God, how I've missed you, Minnie. I'm not going to give you up."

Just for a moment, I'm frozen in disbelief. Then, I

snatch my hand away. "You didn't give me, up. You gave me away. There's a big difference."

Unblinking, he leans toward me. "I screwed up. Now, I want you back, and I'm willing to do whatever you want to make it happen."

Okay, now I get it. He's viewing me as the prize in a new contest. Who gets the girl? Billy or Mick? I am truly so gob smacked, all I can do is shake my head.

Unwisely, he continues, "I know you and Mick have, um, taken it to the next level. He and I discussed it and…"

"You discussed it?" Though I feel like shrieking in outrage, I lower my voice. "What's between Mick and me is clearly none of your business."

He fishes for my hand again, but I slip it under my left bun so he can't get it.

"Here's the deal, Minnie," he says. "Mick and I have a working relationship. We don't want to jeopardize it. We can't be acting like a couple of assholes fighting over a woman. So, we talked it over, and he agrees the decision has to be yours. Totally. We've worked out a plan."

I'm so furious I can barely speak, but I'm really curious about the plan. I part my lips and speak through a clenched jaw. "Lay it on me."

The sparkle in Billy's competitive soul dims slightly, and he squirms in his seat. "Well, we agreed there's only one fair way to do it."

"Which is?" My voice sounds scary, even to me.

"We take turns."

Equal measures of disgust and amazement coalesce into a fiery ball. I can actually feel it bouncing around in my brain, ready to blow. Shall I unleash on Billy? Or save it for Mick? Really, both these idiots deserve the fallout. My first instinct is to flee. I reach for the door handle and then, change my mind.

In order not to spook Billy, I force myself to speak calmly. "I want to make sure I understand what you're saying. I, Honor Melanie Sullivan, would be like a car, or maybe a pickup truck you and Mick share. The two of you schedule equal time behind the wheel, so to speak."

"No, no," Billy protests. "You've got it wrong. We..."

I hold up a hand and glare him into silence. "Let me finish. On week one, you get to take 'er for a spin. Week two, the vehicle, whose name might be Melanie, belongs to Mick. Correct?"

Billy takes a look at my expression and scoots back toward the driver side door. "Mick said you'd be pissed off. You are pissed off...right?"

"Really? You have to ask? Are you guys really so dense you think I'd sleep with both of you and decide which one I like best?"

He flushes. "The sleeping together part wasn't discussed."

"Not part of the plan? So, we do what? Hang out together like beer-drinking buddies?"

He mumbles, "It sounded better when Mick and I talked about it."

"Yeah, I bet it did."

I'm out the door so fast, Billy barely has time to exit the car. His words follow me through the door to Number Ten. "Just think about it. Okay?"

I don't bother to answer as I slam the door and lock it.

Chapter Thirty

Thoroughly disgusted with the entire male species, I stand in the shower until the hot water runs out. I towel off, determined to make Number Ten a man-free zone. My phone alternately rings and buzzes as I dress for work. I glance at the display. Billy. Billy. Mick. Billy. Mick. Looks like Billy called for reinforcement. I decide to cool off a bit before engaging with either one of the testosterone-laden idiots.

Curious, I check Mick's last message. It says:

—EITHER ANSWER YOUR DAMN PHONE OR CALL ME!—

Yeah, right. Like a text written in all caps and includes an exclamation point is going to scare me. I tuck the phone in my apron pocket and head for the pub. Thankfully, I'm so busy delivering orders, I don't have time to brood over boyfriends past or present (one of whom may soon be included in the past category).

The hubbub dies down around ten. The other waitress, Helen, is in desperate need of a smoke break. I tell her to go ahead, and I'll cover for her. She slips on her coat and heads for the door, almost crashing into Billy and Mick in her haste. She does an abrupt about-face and sidles over to me.

With a sly grin, she says, "Hmm, seems like your old boyfriend and new boyfriend have joined forces. Sure you don't want your break now?"

I wave her away. "I'm sure. Take your time."

The men slide into a booth. Mick is grim-faced. Billy gives me a sheepish grin. Without saying a word, I slap menus down on the table. Before I can step away, Mick's hand darts out and traps my hand. His gaze is intense and focused. "There's been a misunderstanding. We need to talk."

"I'm busy. Helen is on her break."

I try to tug my hand away. Mick's grip tightens. "I just drove three hours to talk to you face-to-face because you are acting like a pissed off little girl who wants to punish me by not answering her phone."

"Now it's my fault?"

With a pleading look, Billy says, "No, it's mine. I screwed up. Everything I said came out wrong. Just give us a chance to explain, Minnie. Please?"

Billy saying please? Highly unusual. Despite my resolve, I'm beginning to weaken, even though I'm not happy about the phrase pissed off little girl.

I glare at Mick. "Let go of my hand. When Helen's back, I'll take my break."

Still fuming, Mick releases me and opens his menu.

Nick intercepts me on my way to the kitchen. "Boyfriend problems?"

"Nothing I can't handle," I mutter. "We'll sort it out on my break. Mind taking their orders? I need to calm down before I say or do something I'll regret."

I fantasize about dumping today's special, spaghetti and meatballs, on their stupid heads. The image makes me smile. Maybe I'm a pissed off little girl after all.

By the time Helen returns, the guys have devoured

their dinners and are now bonding over a pitcher of MGD.

Nick says, "Need a private place to talk? You can use my office."

I'm sure he's channeling the bad behavior I'd demonstrated a few months back, when I roughed up a customer who turned out to be my long-lost father. Long story short, in my defense, I didn't know who he was and believed he was a threat to my safety.

"It's okay. No violence. I promise."

I walk over to the booth. Both men slide over to make room for me. Really? Now I have to choose who I sit with? I grab a chair and pull it up to the end of the table.

Billy says, "Since I messed it up, it's better if Mick talks."

I don't bother to answer.

Mick says, "It's not what you think. I know Billy still has feelings for you, and maybe I rushed you into something you're not ready for. He and I talked it over and agreed it should be up to you. No pressure. If you want to spend time with Billy, it's okay with me."

"Define spending time," I say.

Mick scowls. "You're not making this easy."

"Why should I? You haven't made it easy for me. Shouldn't I have been included in the discussion? FYI, I'm not a pissed off little girl. I'm a pissed off, fully grown woman."

Billy looks anxious. He's rubbing the stubble on his chin and glancing at me like I'm a rabid wolverine ready to rip out his throat.

Mick's grumpiness dissipates rapidly. I see his lips twitch and know he's trying to hold back a smile.

"Okay, consider yourself officially included. Billy misspoke when he used the term taking turns. I have a hunch it's what ticked you off. Am I right?"

I look back and forth between the two clueless men and suddenly, the anger whooshes from my body like air from a deflated balloon. The whole situation is so ludicrous I feel laughter bubbling up in my chest. Laughing would probably weaken my position, so I choke it back and try for a mature, reasonable response. "Yes, you're right about that particular phrase. But what ticked me off even more was the fact you guys make decisions about me when I'm not present. Don't do it again."

Both men nod like bobble head dolls.

Billy brightens up. "So, you don't mind if I come back and hang out at Nick's?"

"Of course not. Why would I?"

Unfortunately, Mick still doesn't get it. "So, what's your decision?"

I stare at him. "About what? Billy hanging out at Nick's?"

"Do you want to spend time with him? See if there's still a spark?"

I shake my head in mock despair. "Billy's a friend, and he's welcome here anytime he wants to hang out. But, I'm with you now, dummy. Understand?"

With a gusty sigh of relief, Mick covers my hand with his. "Yes, *malysh*, I understand."

Billy looks a bit crestfallen but rallies nicely. "I respect your decision, but I'm not giving up. Fair enough?"

"Fair enough," I repeat. "Now, if we're done here, I need to get back to work."

Mick says, "I'll hang around until you're off. I have news about Myron."

"I'll hang around, too," Billy says, with a wink. "See if you change your mind. And, fill you in on the Rathjen's. "

I push my chair back and shake my finger at both of them. "Just one rule. Do not discuss Melanie, make decisions for Melanie, or talk about Melanie unless she is included in the conversation. Got it?"

We share a hearty laugh all around. Their laughter is for real. Mine, not so much.

****

I join them again at closing time, exhausted, foot weary, and ready for bed in a man-free environment. I do my best to ignore the hopeful look in Mick's eyes. Billy just looks tired. Or, maybe drunk.

I slide in next to Mick. He wraps an arm around my waist and nuzzles my neck. In light of our previous conversation regarding my choice of boyfriends, it seems like a gross lack of etiquette to flaunt our relationship in front of Billy.

I put some space between us and remind him of his previous reference to Myron.

Mick, looking disappointed, says, "Oh, yeah, Myron," and fishes a folded paper from his pocket. He unfolds it and sets in front of me. "It's your authorized visitor's form for the federal prison in Sheridan. You passed your background check. Let me know when you want to see Myron, and I'll set it up."

An involuntary shiver skitters down my spine. In my mind, he's still wielding his hunting knife over my helpless body. I hate the fact the mere mention of his name holds such power over me. My choice would be

219

to never see him again, but Myron and Eddie are currently filed under the category Unfinished Business. If there's any chance Myron truly has evidence implicating Eddie in Dani's death, I can't let fear stop me.

My hand trembles slightly as I smooth out the paper. "Wednesday is my day off."

Mick says, "I'll drive you. Don't think Old Yeller is up to the job."

"Actually, Kendra wants to go with me. I'll check with her. By the way, my car's name is Buttercup, not Old Yeller."

Mick shrugs. "Just let me know, and I'll meet you there. Make sure you have current I.D. I'm working a case in Eugene, so I'll be close by."

His gaze flicks over my body. "Couple of rules. No revealing clothing."

"Fine," I say. "I won't wear my see-through blouse. Anything else?"

"You'll be going through a pat down and a metal detector. If you have an underwire bra, you'll have to take it off."

I roll my eyes. "No dangerous underwear. I promise."

He pulls me close and whispers, "Maybe I'll get to do the pat down. I promise to be extremely thorough."

Embarrassed, I push him away and glance over at Billy. "So, about the Rathjens?"

He tips his mug up and drains his beer. "Mick said you've cleared Rick Rathjen, Riley, and the daughter. What about the missus?"

"Haven't had a chance to get a good look at her soul. She's a cold bitch, and she's cheating on her husband, but why would she kill Yasmin?"

Billy spreads his hands on the tabletop and leans forward. "Maybe she found out the girl was pregnant and isn't ready to be a grandma."

"Riley told me his folks didn't know about the pregnancy. I guess they do now."

"Yes, they know. I talked to them, yesterday. Apparently, the kid told them the whole story, knowing they'd find out when the autopsy report came out."

I think about my last visit with Riley, how he'd made a connection with his sister. "How did they seem? Mad at Riley, or what?"

"I'd say more sad than mad. Rick Rathjen admitted he lied about Riley's whereabouts the night of the murder. Because of his radical views, he figured he'd be suspect number one and was trying to protect his family."

I turn to Mick. "So, do I continue with the riding lessons?"

"You need to connect with Roxanne Rathjen. Can you arrange a lesson with her?"

I groan. "She hates me, but I'll try."

Our conversation is interrupted by Paco who bangs through the door and scans the room. When he spots me, he stomps over to the booth. His longish hair sticks out in a dozen different directions, and he's sporting a maniacal grin.

"No offense, gentlemen," he tells Mick and Billy. "I need a private word with my niece."

Since I haven't seen him since he bombed out of Goodhart's office in pursuit of Rebecca Porter and friend, I'm both curious and apprehensive. I slide out of the booth and follow him to the deserted bar.

He leans close and lowers his voice, even though we're alone. "Tomorrow morning. 10:00 a.m., stand outside your door. You will see justice in action. I promise, you won't be disappointed."

He drops a kiss on my forehead and leaves before I can form a question.

Chapter Thirty-One

At 9:45 the next morning, I splash cold water on my face, brush my teeth and run a comb through my tangled hair. Grumpy and sleep deprived, I wish Paco had factored in my late night and scheduled his special surprise for noon. I peek through the blinds to check the weather. The snow is gone. Sunbeams dance upon frost covered cars in the parking lot, giving the impression of warmth. But, this California girl knows better.

Thunder Paws, curled up on the pillow next to mine, yawns and stretches. Yes, my newly acquired tomcat companion was the only male welcome in my bed last night.

Clad in jeans, sweatshirt, boots and puffy vest, I step on to my tiny front porch and lean against the door, breathing in the crisp pine-scented mountain air. Soon, I hear the unmistakable rumble of Harley Davidson motorcycles, a lot of Harley Davidson motorcycles, their distinctive sound growing louder by the minute.

Paco's crew, led by Chuy drive slowly past Number Ten. Three pairs of bikers follow him. They pull forward as Paco, astride his bike, leads a black Lincoln Navigator to a stop directly in front of my door. Twelve more bikers crowd in behind the SUV. Paco and the others block the only way out.

I see frightened faces peering out motel windows. A man steps out of Number Twelve and shouts, "I'm calling 911."

Paco steps over to the guy and slips some folded bills into his hand. "This will only take a moment, sir, and we'll be gone like the wind."

Nick bursts from the back door of the pub and trots across the parking lot. "What the hell is going on, Paco?"

Paco clamps a hand on Nick's shoulder. "Sorry, man, should have clued you in." He whispers something to Nick who grins and strides away to calm his agitated motel guests.

Paco walks to the Navigator and bangs on the roof with a ham-sized fist. "It's time, ladies. We're not getting any younger."

The driver side window slides down, revealing Noelle Hoffman's pale face. I see an anxious-looking Rebecca Porter in the passenger seat. A white poster board is lifted to the open window. Printed in block letters are the words, *WE WOULD LIKE TO APOLOGIZE.*

Paco says, "There's more."

Another sign appears. *WHAT WE DID WAS WRONG.*

"Damn straight," I mutter.

Sign number three: *WE ARE MOVING TO CANADA AND WILL NEVER BOTHER YOU AGAIN.*

Paco takes my arm and leads me away from the vehicle. "I had a little talk with the ladies and convinced them it would be in their best interest to leave the country. After they made their apology, of course. My boys are giving them a motorcycle escort to the border."

"You actually trust those two? How do you know

they won't come back?"

Paco pats the pocket of his leather vest from which a folded paper is visible. "Did you know one of my guys, Rocco, is a Notary Public? Comes in real handy."

My mind is boggled. I can't comprehend how Rocco, obviously a gang member, managed to demonstrate the integrity and skills required to become a Notary, so I don't ask.

Paco continues, "This document was signed by these so-called ladies and notarized by Rocco. It describes, in detail, all of their actions, the crimes they committed against you and Ms. Goodhart. If they ever turn up in this area again, they will be prosecuted."

He hands the paper to me. I scan it quickly. It looks legitimate. I'm pretty sure it's not.

I say, "They actually believe this is for real?"

Paco chuckles. "Don't you worry, little girl. They believe it."

He walks me back to the car and rotates his index finger.

The window lowers and the next sign appears. *NOD IF YOU ACCEPT OUR APOLOGY.*

I stare into the eyes of the woman who tried to kill me. "Flash cards? Really?"

"Sweet!" Paco gives me a thumb's up. "I agree."

I take one step closer to the car. Fear is not the emotion I feel when I look at the woman behind the wheel in the deadly vehicle. It's outrage. "The only apology I'll accept is a spoken one. From each of you. You have to look into my eyes when you say it. Then, I'll know if you're telling the truth. Step out of the car, and we'll see how it goes."

I hear a rumble of laughter from Paco. He is so

loving every minute of the pageant he's orchestrated. Noelle and Rebecca? Not so much. I have no intention of making it easier for them. It's my payback, too. Right?

Since they have no choice, they climb out of the car and stand in front of me, all the while casting nervous glances at Paco. He slips an arm around my shoulders. They step back, out of reach. I try not to smirk.

Noelle is immediately disqualified since she gazes over the top of my head as she utters her apology. Paco becomes a human buzzer. "Blaht! Try again. This time, make eye contact."

Reluctantly, Noelle looks into my eyes. I search her soul and see it's riddled with fear. Thank you, Uncle Paco.

She says, "My need to love and protect Rebecca interfered with my better judgment. I'm sorry I injured you. You will never see me again."

The words she speaks are true and, this time, I nod my acceptance.

Rebecca steps forward. Our gazes connect. Her anger is gone. Instead of the fear so predominantly displayed in Noelle's soul, I see Rebecca's is a unique shade of violet. It tells me she's made a decision, and she's content with it.

She doesn't wax eloquent. It's just a simple, "I'm sorry," but it's spoken with sincerity.

I glance up at Paco. "I'm good. Thanks, Unc."

He gives me a squeeze and calls, "Move 'em out, boys."

Chapter Thirty-Two

Kendra and I are on our way to Sheridan, Oregon, home sweet home to the federal prison housing my mortal enemy, Myron. Kendra is beyond excited. After all, it is a day away from multiple kidlets and responsibilities. Can't say I blame her.

She's driving her minivan. I'm half comatose in the passenger seat, exhausted after serving adult beverages into the wee hours. All I want is a few more hours of sleep, but Kendra doesn't get the hint. Her queries slam into me like bullets from a semi-automatic weapon.

"Do I get to go with you to talk to Myron?"

"No."

"Will the hunk be there?"

"If you're talking about Mick, yes."

"Whoo hoo!"

She whacks me in the arm and chuckles. "Maybe after your meeting with Myron, you and Mick can score a room for a conjugal visit."

"Even though I can't imagine a more romantic setting, there are no conjugal trailers at federal prisons."

"And, you know this…how?"

"Research. Internet."

This strikes her as hilarious. "So, you thought about it, too?"

"No," I say. "It was just a random fact I stumbled upon when checking out the website."

"Yeah, right."

She waits until I doze off before blurting, "Billy's really sorry he screwed up. He wants you back."

Abandoning my plan for a nap, I straighten up in my seat and fill her in on the whole "taking turns" fiasco.

"Men can be such idiots." She shakes her head in despair. "So, what are you going to do?"

"Live by my new rule: one man at a time."

"Billy's stubborn. He won't give up."

"I'm stubborn, too. We'll have to see how it plays out."

Kendra reaches over and grabs my hand. "No matter what you decide, you'll always be the sister I never had."

The warmth and sincerity of her words take me by surprise. Hot tears sting my eyes. I dash them away, squeeze her hand, and manage to say, "Thanks."

"Okey, dokey, then," she says. "Take a nap. I'll wake you when we get there."

I close my eyes and try not to think about Myron. Apparently it works, because my next conscious moment is when the car stops.

Kendra gently pats my shoulder. "Wakey, wakey, sleeping beauty. We have arrived."

I yawn, stretch and get my first glimpse of the Federal Correction Institution in Sheridan, Oregon. As a product of watching too many prison movies, I expected to see a grim, gray building behind a concrete wall, patrolled by gun-toting guards and snarling German Shepherds straining at their leashes. Instead, I look across the parking lot and see a square cement block building with a peaked burgundy roof as well as a scattering of attractive red-roofed buildings surrounded by an expansive lawn dotted with trees. Had it not been for the high wall topped with razor wire circling the buildings, the setting could easily be mistaken for a private school campus or senior development.

"Wow," Kendra says. "I hate to say it, but it's kinda pretty."

"Way too good for a creep like Myron," I mutter.

"Are you scared?"

I see no reason to lie to my best friend. "A little. He's still a major player in my nightmares. Myron and his big old knife. I was hoping to never to see him again."

She reaches for my hand. "Just remember, you're doing this for Dani. Our Dani."

Unable to speak, I nod.

She squeezes my hand. "Besides, he's locked up, and you're not."

I give her a weak smile and reach for the door handle. "If you want to go shop or something, I'll call you when I'm done."

With a contented smile, Kendra reclines her seat. "Do you know how often I get to nap in the daytime? Never."

I hurry down the broad sidewalk toward the square building. It is obviously the entrance since it juts out in front of the wall. Printed in block letters over the broad double glass doors are the words

FEDERAL DETENTION CENTER
SHERIDAN, OREGON

A man in uniform holding a clipboard steps through the door. He runs a practiced eye over my outfit, consisting of jeans, T-shirt, running shoes and zip front sweatshirt.

"Your name, ma'am?"

I tell him and his steely gaze peruses the clipboard. He makes a tiny check mark next to what I assume is my name. "Please follow me into the lobby, Ms. Sullivan."

Lobby? Prisons have lobbies? As I step through the door, it occurs to me I'll soon be behind the wall instead of outside looking in. The next fifteen minutes consist of making sure I'm carrying no contraband to pass to my mortal enemy, Myron. First, I hand over my cell phone and then pass through the metal detector. Thanks to my sports bra, I set off no alarms. Next, I'm handed over to a muscular woman with spiky gray hair and a gun who leads me to a private room where I'm instructed to remove my shoes and jacket. I stand with legs spread apart and arms extended while she pats me down. Satisfied I'm as clean and shiny as a newborn babe, she takes me back to the lobby where Mick is waiting, looking hot in a blue dress shirt that matches his eyes and snug Levis. Need I say more?

Disregarding the "no touching" rule and gaggle of uniformed personnel watching us, he pulls me close until I'm pressed against his rock-solid body. "You look pale."

"I'm okay."

"Wish I could be in the room, but he said he'll only talk to you."

It's then I realize I've put the whole talking to Myron thing on the back burner. Just call me the Queen of Avoidance.

"So, it will just be Myron and me? Alone in the room?"

Mick strokes my back. "He'll be in a chair, shackled, cuffed, and chained to the floor across the table from you. Also, there will be a guard outside in the hall, watching through a small window. I'll be there, too."

He gives me a squeeze. "You'll be fine. Word of advice. Don't let Myron pick up on your fear. It will give him the upper hand. Show him tough little Mel, the one who scared the shit out of him at the clinic last June. I know you can do it."

I nod, take a big breath and let it out. "Let's get this over with."

Since Wednesday is a non-visiting day for family and friends, I'm taken down a labyrinth of hallways to a room reserved for prisoners and their attorneys. Thankfully, I'm not led through a cellblock, but I clearly hear male voices, some shouting obscenities, some tinged with desperation. The cloying smell of a pine-scented disinfectant does little to disguise the scent of institutional food. Apparently lunch included a serving of onion-laced mystery meat and beans. As I breathe in the noxious mixture of odors, my stomach reacts with a series of death defying flip-flops. I gulp back the bitter bile flowing upward. It reminds me of a past encounter with Myron when I'd been drugged and spewed the entire contents of my stomach all over him. Am I prepping for a re-run? Somehow, recalling the memory amuses me, and I snicker.

The guard leading me to the room hears me and glances over his shoulder. "You okay, ma'am?"

Mick, who's trailing behind me says, "Are you laughing?"

"I'm fine," I assure them. Much to my dismay, I

can't seem to stop my hysterical giggling fit. I sober up quickly when we reach the appointed room.

The guard says, "The prisoner is already here and secured. I'll take you in, get you settled, and step out into the hall. You'll have privacy, but I'll be watching through the window if you need anything."

He fishes a key ring from his pocket and unlocks the door.

Mick pats my butt and says, "Go get 'em, Tiger."

I follow the guard through the door.

Chapter Thirty-Three

Myron is clad in khaki pants and shirt and sprawled in his chair, at least as much as he was able, considering all the cuffs, shackles, etc. attached to his body and, in turn, fastened to the metal loop on the floor. Obviously, he's had more time to work out. His shoulders are broader. Even his neck has muscles. His legs are spread like he's giving me a special view of his disgusting package.

"Hey, there she is," he says with a smirk. "The girl with the sweet little round ass. Unfortunately, I didn't get a chance to fully appreciate it, if you get my drift. But, hey, who knows? If our deal works out, maybe I'll look you up when I get out."

I know he's pushing my buttons. I stand behind the chair opposite him and look into his flat gray eyes and grimy soul.

He says, "Have a seat, sweet cheeks. Then, we'll talk."

"This shouldn't take long. I'd rather stand."

A red flash rockets across his soul. "Sit, or no deal."

I pull the chair back and perch on the edge. "So, talk."

He loses the smirk and straightens up in his chair. "No matter what you think, I'm not stupid."

He pauses and stares at me.

"Never said you were," I lie.

"What I'm about to tell you will implicate Eddie Morgan in the death of his wife. That's why you're here. Right?"

"Yes, and it will also get you a shorter sentence."

With a menacing glare, he leans forward. I can tell he expects me to shrink back. Instead, I scoot my chair closer to him and narrow my gaze. "So," I say. "Why me? Why not just tell the 3 Peaks cops? You'd still get your deal."

His cockiness vanishes. He pinches his lips together and avoids my eyes. "It's not just about my sentence. It's about stuff you said back then. When, you know…" His voice trails off, forcing me to read between the lines.

Last June, when Myron had me bound and helpless, he threatened me with rape before he killed me. I was winging it and told him whatever he did to me would happen to him in prison, three times over. He didn't know I was totally bluffing.

I say, "I'm guessing you want to see if I still have my mojo. I do."

Myron risks a glance at me. "I did some checking up on you. Got lots of time now. Read the 3 Peaks newspaper."

He pauses and stabs a finger at me. "It's what I thought. You're some kinda witch."

If Myron thinks I'm a witch, it's okey dokey with me. I'm feeling a power surge. Yes! I have gained the upper hand.

I give him a brief smile. "Myron, I'm so glad you finally recognized my abilities. If we work together, your life inside prison walls will be so much better."

234

I can't believe he falls for this line of bullshit, but he does.

He heaves a sigh of relief. "Okay, I'll give you the goods on Eddie, but you have to promise you'll reverse the spell, or whatever it is you did to me."

"It depends on your information. If it pans out, and Eddie is arrested, I'll be happy to lift the burden from your soul."

This sounds so good, I'm almost tempted to pat myself on the back.

Myron says, "Okay, it's a deal."

I agree.

When Myron spills the beans, I discover his loving mother, Harriet McGraw, (probably not related to Dr. Phil) has a storage unit. Within this unit are tapes from an answering machine containing several messages from Eddie Morgan. The first one describes Eddie's attack on his wife, Dani. Unfortunately for Eddie, she does not die from his blows. He panics and calls 911. When the medics arrive, he concocts the accident scenario. The second message is Eddie's plea for help. He can't risk Dani waking up. Myron tells him, "No problem," and sets up a time to meet with Eddie. Although Myron won't admit it was his idea, he says Eddie went to the hospital late at night, sneaked into Dani's room and injected an air bubble into her IV tube, thus causing the embolism leading to her death.

Though I've long suspected Eddie killed my best friend, hearing the act described in Myron's flat, uncaring tone triggers a tsunami of emotions. Overwhelming sadness mingles with rage as memories of sweet Dani and baby Destiny flood my mind. I bite my lip and fight back tears, not wanting to lose my position of strength. I promise myself a good cry later.

"Why now?" I ask. "Why didn't you bring this up when you were arrested?"

His lips curl upward in a familiar sneer. "Always hold something back. That's my motto. Bring it out when it will do the most good. Like now."

My first instinct is to get up and walk out, let him stew in his own juice. If I don't, at some point Myron will be a free man. Before he's set loose on society, his years behind bars will help him sharpen his criminal abilities to a fine point. But, this is about justice for Dani, so I wrap my fingers around the edge of the chair and force myself to stay put.

"How do we get in touch with your mother?"

"The cops have her address. She visits me on Saturdays. I'll tell her to hand over the tapes."

I nod and stand.

He straightened in his chair and smirks. "Aren't you going to thank me?"

"You helped Eddie kill my best friend, so, no, Myron, I'm not going to thank you."

Disgusted, I head for the door.

"Hey," he calls. "Don't forget about the other thing we talked about. You know."

"Like I said before, I'll think about it after Eddie is arrested. In the meantime, you best take care in the shower."

I hear a click as the guard opens the door and ushers me into the hall. Mick places his hands on my shoulders and gazes into my eyes. "How did it go? Do we get to nail Eddie?"

"Oh, yeah." I smile up at him. "I have one request. I want to be there when it happens."

Chapter Thirty-Four

Back in 3 Peaks, I desperately need a distraction until I get my grubby little hands on Myron's incriminating tapes. Since it's Wednesday, it will be at least four days until Mama Mildred visits her son at Sheridan. Hopefully, Myron will be able to convince her to hand them over.

Who am I kidding? Once the bureaucracy is involved—Homeland Security and the 3 Peaks police department—I'll be lucky to get anywhere near the evidence. And, they are already involved. Before Mick left to go back to whatever he's doing in Eugene, he called Billy to coordinate the course of events. To his credit, he did ask Billy to include me in the action. Whether or not this will happen remains to be seen.

All I can do now is wait. Since it doesn't take much time to perfect the happy dance I plan to perform for Eddie's perp walk, I decide to finish up my business with the Rathjens. Once I determine whether or not Roxanne Rathjen had any involvement in Yasmin's death, I can submit my timesheet to DHS and get paid. This probably sounds crass, but I'm itching to get out of Number Ten and into an apartment of my own. The check I received from Louise Goodhart is now residing in my bank account along with whatever I manage to set aside from my waitressing job. I'm hoping the Homeland Security money will put me over the top.

Both Steve and my mother frequently offer to bankroll the deposit, but I've stubbornly turned them down. I want to do it on my own.

Factoring in the above information, I give Riley Rathjen a call. He answers on the first ring.

"Hey, cowgirl," he says. "Sugar Lips misses you. Coming back soon?"

He has a lilt in his voice, totally missing in our previous conversations. I take this as an encouraging sign of healing. Though I want to pelt him with questions, I hold back.

"Actually," I say. "Your dad put me on Bella the last time I was out. I seem to be a great source of amusement for your entire family when I'm astride Sugar Lips. What do you think?"

He chuckles. "You ready for Sneaky Pete?"

I hold back a shudder. "No way. Would your mom mind if I rode Bella again?"

"She's home for a change. I'll go ask her if it's okay."

I hastily add, "Do you think she'd be willing to give me some pointers about riding Bella? Like maybe there's girl stuff I need to know."

I know this sounds incredibly ridiculous, but I'm making it up on the fly.

A long silence ensues, and I try to imagine what is going through Riley's mind. Things like bouncing boobies, tampons versus pads, virgins versus non-virgins, potential pregnancies, etc.

Finally, he says, "Well, um, I guess I can ask her. Does this mean you don't want a lesson from me?"

Okay, now I know what he's thinking about. Rejection. Not all the other stuff floating through my overactive mind. "Of course I want you to be there, Riley. Since Bella is your mother's horse, I thought maybe she could give me some pointers."

"Hang on a sec."

Apparently, he doesn't want me privy to their conversation, because I hear a clunk as he places the phone on a hard surface and the sound of receding footsteps. I strain to make sense from their muffled words. Riley's voice is steady and insistent. Roxanne's is a bit shrill. Is she angry? Protesting? Riley persists and I hear Roxanne's tone level off and die down.

Riley picks up his phone. "Mom says she can give you some time, but it depends on when you're coming out."

We settle on Friday morning at eleven, which means I'll be able to log some solid slumber time after my shift ends at 2:00 a.m., providing all goes as planned, and Mick doesn't show up. I'm learning a great deal about having a boyfriend who works for Homeland Security. They come and go like phantoms in the wind. Good or bad? I haven't decided yet.

And, wouldn't you know, just as Mick goes missing, Billy starts hanging out at Nick's again, looking hopeful. Even though I'd told he was welcome to return, I do my best not to encourage him.

The locals spot him and call, "Hey, kid, welcome back!"

After casting a lustful glance in my direction, he joins his pool shooting buddies in a section of the bar we call the Corral. It's a bit rowdy there, but I can usually handle it on my own. Occasionally, an obnoxious drunk who doesn't play by the rules, gets too frisky. When that happens, a couple of my regulars march him to the front door and toss him unceremoniously into the parking lot. Works for me.

Billy approaches me during my break. He touches my arm. "You got a minute to talk about Myron?"

We head for an occupied booth. I sip ice water and wait for him to talk. Instead, he reaches across the table and takes my hand. "Mick around?"

"Maybe," I say, pulling my hand free. "How's the Backwoods Princess?"

His brow furrows. "Who?"

"Haley McFadden. She has a sticker on the back end of her Jeep. It says Backwoods Princess. Guess you never noticed. Maybe you were too busy looking at her back end."

He shakes his head and bites his lower lip like he's trying not to grin. "Jesus, Minnie, do you always go for the throat?"

"Balls to the wall."

His right hand drops below the table. "Shoulda worn my jock. Thank God there's not a steak knife on the table."

I peek under and see he's covering his privates. We lock gazes. His eyes crinkle in amusement, and we both bust out laughing.

We sober quickly. I sip more water. He places his hands on the table and says, "Haley is no longer in the picture.."

"What happened? Did she get pissed off when she found out you already had a girlfriend?"

"No. Every time I looked at her, I wanted her to be you. She figured it out and told me to fuck off."

"Oh."

I don't want to believe him, but a quick glance into

his soul tells me every word he's uttering is the truth. Well, damn. I'm not ready to go there.

"About Myron?" I prompt.

"Mick told me about the tapes. Once we get the green light, we'll pay a visit to his mom. I've talked to my captain and told him about your involvement, if not for you, we'd never get to nail Eddie Morgan."

"And?"

"He said you're a civilian, but he'll take it under advisement."

I groan. "Double speak for, 'no way.'"

He leans forward, his gaze focused and intense. "I won't let it go, Minnie. I want you there. I'll figure out a way."

I nod. "Let me know. Gotta get back to work."

When my shift is over, I slip out the back door, carrying a carton of leftover tuna and noodles. Thunder Paws trots next to me, periodically leaping into the air in an effort to bat the carton from my hand. Despite his ominous growls, I lift the carton high above my head until we're inside Number Ten. He can scarcely wait until I deposit the food into his dish before diving in.

Tom cats. Men. The similarity is amazing. As the thought drifts through my mind, Mick calls.

"*Malysh*," he growls, sending little waves of heat spiraling through my body. "Too tired to talk?"

I assure him I'm not and flop down on the bed. Thunder Paws, having devoured his tuna noodle casserole, joins me, purring loudly while scrubbing his whiskers with one enormous paw.

"I hear something. Sounds like a motor. Do you miss me so much you now have a vibrator?"

"It's the *kotik*, dummy."

His deep chuckle triggers one of mine.

"This is good," he says. "You now know the Russian word for cat. Stick with me and you'll soon be multilingual."

I tell him about Billy's visit.

He stays silent for a while. Finally, he says, "I meant what I said earlier. If you still have feelings for Billy, you need to tell me. I'm not saying I would like it, but you are so young, *malysh*, it is not right for me to control you. You must make up your own mind."

Unexpectedly, hot tears spring into my eyes. I wipe them away. "Like I said before, I'm with you now."

Our conversation veers away from the hot button issue. We chat a few minutes more about insignificant matters before saying, "Good night," and making kissy sounds into the phone.

Later, with Thunder Paws curled up next to me, I stare into the darkness thinking about my life, my loves and the decisions lying ahead. I care deeply about Billy, but my broken heart hasn't yet healed. Is it possible to love more than one man?

Chapter Thirty-Five

When Friday morning arrives, the very last thing I want to do is go for a brisk ride aboard a horse. As I lie snuggled beneath the down comforter my mother sent via one of Abel's trucks, I hear wind whistling through the parking lot. A hopeful thought flits through my mind. Maybe, it's snowing and it would be unsafe to drive Buttercup on slick roads. I slip out of bed and peek out the window. Damn, no snow. Just dark, leaden skies and a brisk wind.

Thunder Paws emerges from the depths of my bed covers, stretches and trots hopefully to his bowl. Discovering it empty, he turns, fixes me with an evil glare and growls.

"Sorry, buddy, all I've got is kibble."

In an attempt to get T.P. on a healthier diet, I'd actually forked over a few bucks for cat chow. He hates it. Apparently he's always been an alley cat, feasting on leftovers from garbage cans. The first time I put kibble in his bowl, he gave it a sniff, turned up his nose and stalked to the door.

Now, to make my point, I pick up the cat food box and shake it. Thunder Paws gets the message. He trots to the door and demands to be let out, using his paw-pounding technique. I open the door, and he scoots out, heading for the back door of the pub. We both know he'll wait outside until one of his well-trained kitchen minions emerges with a greasy, unhealthy treat. The cat and I have a lot in common.

Even though I long to slip back under the covers for a long, uninterrupted snooze, it is not to be. I want to be paid, so I need to complete my assignment from D.H.S. After once again checking the weather, I pull on the long johns and flannel lined jeans I'd scored at the thrift shop for five ninety-nine, plus a Nick's Place T-shirt, a hooded sweatshirt and a butt-ugly water-proof jacket—courtesy of my mother who thinks it rains non-stop in Oregon—and my black high-top tennis shoes. Quite the fashion statement. At least, I won't freeze to death astride a tall horse.

I arrive at the Rathjen's fifteen minutes early, hoping to catch Roxanne in an unguarded moment, before she puts on her public face. In my previous encounters with her, I'd found her difficult to read. Obviously uncomfortable in my presence, she's reluctant to make eye contact. It's almost as if she knows I'm trying to ferret out her secrets. I don't believe Roxanne is a killer, but I'm certain she's hiding something. My task it to discover whether or not it's related to Yasmin's murder. Definitely not easy to do with someone as slippery-souled as Roxanne. So, since she's such a hard case, whatcha gonna do, Mel? Suck up, of course. If Roxanne is as shallow as I suspect, sucking up might work.

I park Buttercup and look around for Roxanne. But, it's Riley I spot. He's in the barn putting a bridle and saddle on beautiful Bella. When he walks out to greet me, Bella plods along behind him like a faithful German Shepherd.

Much to my surprise, Riley wraps his arms around

me and pulls me in for a hug. He smells of teenage boy testosterone, fresh air, pine needles, and hay. Mesmerized, I breathe in the dizzying array of scents. He releases me, blushes, and puts some space between us. "Hey, girl, I've missed you. Glad you're back."

He takes my hand and leads me into the barn. Bella follows.

I'm a bit embarrassed by the fact I've so enjoyed the assault on my senses precipitated by Riley's hug. I take a step back and study him. "Thanks, I've missed you too. Looks like you're feeling better. I was worried about you the last time we met. How are things going?"

The expression on his face grows hard. "Better. Rachel and I talked. We came to the conclusion we're way more grown up than our mom and dad, and if this family is going to be fixed, it's up to us. Pretty lame, huh?"

I nod. "It happens."

"We told them we needed to talk. Really talk. I guess you know I was pretty depressed. I owe Rachel big time. She talked me down. Apparently, my mom is screwing around, and Rachel knows about it. She threatened to tell Dad."

I don't mention the fact I already know this, since I'd been blatantly eavesdropping when I overheard the previous mother-daughter shouting match.

"How did your mother react?"

"She poured herself a big old glass of wine and chugged it."

"Then," Riley continues, "We cornered Dad. Rachel told him the two of us were going to move out and live with our grandparents if he and Mom aren't able to get it together."

He pauses and gazes over my head at his family home. "Dad got all red in the face and yelled a lot. Rach and I just stood there. Didn't say a word. Finally, he talked to our mom and they both agreed to a family meeting. I told them everything."

He looks away and gulps back tears. "About Yasmin. About the baby. How much we loved each other and planned to get married."

"And now?" I prompt.

He shrugs. "Remains to be seen. They didn't have much to say. Now, we're all tiptoeing around each other. Know what I mean?"

"Family counseling would be good."

He heaves a heavy sigh. "Yeah, it would. My dad thinks it shows weakness…like he can't take care of his family. We're working on him."

He flashes a brief grin. "Fingers crossed."

"Would you really move out? You and Rachel?"

"Absolutely."

"Then you're holding all the cards. Keep the pressure on. Set a date. Tell them if they don't make an appointment for counseling by the deadline, you and Rachel are gone. Trust me, they don't want to lose either one of you."

Riley looks puzzled for a moment. Then I see a sparkle of light flicker across his soul. Riley finally understands there's been a shift of power in the family dynamics.

He smiles and nods. "Thanks, I'll talk to Rachel. We'll work it out."

"Work what out?"

Roxanne's voice precedes her. She steps through the barn door, eyes narrowed in suspicion. The woman is like a Prius. Neither of us had heard her approach. Riley and I are struck dumb for a moment.

I rally quickly and step between mother and son. "I was just telling Riley I'm looking forward to riding Bella again, you know, after learning on a Shetland pony, it's a whole new experience."

I realize I'm babbling but I need to give Riley time to get it together.

Roxanne gives me her frowny face. "I thought I heard Rachel's name mentioned."

"Riley said Rachel thought it was ridiculous for me to ride Sugar Lips."

Her gaze flicks up and down my outfit. "Well, she's right about that."

I give her an ingratiating smile and gaze into her eye. She stares unblinking into mine as if to determine if I'm lying. Yes! Exactly what I'd hoped for. I get a good long look before she turns away and speaks to Riley.

"Your dad needs help changing a tire. He's in the garage. Be back in ten minutes."

Riley nods and makes a hasty exit.

Roxanne ignores me and walks to Bella. Moving slowly, she reaches up and strokes the Palomino's velvety nose. She croons, "How's my beautiful girl today?"

The skeptic in me wonders if she shows the same affection to her children. I shift my weight from foot to foot, trying to figure out how to proceed. Silently, I check out her attire. She has to be the best-dressed horsewoman in Oregon, or possibly the entire United States. Form-fitting tan suede trousers cling to her long, shapely legs and terminate inside hand-tooled leather boots. A black turtleneck sweater peeks out of a deep fuchsia puffy zip-front jacket, the kind you can fold up and store in a little bag. Her wavy blond hair is pulled back and fastened with a jeweled clip, the same color as her coat.

Acutely aware of my fashion shortcomings, I pull up my hood in an effort to conceal messy, bedhead hair. Then, I remember why I'm here. Screw it, Mel. You're not interviewing for a modeling job. Get it done, and you'll never have to see the woman again.

Since most people grow uncomfortable when a silence grows too long, I wait her out.

With one hand on the horse's bridle, she finally turns to face me. "What can I do for you? Riley said you had some questions about Bella."

Since I hadn't really thought this through, I struggle to come up with relevant, horse-related questions.

"Well, um," I begin. "Since Bella's your horse, I thought you might have some tips for me. Like things I should avoid. She's used to you. Maybe she doesn't like me riding her."

I know this sounds incredibly lame, but it's the best I can come up with at the moment.

She looks puzzled, as if this is a difficult question to answer. Finally, she says, "I don't think it will be a problem as long as you don't act afraid. Horses know when you're afraid."

"Okay. Anything else?"

She glances toward the door, clearly wanting to get back to whatever she was doing "She has a soft mouth, so don't yank on the reins."

I'm all out of questions and, besides, I have what I

need, soul-wise. "Alrighty then, thanks."

She hands me Bella's reins and moves toward the door. Before she steps out, she stops abruptly and turns to face me. "A word of caution," she says.

"About Bella?"

"No, about my family."

Startled, I repeat, "Your family?"

She folds her arms across her chest. Her eyes glitter with hostility. "I know you've wormed your way into Riley's affections. The question is why? I know you know about Yasmin and the baby. Let me remind you this is our family's business, not yours."

The worm reference really frosts my cookies. It brings to mind a nocturnal invertebrate emerging from the bowels of the earth and wrapping its slimy self around Riley in order to extract his secrets.

I draw myself up as tall as possible. "I've done absolutely no worming. Your son knew I was acquainted with Yasmin. He initiated the conversation. Do you have any idea how much Riley was hurting? How depressed he was? Probably not since your family was too busy closing ranks and deflecting blame to listen to him, to support him. So, he talked to me instead."

Two spots of red burn high on her cheeks. She opens her mouth and then closes it again.

I decide to go for broke, knowing it's probably my last trip to the Rockin' R Ranch. With any luck, I'll never see Roxanne again. "Riley's a good kid. So is Rachel. Word of advice, start listening to them if you want to keep your precious family together."

After two long steps, she looms over me and snatches Bella's reins from my hand. "No way are you riding my horse. Get out."

I don't bother to answer. I step around her and stride out the door.

Before I can slip into Buttercup and drive away, Riley catches up with me. "What's going on?"

Roxanne calls, "Let her go, Riley. She doesn't belong here."

Riley's back stiffens. He turns and snaps, "Not for you to decide, Mother. She's my friend. If she's not welcome here, I'll meet her somewhere else."

Her eyes widen in surprise. I wonder if this is the first time he's ever stood up to her. Rather than making a fuss, she rolls her eyes and mutters, "Whatever," before marching toward the house.

Riley takes my hand and murmurs, "Sorry."

I squeeze his hand. "I'm the one who's sorry. After she told me to butt out of family stuff, I lost my temper. Told her she'd better start paying more attention to her kids or she'd lose them."

"No shit?" His eyes light up followed by an authentic full out, joyful Riley grin. Seeing him smile again makes my heart happy.

"No shit," I say, tugging my hand free. "Gotta go."

I slide into Buttercup. Riley catches hold of the door. "Sorry about the riding lesson."

"It's okay," I say, trying to look disappointed. I silently vow, I will tell Riley the truth at some point. I feel bad about deceiving him. Maybe when we're both older and wiser.

I crank up the motor. Riley doesn't budge. I sense he's got something else on his mind. I think I know what it is and hope I can handle it tactfully. I truly don't want to play the boyfriend card.

He leans in close, eyes bright with hope. "I'll miss seeing you. Think we can hang out sometime?"

I pat his cheek in a sisterly fashion. "Sure. We should meet for coffee."

"Maybe dinner and a movie?"

"Riley," I say. "Dinner and a movie sounds like a date. I'm twenty-three. You're nineteen. Let's settle for friendship."

He looks a bit crestfallen. "I guess so."

Before he closes the door, he mutters, "Four years isn't so much."

I smile. "Still puts me in cougar territory."

Another Riley grin appears. "Rowr," he says, closes the door and lifts a hand in farewell.

Chapter Thirty-Six

It's Sunday and things are slow at the pub. The dinner crowd is gone, and the hardcore drinkers are taking the night off. I'm feeling antsy, waiting for a call from Billy or Mick, telling me Myron's mother followed through as planned and visited her creepy son at Sheridan over the weekend. If so, I need to know if she's cooperating and ready to hand over the incriminating tapes. But, the cell phone in my apron pocket remains silent. If they leave me out of the loop, as usual, I will be royally pissed off.

Nick beckons me to the bar. He looks as bored as I feel.

"Not much action tonight," he says. "Go ahead and take off. I'll give you a jingle if I need help."

I thank him and sidle to the door before he can change his mind. I'll use the time to put the finishing touches on the Homeland Security report since I've reached my conclusions about the Rathjen family.

Coatless and shivering in the chill night air, I scurry across the parking lot, toward the warmth of my haven, Number Ten. I'd left a lamp on, and a rosy glow leaks out from beneath the blinds. I reach for my key and then, stop, dead in my tracks. I always park Buttercup outside my door and now, she's gone. I look around the parking lot. Maybe I'd absent-mindedly parked her in front of the wrong room. Feeling slightly panicky, I scan the area. No Buttercup. This can't be happening. Why would anyone steal Buttercup? She's an ugly old clunker, but she's my ugly, old clunker, paid for with hard-earned money.

I reverse course and trot back into the pub. Nick, still behind the bar, doesn't look surprised to see me. He winks and says, "Thought you'd be back. Are you missing something?"

"Somebody stole my car," I gasp. Then, his words penetrate my brain. I gaze at him through slitted eyes. "You knew? What's going on?"

"Call your boyfriend."

Stupidly, I ask, "Mick?"

He chuckles. "Got more than one?"

Flustered, I feel a blush warming my cheeks. I turn away and reach for my phone. Before I can place the call, the door flies open. A guy in a black hoodie pushes through and stops, scanning the bar. The hood obscures his face, but his body language is menacing.

Oh, shit, we're being robbed!

"Nick," I whisper. "This guy is bad news. Do you still have a baseball bat stashed behind the bar? Give it to me and call 911."

"It's fine, Mel."

Outraged, I hiss, "Fine? Look at him. He's about to pull a gun and take all your cash. Plus, he might shoot somebody if we piss him off."

Nick, still majorly unperturbed, continues to chuckle. What the hell?

I stand and reach behind me until I'm able to wrap my fingers around the handle of a heavy glass pitcher filled with beer. With a little luck, I can throw the beer in his face and, while he's blinded, whack him in the head.

He walks slowly toward us. His face is in shadow but light bounces off the silver ring piercing his slightly crooked nose. My heart hammers in my chest. I slide the glass pitcher to the edge of the bar. I gather myself, weight forward. I'm ready to pounce.

The man takes another step and reaches out a hand. From beneath dark brows, his bright blue gaze sweeps over me. He says, "Come with me, *malysh*."

"Mick?" Weak in the knees, I push away from the bar. "What the hell?"

He pushes back his hood revealing dark, spiked hair and a two-day beard stubble. "Undercover," he says with a grin.

Nick's chuckle blossoms into a belly laugh.

I turn and glare at him. "Not funny. I could have hurt him. I might have even killed him."

"I sincerely doubt it. I think Mr. Homeland Security can take care of himself."

"Nevertheless," I begin.

Before I can finish my thought, Mick grabs my hand. "Come with me."

The fight or flight instinct leaks from my body, and I'm beginning to connect the dots. I fish the car keys from my jeans' pocket and dangle them in the space between us. "This better be about my car."

With a lightning fast move, he grabs the keys, takes my hand, pulls me through the door and drags me across the parking lot. I have to trot to keep up with his long-legged stride. Buttercup is back in her usual spot.

"You stole my car?"

"Yeah."

"But, why? How? I had the keys."

"I'm a man of many talents."

I fold my arms across my chest and stare up at him. "So, you hot-wired it? I assume there's a good reason for your thievery."

With a self-satisfied smirk, he nods.

I blow out air. "Okay, enough with the guessing game. Why did you steal my car?"

His smirk disappears. "Thought you'd notice."

Oops, I get it. He's done something nice for me and, I'm such an ungrateful wretch, I've failed to notice. Peering through the windows, I see the same old ratty upholstery and mud-colored floor mats.

"Lower," he says.

Lower? I already checked out the floor mats.

"Not inside the car," he hints further.

I use the flashlight app on my phone and shine it over Buttercup's dented exterior. Mick takes my hand and directs the beam downward. A Firestone sticker clings to the left front tire.

I'm torn between anger at his deception, laughter, and gratitude. I pick the latter. "You bought me new tires. Thank you so much."

"Snow tires," he proclaims. "Can't have you driving around 3 Peaks in the winter on bald tires. Not safe."

I wrap my arms around his waist and smooch his bristly cheek. "What's the occasion?"

He cups my face in his hands and brushes his lips across mine. "Late birthday present."

I place my hands on top of his and notice, for the first time, he also has a small ring in his left eyebrow. "But we weren't even together on my birthday."

"Doesn't matter."

I push away from him. "Don't tell me you've been talking to my mother."

"No worries. Your dad told me when I talked to him this morning."

"So," I say. "You, my dad, and Nick all colluded in a scheme to steal my car."

He nods and hands me the keys. "Wanna try 'er out?"

What I really want to do is take a hot shower and curl up under my down comforter, preferably alone, but I can't ignore his hopeful expression. Will I be able to tell the difference between my old bald tires and the new Firestones? Probably not, but I'm prepared to lie. "Sure, let's do it," I exclaim, scrambling behind the wheel.

Mick trots to the passenger side and climbs in. "My place," he says. "I cooked."

Whoa, snow tires and a home cooked meal? I'm impressed, even though somewhat anxious about visiting Mick's apartment. I haven't been back since that fateful night last June when he plunked me down on his couch with my injured right arm in a sling, my ankles bound together, and my left arm tied to my thigh. Determined to escape, I inched across the living room on my butt until I reached a phone. I paid the price in pain and still have a hard time believing I managed to escape. Neither can he.

Even though I now know Mick is a good guy, the reptilian part of my brain does not want to believe it. Not for an instant. It's taken time to trust Mick, more time to invite him into my bed. The next logical step is to confront the scene of my agony and put it behind me.

I fire up Buttercup and merge into the traffic

whizzing by the pub. I glance over at Mick. His head is cocked to one side like he's listening for something. I mimic his action. Do new snow tires make a special sound? I curse myself for being so ignorant. Time to fake it.

"Oh, yeah," I squeal, as if I'm in the throes of an especially wonderful orgasm. "Listen to those tires hum!"

One unnaturally dark eyebrow shoots up. "You're so full of shit. It's not the sound of the tires, it's the way the car handles."

"I knew that," I huff. "I was just testing you."

From the way he pinches his lips together, I know he's trying not to laugh. He says "Sure you did."

I decide the best course of action is to keep my mouth shut since Mick's bullshit meter is so finely tuned. I don't speak until we pull into his apartment complex and park. I reach over and squeeze his hand. "When I scraped together enough money to buy Buttercup, it never occurred to me to check the tires and, being a California girl, I didn't factor in snowy winters. Anyway, what I'm trying to say is I truly appreciate you looking out for my safety. If you give me the bill, I'll pay you back."

Mick glowers at me. "Is there something about the word gift you don't understand?"

Seemingly, I've just made it worse. I throw my hands in the air. "Sorry. I'll just say thank you and let it go. Okay?"

He still looks pissed off, but exits the car, strides to the driver's side and opens my door.

I step out of the car, my gaze fixated on the sign, High Desert Pines. A series of flashbacks flit across my mind. Me, woozy from a head injury. My broken elbow throbbing to the beat of my heart. Mick, propping me up with his body as he unlocks the door to apartment 110.

Mick takes my hand. I take a deep breath and let him lead me through the door.

Chapter Thirty-Seven

He squeezes my hand. "You're shaking.

"I'm fine."

His brows draw together. "Don't lie to me, *malysh*. What is bothering you?"

"I've only been in your apartment once, and all I remember is a whole lot of pain."

"Ah," he says. "That was quite a night. Never thought you'd manage to get away."

Somehow, his words make me swell with pride. I cop a little attitude. "Guess you found I'm tougher than you thought, big boy."

He trails a finger across my lower lip, smiling when I shiver. "I promise. Tonight will be about pleasure, not pain."

Pleasure has many definitions, many connotations. Right now, it's olfactory, a fancy name for breathing in the aroma of home-cooked food. I breathe in the heavenly smells wafting through the air, practically drooling in anticipation. I can't categorize the ingredients, but I get a whiff of sugary baked goods along with a mixture of meat, subtle seasonings, fresh vegetables and vinaigrette.

The angst I was feeling about entering Mick's apartment vanishes. I lick my lips and head for the table set for two.

Unfortunately, Mick gets the wrong idea.

Following close on my heels, he slides his arms around my waist and presses his body against mine. He nuzzles my neck, his breath warm against my skin.

"My *maylsh*," he says, "Beautiful girl. Dinner can wait."

I twist around in his arms. "Are you kidding me? Do you want to hear my stomach make bizarre noises while we're doing it? If you don't feed me, now, you're probably not going to get lucky later."

Mick looks disappointed, but is gracious about my rebuff and guides me into a chair. We start with Grey Goose vodka and a splash of lemon juice over ice followed by a vinaigrette salad of beetroots, carrots, peas, pickled cucumbers and smoked salmon.

Mick clears our salad plates and places a wooden cutting board in the middle of the table. Wearing oven mitts on both hands, he pulls a covered dish from the oven and places it on the table.

"I confess I did not cook this," he says. "There's a Russian market in Eugene whose specialty is Meat a la Peter."

He pauses and gazes down at me. "In case you don't know, it refers to Peter the Great. This dish was his favorite meal and very difficult to make."

He lifts the lid, and I see meat baked with onions and mushrooms, bubbling in a savory sauce. I breathe in the aroma and sigh with pleasure. It's all I can do to keep from grabbing a fork and digging in.

We devour Meat a la Peter the Great. For the record, it's pretty darn great. When we come up for air, Mick reaches over and mops my chin with his napkin.

"Very good, *kotik*, you eat like a Russian woman."

I'm slightly alarmed. Should I be flattered or

offended? Images of large muscular women with hairy armpits bench-pressing barbells appear in my mind. Not sure how to respond, I say, "Well, um, I guess I was pretty hungry."

He raises a finger and shakes it. "When I say good, I mean good. Most American women eat like little bunnies. A carrot for lunch. A salad for dinner. Always worried about their weight. You eat like a real woman. I like it."

He pushes his chair back and stands. "Now, are you ready for *Syrniki*? I made it myself."

I don't have a clue what *Syrniki* is, but in the spirit of eating like a Russian woman, I say, "Of course. Bring it on."

He carries a foil-covered tray and small plates to the table, removing the foil with a flourish. Upon the tray I see a stack of what looks like crisp, brown pancakes.

"These," he says, "I made myself."

When I give Mick a questioning look, he says, "One moment." He returns with a jar of honey.

He slides two *Syrniki* onto a plate, garnishes it with honey and places it in front of me.

"Eat," he commands.

I sense this is important to him, so I take a big bite. Oh. My. God. The combination of flavors, brown, crispy crust and warm, creamy filling explodes in my mouth. I moan in ecstasy. I may have even spoken in tongues. Embarrassingly, the two *Syrniki* are inhaled in record time.

I lay down my fork and smile up at Mick. "You actually made these?"

He nods. His gaze is intense and fixed upon my

mouth.

"Who taught you?" I whisper, even though I'm fairly certain culinary matters are not uppermost on Mick's mind.

He doesn't answer. Instead he places his hands on my shoulders and slides them upward to cup my face. He leans close, his tongue sweeping across my lower lip. He murmurs, "You taste of honey. I want to taste more of you."

I gaze up at him. With his two-day growth of beard, black, spikey hair and piercings, he isn't the Mick I know. It's like looking into the face of a dangerous, dark-haired stranger who wants to do outrageous things to my body.

He brushes the back of his hand across my breasts, glances down at my traitorous nipples clearly visible through the thin material of my shirt and gives me a knowing smile. "I think you like the new me."

Suddenly, I'm on fire as the heat in his eyes ignites an answering flame deep within me. I want his warm, bare skin pressed against mine. I want to match my breath to his. Feel him deep inside me, loving me. I stand, grab his shirt with both hands and pull it over his head. His nimble fingers remove my shirt and bra and soon, we're both bare from the waist up. He lifts me up until I wrap my legs around his waist, my arms around his neck.

I bite his lower lip, ravenous for him.

He yips in surprise and mutters in Russian. I see him eyeing the table and deduce, in his haste, he's about to clear it off with one sweep of his hand. In spite of my lustful yearnings, I can't bear to see what's left of the *Syrniki* fly through the air and land on the floor.

"Not on the table," I gasp. "Leftovers later."

I feel a rumble of laughter deep in his chest. "We shall commence our proceedings in the bedroom as madam requests." His hands encircle my waist, and he tosses me over one shoulder, caveman style.

The bedroom is dimly lit, but smells of fresh, clean sheets and the scent I've come to associate with Mick, that of a pine forest, juniper, and lemon-flavored vodka. I sigh with pleasure as he gently places me on the bed and strips off the rest of my clothes.

"Now you," I say, reaching for the metal fasteners on the front of his jeans.

When his erection springs free, I slide my hand up its length and follow with my tongue.

"Oh, sweet Jesus," he moans, reaching for the rubber on the bedside table. "Don't think I can wait."

"It's okay," I say. "I want you inside me. Now."

He flashes a wicked smile. "I was born to serve."

In spite of my body's urgent demands, I take a moment and grin up at him. "Oh, yeah? I'll remember those words."

He lays a finger across my lips. "Hush, *maylsh*."

Later, much later, we're spooning. Unlike Billy who is a restless sleeper, Mick likes to spoon. I fill him in on my last visit with the Rathjens.

"And," I say. "The report is written."

He promises I'll be paid soon and yawns. I snuggle against him, trying to summon the energy to get dressed and drive home. But first, I have questions.

"Who taught you to cook?"

"My mother."

"Oh," I say, faking surprise. "And, does she live nearby or in Russia."

"Classified."

I turn to face him and peer into his untroubled soul. "Classified? Are you kidding me? Doesn't seem like the whereabouts of a person's mother should be classified information."

"Would you like to share your opinion with my boss?"

Really, I have no answer, and his next statement chases all fatigue from my body.

"Speaking of mothers," he says in a casual tone. "Myron's mother says she won't talk to anybody but you."

It takes a moment for his words to sink into my foggy brain. When it does, I spring from the bed and stare at him in amazement. "You waited all this time to tell me? What's wrong with you?"

He rises to a sitting position, arms folded across his muscular chest, and glowers at me. "Perhaps I had more pressing matters on my mind."

I can scarcely believe what I'm hearing. "Perhaps you chose to wait until after we had sex to tell me. You know how long I've waited to nail Eddie?"

He brushes the question aside and narrows his eyes. "Seems like you enjoyed it, too."

I stamp my foot. "So, not the point, Mick, and you know it."

He sighs and holds out his arms. "Ah, *maylsh*, you know you drive me crazy. I look at you and lose my mind. Come back to bed."

I feel myself weakening, so I take a step back. "Not until you tell me every teensy, little detail."

He complies, but it occurs to me he may have an ulterior motive. He does and, though I'm loathe to admit it, my angry rant dissipates quickly. Apparently, I'm a sucker for charming, sexy Russians. It's a lame excuse, but it's all I've got.

Chapter Thirty-Eight

I'm standing in the street in front of Harriet McGraw's neat, tan bungalow, reluctant to take my first step toward the tiny front porch topped by a peaked roof. I try to puzzle out what's giving me bad vibes and decide it's the windows. Identical bare windows flank the front door, giving the impression of a pair of knowing eyes peering at me, studying me. Or maybe it's the overgrown trees closing in around the back and sides of the house, shrouding it in darkness. I indulge in a little self-talk. You're being silly, Mel. Don't chicken out now.

I ignore the creepy window eyes and walk briskly onto the front porch. When I raise my hand to knock, the door flies open, and a tall, spare woman with steel-gray hair, thin lips, and black suspicious eyes looks me over. She's wearing gray slacks, sensible shoes, and a navy long-sleeved shirt. The contrast between the dark shirt and her colorless face is startling. It feels like a disconnect between her body and soul. I want to reach over and pinch her cheeks to see if blood flows through her veins.

"I am Harriet McGraw. You are Miss Sullivan, I presume," she says. Her voice is deep, her diction precise. So not what I expected when I visualized Myron's mother. I'd pictured a slatternly woman puffing on a cigarette and swilling cheap beer.

"Yes, I'm Mel. Thanks for meeting with me."

She steps back and waves me into a small, gloomy living room. The walls are beige. The rug is dark brown. The furniture, a straight-backed sofa and two wing chairs are a lighter shade of brown. A large crucifix featuring a suffering Jesus is prominently displayed on the wall above a flat screen television. His eyes are not closed in agony, but wide-open and all seeing. I try to imagine growing up in this environment. Would it be an act of blasphemy to laugh at a silly bit on TV with the gaze of Jesus upon you? I almost summon a tiny shred of sympathy for Myron. Almost.

Harriet perches on the edge of the couch, her back ramrod straight. "Sit," she says.

I obey and plop down on the wing chair opposite her. She cocks her head to one side and studies me. I'm acutely uncomfortable, and the creep factor makes me want to flee.

She folds her hands, places them in her lap, and clears her throat. "I tried to guide Myron down a righteous path, but he rebelled and chose the devil's way. However, I do visit him in prison like a good mother should. My hope is that he will come to the light."

Wow, sounds like she's been listening to country music. Although I know Myron's main focus is to learn how to become a better criminal, I manage to say, "It could happen."

She leans forward. Her dark eyes look like tiny hot coals burning in her pale face. "He told me you've cast some sort of a spell on him. Do you practice witchcraft?"

Part of me wants to say, Yes, and how do you feel

about becoming a frog? I resist the urge, draw myself up and say, "I assure you I do not practice witchcraft. Myron has an overactive imagination."

She persists. "But, there is something wrong with you. You have power derived from the occult. I read about it in the paper. I must warn you, you're treading in dangerous territory."

I struggle to tamp down the anger and outrage her words evoke. I spent the first twenty-one years of my life thinking something was wrong with me. When I met my biological father and together, we helped save innocent lives, I realized I've been blessed with a gift. Rather than go into a long explanation of my soul reading ability, which I know she will misinterpret, I silently vow not to let the words of this judgmental fanatic take root in my heart.

"You're entitled to your opinion, Ms. McGraw. Can we talk about the tapes? I believe Myron asked you to give them to me."

"Ah, yes, the tapes." Her thin lips lift in a brief triumphant smile. "I've decided to hang on to them until you answer my questions."

Patience is a virtue, Mel. "The only question you asked me was about witchcraft and I answered it."

She pinches her lips together and gazes at me through hooded eyes. "If I give you the tapes, will you help my son?"

"Help him, how?"

"The mind is a powerful thing. Myron is easily swayed and believes you can make his life easier in prison. I will give you the tapes on one condition."

I remind myself I'm doing this for Dani. "Okay."

"Promise me you will meet with him face to face,

offer your forgiveness, and lift the curse you placed upon him."

Lift the curse? Don't go there, Mel. It would be a waste of perfectly good air. "Myron knows that will happen when Eddie Morgan is arrested for his wife's murder."

I hope she doesn't notice the parsing of my words. If Eddie isn't arrested, Myron's imaginary curse remains firmly in place.

Apparently, my word isn't good enough for the old bat, because she makes me stand in front of the crucifix, look into the eyes of Jesus, cross my heart, and repeat my promise before she hands over the tapes. Once they are in my possession, I dash for the door.

With one hand on the knob, I turn and ask, "Have you listened to the tapes?"

"Oh, no," she says. "I don't want to get involved in all that nonsense."

I swallow my response and push through the door. To Harriet McGraw, Dani's death, aided and abetted by her son, is nonsense. Maybe her Jesus will forgive her. I can't.

****

Billy presses the tape recorder's off button. We're sitting in a small interview room at Billy's work place, the City of 3 Peaks Police Department. Because Mick had to resume his undercover, dark stranger identity somewhere in the state of Oregon, he reluctantly handed me over to the locals, aka, Billy the Kid.

We'd just listened to the somewhat incoherent ramblings of Eddie Morgan as he describes his attack upon Dani. According to Eddie, it started as an argument between husband and wife. At one point, he whines, "I didn't set out to hurt her, man, but she wouldn't shut the hell up, so I sorta punched her. She fell and hit her head. I called 911."

He grows increasingly panicky during his conversation with Myron. "You gotta help me, dude. If she wakes up, we're all screwed."

Myron is careful not to incriminate himself, but tells Eddie he has the answer to his "little problem." They arrange a time and place to meet.

"So," I ask Billy. "When are you going to arrest Eddie? Has to be soon, or he'll be in Idaho."

Billy says, "I have to run it by the captain. He'll take it to the district attorney. And, a lot will depend on whether or not Myron will cooperate and testify against Eddie."

I think about the oath I was forced to take by Myron's creepy mother. "I promise you, he will. I'll make it happen."

Billy stands and places his hands on my shoulders. He gazes into my eyes. His soul looks pretty damn spiffy compared to a few weeks ago. It still has a few burning embers, but they've probably always been there due to his competitive nature.

"What do you see, Minnie?"

"I see you're in a good place."

A little spark of heat passes between us. It feels like a jolt of electricity. I'm totally mortified and pull away. What the hell is the matter with me?

Billy grins. "You still feel it, huh? Me, too."

I hold up a hand. "Not going there."

I back away from him. "Now, about Eddie. Fast track. Either you get it done, or I'll be parked outside the D.A.'s door until the end of time. Might be a little embarrassing for 3 Peaks P.D."

Billy sighs. "God, you're like a pit bull when you have an agenda."

"Why shouldn't I be? Nobody else cared enough to find out what happened to Dani. She's the forgotten one. Eddie needs to pay for what he's done."

I gather my things and head for the door.

"Minnie Mouse," Billy says softly. "I'll do my best. I promise."

"If I don't hear from you within twenty-four hours, I'll be back. And, that is a promise."

I'm not proud of it, but I slam the door.

Chapter Thirty-Nine

It's payday for a bunch of our regulars, and Nick's Pub is packed. I'm so busy filling orders and delivering food and drinks, I don't have time to fret about the Eddie Morgan issue.

Around 9:00 p.m. I glance over at the door and see a morose-looking Rick Rathjen wander in. He makes a beeline for the bar, settles on a stool, and places an order with Nick. I remember Nick's rant about Rathjen's blog, "Americans First," and wonder if he knows who he's plying with liquor. Knowing Nick as I do, I doubt it would matter. Rathjen is a paying customer and, unless he creates a fuss, he's welcome to drink at Nick's.

Rathjen spots me when I bring my tray to the bar for re-fills.

He lifts his glass in salute and drawls, "Hey, lil' Queenie. I didn't know you worked here."

If Harriet McGraw's life is country music, mine is a Chuck Berry song. The notion makes me smile.

"Hi, Rick. How are you doing?"

He motions Nick over, points at me and says, "Bet you didn't know your barmaid took riding lessons on a Shetland pony."

Nick places the glass he's polishing on the bar and looks over at me, his eyes dancing with amusement. "No way. A Shetland pony, Mel?"

I set my tray down. Hands on hips, I fake glare at Rathjen. "You know perfectly well I transitioned to Bella and no longer need lessons because I'm such a skilled horsewoman. Or, perhaps you're out of the loop."

Rathjen winks at me, and tells Nick, "She also swears like a sailor."

"I hear ya, man."

He holds out a fist to Rick who gives it a bump.

Fun and games over, Nick gets busy and fills my order.

Rathjen's expression is once again glum. He motions for me to come closer.

"You got a break coming up? I need somebody to talk to."

Besides your wife and kids? I can't tell if he's coming on to me or simply needs a friend.

"It will be a while. We're swamped right now."

"I'll wait."

An hour later, the crowd thins out and my feet need a rest. Under Nick's watchful eye, Rathjen and I move to an empty booth. His eyes are bloodshot, and he's staggering a little. He's clutching a mug of black coffee since Nick cut him off a few drinks ago. I doubt he could do the heel-toe sobriety walk should he get pulled over on the drive home.

He takes a big slurp of coffee. "My life's a God damn mess," he mutters. "My kids hate me, and Roxanne is screwing my best friend."

His words remind me of the sign hanging on the wall above the bar. It's written in Latin and says, In Vino Veritas. It means, "In wine—truth."

I'm far from an expert in relationships. Sympathy

is all I have to offer.

"So sorry, Rick." I reach over and pat his hand. "Your kids don't hate you. I bet if you patch things up with your wife, they'll come around."

His eyes brighten. "You think so?"

"It's worth a try."

He stares into his coffee and thinks it over.

Do I dare mention Riley and Yasmin? I take a big breath and dive in. "Have you and Riley talked about Yasmin and the baby?"

He won't look at me but mutters, "No."

"I know it's is none of my business, but Riley really loved Yasmin. It wasn't teenage puppy love, Rick. She was going to have his baby. He's not only grieving for Yasmin, he's sad about the baby. His flesh and blood. Your flesh and blood."

His head is still down, but I see a tear roll down his cheek.

He glances up at me. "One night after Riley went to bed, I looked at the pictures on his phone. They were mostly all of her. Yasmin."

"She was a beautiful girl, inside and out."

When he speaks again, his voice is choked with tears. He swipes at his eyes. "Some of the pictures were of the two of them together. The way Riley looked at her, my God, the love in his eyes. Then, I knew it was for real."

He shakes his head. "God forgive me, we made them sneak around. Me and my wife. Her family, too."

"Talk to Riley. Tell him what you just told me. He needs to hear it. And, take your wife somewhere nice, maybe on a shopping trip to Portland or Cannon Beach. Things will get better, you'll see."

He nods and fumbles in his pocket for his keys. I snatch them away. "You're not driving. I'll get you some more coffee."

He sits back down. The corner of his mouth lifts in brief smile. "Damn, Queenie, but your bossy."

I fill his coffee cup and tell Nick to keep an eye on Rathjen while I phone Riley. He answers after three rings. "Mel? What's up?"

"Your dad's at Nick's Sports Bar. I don't think he should drive. Can you come and get him?"

"Aw, shit, is he drunk?"

"Pretty much. Want me to bring him home?"

"No, I'll be there in a few."

Thirty minutes later, Riley and Rachel show up. They step inside the door and gaze around the room until they spot their dad sitting alone in a booth. Rachel is wearing sweatpants, a pink T-shirt and flip-flops. Her face is pale, and she looks scared. Riley's expression is grim but determined, as he strides toward his father. Rachel hurries to keep up.

We've been pouring coffee down Rathjen's throat, but he's still pretty loopy. When I refused to return his car keys, he turned belligerent, and Nick had to apply a little muscle to get him to settle down. His anger soon petered out. He's now in what Nick calls, the crying in your beer mode, although in Rathjen's case, the tears are falling into a coffee mug.

When he sees his kids, he's still weepy. As they approach, he stands and holds out his arms. "Get in here, you two. Daddy needs a hug."

They sidestep the hug and, instead, flank their father, each gripping one of his arms. Riley says, "Let's get you home, Dad."

They march him toward the door. Suddenly, Riley changes course, and he leads his father to the bar. With his free hand, he pulls a wallet from his back pocket and asks Nick, "How much does he owe you?"

Nick waves him away. "No worries. He settled up. Just get him home safe."

Riley looks at me. His blue gaze is steely, but his soul is streaked with dark patches of sadness and disappointment. I want to kick Rick's butt. The poor kid is just getting his act together, and now he has to be the grown-up in the family.

I lean over and smooch him on the cheek. "Hang in there, sweetie."

He tries to smile. "Thanks, Mel. I'll call soon."

I scurry ahead to hold the door open. Before they pass through, Rathjen says, "Hold it. I have something to say to Queenie."

Riley and Rachel exchange a puzzled glance, but stop.

With effort, Rathjen pulls himself up to his full height. He leans close and whispers, "I'm going to do what you said. Take my wife for a special weekend. And, about the other situation we talked about too. With Riley and the girl. Okay?"

I nod. "Good."

As Riley and Rachel guide their father into the parking lot, I say a little prayer for them. I've done all I can do.

I think about my stepfather, Abel, and his ministry in the back of the Godmobile. His down-to earth message to fellow truck drivers often includes the words, "You think God is a hot shit CEO who sits behind his big desk twenty-four-seven and watches us make a mess of our lives? No way! He's right here, right now, ready to help. If you're in need of a miracle, ask him. A loving God has no problem inserting himself into the human condition, and it's called divine intervention."

If ever a family was in need of divine intervention, it's the Rathjens.

Chapter Forty

The next day, Billy's twenty-four hours have expired, and I'm working up a head of steam, ready to take up residence outside the D.A.'s office. My mind runs a little amuck. I even consider calling the local paper. I can see the headlines. *Local Woman Demands Justice for Murdered Friend!*

Fortunately for Billy and the 3 Peaks Police Department, he texts me the following message:

—*Whatever you're planning to do, don't! Will call soon.*—

He includes an emoji of a smiley face. I assume this is a good thing and pursue my weekend tasks.

1. Put clean sheets on the bed.
2. Scrub the toilet.
3. Wash clothes.

As promised, he calls a couple of hours later.

"Hey, Minnie, my captain is on board. He handed the tape over to the D.A.'s office. It looks good, but remember, it's Friday and the wheels of justice turn slowly."

"How slowly?"

"Can't exactly say, but keep your fingers crossed. It will probably be next week before something happens.

"Damn, Billy! Eddie's moving at the end of the month, next Wednesday. You can't let him get away."

"No worries. If he's involved in a serious crime, he'll be extradited."

"But I want to see the perp walk, and I can't if he's in Idaho," I wail.

I hear Billy chuckle. "No matter what happens, I promise you'll get to see Eddie in handcuffs. Okay?"

"For sure?"

"I'll make it happen."

"Nevertheless, I'll be parked outside the D.A.'s office on Monday, just in case."

Billy groans. "Yeah, I figured. Talk soon."

I thank him and get ready for work. The night is uneventful, just the way I like it. The Rathjen family is still on my mind while I work my shift the next day. At 10:30, I catch a breather and text Riley.

—Everything okay?—

He doesn't text me back. He calls instead. "Mel? You working tonight?"

"Yeah."

"Something weird is going on. Can you come out?"

"Weird how?"

"Don't want to say over the phone."

"Are your mom and dad home?"

"No," he says. "Dad was all pumped up after he talked to you. Told Mom to pack for a special trip. He called it a second honeymoon. Weird, huh?"

"Is this the weird thing you don't want to talk about on the phone?"

"No, no, it has to do with Yasmin's family. So, can you come out?"

"I'll check with my boss and let you know."

When I tell Nick it concerns the Rathjens and promise to work a couple extra hours on my day off, he gives me his blessing. "No problem. I can manage."

I thank him and dart through the kitchen, snagging a leftover toasted tuna sandwich for Thunder Paws on the way to the door. The cat is outside Number Ten, curled up on my tiny front porch. He greets me with a throaty yowl, gathers himself, and springs into the air in an effort to bat the sandwich from my hand. Once again, I hold it over my head where he can't reach it. Forgiveness is not his strong suit. He hisses and growls while he waits for me to unlock the door. Once inside, I toss the sandwich into his bowl, grab my coat and head for Buttercup.

An icy wind sweeps through the parking lot, carrying the scent of fresh snow from the three mountain peaks west of the city. A full-faced moon peeks out from behind scudding clouds, alternately bathing the landscape in shadow and light. Dried leaves, plastic grocery bags, and Big Gulp cups tumble across the asphalt, coming to rest against the foundation of Nick's Pub.

An unexplained feeling of apprehension steals over me. I gaze around, looking for possible danger, and see nothing menacing. Not able to shake the feeling, I return to Number Ten and retrieve the red balloon still bobbing above my bed. Maybe it's silly, but I like to think the balloon holds the spirit of my sister, Hope, and she's watching over me, as Steve suggests. What other explanation could there be? The red balloon is the only survivor of the balloon bouquet Steve brought to the hospital after my near-fatal accident. The other balloons slowly lost their short lives, shriveled up and died.

Feeling a little foolish, I stuff the red balloon inside

Buttercup, rev her up and merge into the traffic heading north, toward Red Ridge. When I arrive at the ranch, the house is ablaze with light. The door flies open and Riley trots to the car.

"Hey, Mel, thanks for coming."

He leads me into the house with one arm slung around my shoulders in what I hope is brotherly fashion. Once again intimidated by the pristine white carpet in the family room, I remove my shoes and tiptoe to the couch where I join Rachel.

She glances away from the blaring TV and gives me a wan smile. "Hi, Mel."

Riley picks up the TV remote, hits the off button and sits in the chair across from us.

He squirms a little like he doesn't know where to start.

I decide to help him out, and say in a joking manner. "So, what's the deal? No parents. Nice house. Most kids would be inviting all their best buds over for party time—not a good idea, by the way—yet, here you are, watching old movies on TV."

Rachel nibbles her fingernails and glances over at Riley. His face is grim, and he looks older than his nineteen years.

He leans forward, bracing his arms on his knees. "Not sure what to do. Yasmin's brother called me."

"Darrak?"

"Yeah, Darrak. He tells me their dad wants to do some kind of a blessing at the place where Yasmin's body was found, and it has to be Saturday night at midnight. Tonight. He wants my family there. I told him it would just be Rachel and me."

"This could be a good thing, Riley," I say. "Bibi is

reaching out to your family, trying to make peace. Too bad your parents aren't here."

When he doesn't respond, I say, "You are going, aren't you?"

"We're trying to decide. The whole let's meet at midnight thing seems strange."

"Maybe the timing of the ritual has something to do with their religion," I say. "For what it's worth, I think it could be a healing experience for all of you."

Rachel says, "Darrak sounded super stressed. Riley put him on speaker phone."

"Yasmin's death has been hard on him. He's been in Nick's a couple of times, drinking. Totally surprised me because Muslims usually don't drink. Do you want me to go with you?"

"Darrak said just family."

I look back and forth at Riley and Rachel and realize the problem. They're two scared kids. I understand their reluctance about visiting the site where Yasmin's body was dumped. Especially in the middle of the night. Still, if Bibi is sincere about extending an olive branch, they should take advantage of the opportunity.

"How about this?" I say. "I'll go with you and wait in the car. It's dark. They won't see me, but I'll be there if you need me."

Rachel nods. Riley's expression lightens. "Sounds like a plan."

Chapter Forty-One

At 11:45 p.m., we set out for the short drive to the designated spot. I insist on bringing the red balloon and tell them it's my good luck charm. Not exactly a lie. The three of us are crammed together in Riley's pick-up, me in the middle, and we're bouncing down a rutted dirt road that winds through Rathjen land. The road ends in a T and we make a left turn.

"Are we still on your property?" I ask.

"No," Rachel says. "This is BLM land. Bureau of Land Management. Dad wants to buy it, but they won't sell."

Yet another reason, I think, for Rick Rathjen's simmering rage.

The night is pitch black, the moon having disappeared behind a bank of thick clouds. Tumbleweeds, driven by a gusty wind, do an erratic dance, bouncing off the grill of the truck. A few minutes later, the high beam of our headlights illuminates a white van pulled off the side of the road. Riley hits the brakes and pulls in behind it. I scoot down in the seat in case Bibi and Darrak are scoping us out.

I grab Riley's right hand and Rachel's left, and give each one a smooch. I whisper, "Good luck."

They exit the truck and slip into the night's dark embrace. I, of course, have no intention of remaining in the truck. After removing the keys from the ignition, I exit through the passenger side window so the overhead light doesn't come on. I set off in the same direction as Riley and Rachel, immediately trip over a rock and sprawl, face-first, in the dirt. I stifle my cry of pain with a soft *ooph* and lie still for a moment assessing the damage and listening for approaching footsteps. I hear voices in the distance and struggle to my feet. This time, I proceed with more caution, feeling my way through the darkness one stealthy step at a time.

As I grow closer to the sound of voices, a light flicks on. Darrak's thin face is illuminated in the glow of large battery-driven lantern. Bibi is standing next to him, holding a scarf I recognize as Yasmin's. Riley and Rachel come into view and stop a few feet away from Bibi and Darrak. I creep closer, in an effort to pick up their conversation.

Bibi drapes the scarf around his neck and points to the ground. "This is where my beautiful daughter ended her days, on this patch of dirt. It must be consecrated or her soul will not rest."

Riley says, "What do you want us to do?"

I see a flash of white teeth in the darkness as Bibi forces a brief smile. "First, thank you for coming. Your presence is important if we are to complete the ritual. You ask why you are here. You will find out soon." He runs his fingers over the scarf. "This *hijab* was Yasmin's favorite. Consequently, it is special to me."

"Now," he continues. "I will show you where to stand, and we will begin the consecration."

He takes the lantern from Darrak and points to the spot he wants Rachel to stand, facing east. He places Darrak three feet to Rachel's left. Riley completes the semi-circle.

"Now," Bibi says. "Kneel, if you please, and close your eyes. I will bless the *hijab* and ask Allah to welcome Yasmin into his loving arms."

Riley and Rachel follow Bibi's order and drop to their knees, bowing their heads like the good Catholics I suspect they are. Darrak, the traditional Muslim, kneels with arms extended and his face down. Bibi sets the lantern on the ground and stands behind the three, the *hijab* clutched in his right hand. I'm getting a bad vibe. Something seems off to me. A little tickle of alarm zips through my consciousness. The open-heart pendant vibrates against my skin. Why didn't he bring prayer rugs? Why midnight? Why isn't he joining the others?

I take a step closer, my gaze fixed on Bibi who's now positioned himself directly behind Rachel. He's bathed in an alternating pattern of darkness and light as the wind pushes the clouds across the face of the moon. He grips the *hijab* in both hands. With the speed of a striking snake, he wraps it around Rachel's neck and jerks her to her feet. The scarf is twisted into a garrote. The only sound Rachel can manage is a startled gurgle.

Riley and Darrak leap to their feet.

Darrak says, "Papa, no!"

Riley yells, "Let her go!" and starts toward Bibi who twists the scarf even tighter. He grips it tightly in his left hand. A large knife appears in his right.

He waves it at Riley. "One more step and I'll cut her throat."

Rachel eyes are wide with terror. Her fingers dig at the scarf. She's desperate for air.

Bibi says, "Riley Rathjen, your actions caused my

daughter's death. Now, your family will know what it's like to lose a child. An eye for an eye. A death for a death."

I don't stop to think. I charge into the fray, first kicking the lantern directly at Bibi. By some stroke of luck, it clanks against the knife. He doesn't drop it, but the distraction causes his grip on the scarf to loosen. Rachel wraps her hands around it and takes a gusty life-giving breath. I dive for Bibi's ankles and jerk. He flies backward, arms flailing, the knife still gripped in his right hand. Rachel is free. Darrak is wailing. Riley lands on top of a thrashing Bibi and tries to pin down the hand with the knife. I'm still clinging to Bibi's ankles. With one final burst of strength, he slashes at me. The blade whizzes by my ear and passes through my coat before plunging into the ground.

Riley jerks Bibi to his feet. "What the hell, man? Are you crazy? I didn't kill your daughter."

I pull the knife free, roll to a stand and pick up the lantern, still burning brightly. Ashen-faced, Rachel's trembling legs can no longer hold her. She sinks to the ground and buries her face in her hands.

With sobs racking his body, Darrak says, "Papa, you had no right. Not after what you did to Yasmin."

Riley freezes, his eyes filled with dread. "What did he do to Yasmin?"

Bibi stabs a finger into Riley's chest. "She was pregnant with your child. You ruined her innocence. You took away the honor of our family."

Riley's voice is deadly quiet. "So you killed her?"

Darrak waves a hand. "No, no, no! He did not mean to kill her. It was an accident. He was angry. He put his hands around her throat to shake her. Yasmin was a small girl. Papa grabbed her too hard, and she died."

"And you dumped her body out here to incriminate the Rathjen's?" I ask.

Darrak hangs his head. "Yes, I am ashamed to say so."

His explanation sickens me. I pull the phone from my pocket. "I'll call 911."

Before I can punch in the numbers, Riley says, "No. Wait."

He demands the key to Bibi's van and orders them to sit in it.

"But, Riley," I insist. "He was going to kill Rachel. He took Yasmin's life. He tried to stab me."

I glance down at my arm and see blood oozing through my coat. "Actually," I say, "I think he did stab me."

I'm feeling a little woozy. My knees buckle. Riley picks me up and sets me on the tailgate of the pick-up. He gathers Rachel up and places her next to me, the lantern between us. He unzips my coat and checks the gash on my arm.

"Be right back," he says and walks to Bibi's van. He returns with the *hijab* and ties it around my wound. He murmurs, "Yasmin would want you to have it."

I'm still bummed. "Why won't you let me call 911?"

"Yeah, why?" Rachel says.

He says, "Think it through. Bibi goes to jail. Probably Darrak too since he knew about it. Then, what happens to the Ayoobs? Their business will fail. The family will be ruined. I have to think about Yasmin, what she would want me to do."

Rachel cries, "They should be punished for what they've done."

"They know what they did," Riley says. "They'll be punished every day for the rest of their lives."

"So, you're just going to let them go? Forgive them?" Rachel asks.

Riley's eyes are bright with tears. "To the best of my ability."

When I look into the face of this nineteen-year-old man child, I'm awed by the maturity of his decision-making. How many months have I spent obsessing over Eddie Morgan, longing to see him punished for his involvement in Dani's death? And here's young Riley, who lost the love of his life as well as his child, and he's able to see the big picture. Shame on me.

When Riley hands over the keys to the van and tells the two to go home, Darrak is overcome with emotion and chokes out a brief, "Thank you."

Bibi doesn't waste words. He manages to say, "May Allah bless you," fires up the van and takes off like a gut-shot gazelle. Maybe he fears Riley will change his mind.

Back at the Rathjen ranch, Rachel removes the blood-soaked *hijab* from my arm and gently cleanses it with antiseptic. "You need stitches. We'll take you to the E.R."

On the way to the hospital, we talk about how much information we should share with Rick and Roxanne Rathjen. Rachel is all for telling them the whole story, and how Riley and I saved her from certain death.

Riley and I agree this is not the best course of action.

"Think about it, Rach," Riley says. "You want Dad to have another reason to hate foreigners? We're just getting our family back the way it was before. Let it go."

It seems like truth-telling time, so I fill them in on my role in proving none of the Rathjen family was complicit in Yasmin's death. The hardest part to explain is the soul-reading bit.

Rachel exclaims, "You can actually look into our souls? Cool!"

Riley is not happy. He frowns at me. "So, you really didn't want to learn how to ride? It was all fake?"

I do a lot of fast-talking to convince him that, for me, it started out as a job, but now feel our friendship is real, not fake. I take a big breath and end by saying, "Maybe I could try a few more lessons, but not on Sneaky Pete."

Riley nods. "But, what about the guys you're working for? The cops."

I assure him I'll figure out a big, fat, but believable lie to tell my law enforcement friends. Not sure what, but I'll come up with something.

I ride to St. Peter's with Riley. Rachel follows in Buttercup. The E.R. doc is none other than Dr. Pritchard who took care of me after my close encounter with a Lincoln Navigator.

He remembers me. "You again?"

He injects a local anesthetic and puts six stitches in my arm "Are you accident prone or do you have a death wish?"

Adrenaline rush over, Mel's brain has left the building. All I can do is shrug and shake my head.

Clutching a bottle of pain meds, I climb into

Riley's truck for the short ride to Number Ten. As Rachel pulls up in Buttercup, the door to Number Ten flies open and Mick steps through. He doesn't look happy.

So much for lying my ass off.

Chapter Forty-Two

The word awkward does not adequately cover this situation. I tell Riley and Rachel to grab a chair and introduce Mick as my law enforcement boyfriend. Then, I drag Mick into the bathroom for a private chat.

Hands on hips, his frosty gaze pins me to the floor. "What the hell is going on, Mel?"

"Just listen and try not to be judgmental. I'll explain the situation, but you have to promise not to go tearing out of here to make an arrest until you hear the whole story."

He doesn't exactly agree, but dips his chin slightly.

I use every one of my limited charms to convince him to see it my way, including the Big Kahuna. I hint our relationship may be in jeopardy if he doesn't agree. I'm not proud of them, but here are my exact words.

"Mick, what we have between us is special. I would very much like it to continue. However, if you feel compelled to rush out and arrest Bibi, I'm afraid we are finished."

He stares at me for a long moment while he processes my words. Finally, he says, "Correct me if I'm wrong. You want me to overlook a major crime and, if I don't, you will cut me off."

I give a little snort of disgust. As previously stated, I did not say, "I'm going to cut you off." But, being of the male species, nookie, or lack thereof, is uppermost in his mind.

No sense in pointing out the obvious, so I say, "Pretty much."

His face looks carved in stone, and I see a flare of anger flash through his soul. "You drive a hard bargain, *malysh*."

Suddenly, my brain wakes up and everything is crystal clear. Why didn't I think of this earlier? I could have saved myself the humiliation of using my body as a bargaining chip. "Think about it this way, Mick. It's a no-brainer for you. Since Yasmin's death wasn't a hate crime, Homeland Security has no authority in 3 Peaks."

He gives me a humorless smile. "Have you forgotten we have no rules?"

I decide to ignore the question and head for the bathroom door.

He holds up a hand. "You have another problem."

"I do?"

"Billy and the 3 Peaks Police Department. The last I heard, they're still following up on Yasmin's death. What do you plan to offer Billy in exchange for him dropping the case?"

I know what he's implying, and it ticks me off. However, since I've already pulled out all the stops, bargaining wise, I decide not to go there. Instead, I say, "You need to hear what Riley and Rachel have to say."

We join the Rathjens who look scared. I perch on the end of the bed. Mick leans against the wall, arms folded across his chest, gazing coldly down at me. Riley and Rachel, seated in my only two chairs, look first at me, then Mick. Extremely annoyed by having his slumber interrupted, Thunder Paws stalks to the door and demands to be let out.

"Okay, kids," I say. "Special Agent Petrov is prepped and ready to listen. Tell him what happened tonight. Start with the phone call from Darrak Ayoob."

Riley and Rachel take turns speaking and do a credible job. When we get to the part where Riley refuses to call 911, Mick stops them.

"Hold it," he says, lifting a hand. "This man, Bibi Ayoob, broke his daughter's neck, killing her and your unborn child. Correct?"

Rachel stifles a sob. Riley stands and takes a step toward Mick. "Yes, it's true, and he also stabbed your girlfriend, the one you've been glaring at ever since we got here. So, maybe you'd like to chill a little and listen to the whole story."

Mick looks over at me, and I see the shock in his eyes. "Is this true?"

I nod.

He joins me on the bed and wraps his arms around me. "*Maylsh*, are you okay? Do you want me to kill him for you?"

I hear Rachel gasp and say, "He's kidding."

Actually, after looking at his expression, I'm not sure he is. I roll up my sleeve and point to the stitches. "I'm perfectly fine. Okay?"

Still holding me close, Mick looks over at Riley. "Please continue. I will not interrupt again."

Riley talks about the Ayoob family and his desire not to cause them any more pain. He grows emotional when he speaks of Yasmin, eloquently describing her gentle, forgiving nature. Rachel slips an arm around his shoulder as he wipes away his tears. He ends by repeating what he's said to me. "It's what she would want me to do."

Mick remains silent for a moment. Finally, he rises, walks over to Riley and shakes his hand. "You are a remarkable young man. I'm pleased to make your acquaintance."

Riley and Rachel each give me a hug.

Riley whispers, "I'm so sorry you got hurt. Thanks for everything."

Rachel says, "You're welcome at the Rockin' R anytime. You can even ride Sugar Lips if you want."

After they leave, Mick paces back and forth across Number Ten. Three strides to the table, about face, three strides back. I stay quiet and watch him, knowing he's working something out in his head. Five minutes later, he stops

"I'll talk to Billy."

"And, tell him what?"

"I will tell him D.H.S. received an anonymous tip, and it has far-reaching implications. The case, once again, will be under our auspices."

"Will he believe you?"

"Trust me, 3 Peaks P.D. will be more than happy to relinquish the case. And, from what our friend Riley told us, Bibi will not be pushing them for action."

A gush of relief sweeps through me. I stand and hold out my arms. "Thank you."

It's truly amazing what nookie, or the lack thereof, can accomplish.

Chapter Forty-Three

It's Monday, and Mick is off doing his thing. Is this a harbinger of the future? Then, I get a call from Billy.

"Good news," he says. "Your fairy godmother, aka the district attorney, reviewed the tape and has granted your wish."

I gasp in surprise. "So, Eddie will be arrested?"

"Yes, a warrant has been issued to arrest Edward Morgan for questioning regarding his wife's death in May."

"When and where?"

"We're working out the details. I'll let you know."

I'm suddenly gripped by anxiety. "What if he hires a good lawyer and gets off?"

"Minnie," Billy says. "Stop worrying. Let the system work."

"But…"

"I know Eddie Morgan, and I think he'll cave, especially when we tell him we have the tape. It's clear he hit Dani, knocked her out, and wanted to finish the job. Like Myron, he'll look for a deal. I can't promise you he'll be convicted of murder one, but he'll serve some time."

"He's a cold-blooded killer. He should be locked up for the rest of his life."

"We're getting into a gray area here. The taped

conversation implies Eddie is looking for a way to kill Dani and make it look like an accident. But, Dani was cremated. No body. No evidence. Unless he confesses, he'll probably be charged with voluntary manslaughter."

"What about Myron? He said he'd testify against Eddie in exchange for a reduced sentence."

Billy says, "I know you don't want to hear this, but the D.A. said the reality of the situation is this: Myron's a hard-core criminal serving time. He's looking for a better deal. A judge and jury may not find him credible."

"Well, damn," I mutter. "You mean my visits with Myron and his weird mother served no purpose?"

"You're looking at this upside down. You got the tape. Without it, we wouldn't be able to make the arrest. Trust me, Minnie, we won't go easy on him. We'll scare the crap out of him with the tape."

I remain silent as I mull over Billy's words.

"You still there?"

"Yeah."

"I'll call you soon with the time and place."

Before he clicks off, I remember my manners. "Billy? Thanks for following through."

"Welcome," he growls.

I sit on the edge of the bed and try to analyze my feelings. For the last five months, I've been obsessed with seeking justice for Dani. Now, with Eddie's imminent arrest, it's actually happening. Shouldn't I feel euphoric? I don't. A bajillion thoughts race through my brain and finally, the light bulb flickers to life. Riley Rathjen. If anyone has a right to be consumed with anger and a desire for vengeance, it's Riley. Instead, he channeled the beautiful spirit of the girl he loved, enabling him to release the despair and anger ravaging him. I like to think certain events unfold as if directed by the big conductor in the sky. Perhaps, I've been part of Riley's life for reasons I truly didn't anticipate or understand.

I need someone to talk to, someone I trust. I reach for my phone and punch in a number.

He picks up on the first ring and speaks my name with a slight accent. "Honor Melanie Sullivan, *mi hija*, I was just thinking about you. You are okay?"

"Hi, Steve. Yes, I'm fine. I have something on my mind. Do you have time to listen and, maybe, give me some advice?"

"For you? But, of course."

The story spills out of me like water gushing from a broken pipe. Steve listens attentively, murmuring encouragement when I pause to take a breath. He asks for clarification on a couple of points before lapsing into silence.

"So," I say. "What do you think I should do?"

"The decision is yours. From what you've told me, I believe you already know the answer. Of one thing I'm absolutely certain, as anger and the desire for revenge build, it's akin to holding a burning ember in the palm of your hand. The object of your grudge is unaffected. You become the damaged one."

His words circle through my brain and settle into my heart. "Thank you, Steve."

"*De nada.* Come and see me soon. I have work for you."

Before he clicks off, I say, "I have another question."

"Yes?"

"What does love look like in the soul?"

He chuckles. "Ah, my dear, I wondered when you would ask me that question. I assume you are referring to romantic love."

"Yes."

"It's the color of a deep crimson rose in full bloom and may vary in size and shape. In the early stages, it floats across the soul much like a wind-driven leaf in a pond. In a committed relationship, it's in a fixed position and takes on a golden hue as if touched by a multi-colored sunset."

"Wow," is all I can manage to say.

After a long moment, Steve says, "Have you seen it?"

"Yes, I think I have."

Steve is too much of a gentleman to question me further. I thank him again and promise I'll be in soon.

I set the phone down and think about his words. I have much to reconsider.

****

Eddie's arrest happened the next day at his work place. I wasn't present. Though I may never totally forgive Eddie for taking the life of the best friend I ever had, I feel a sense of freedom, as if something dark and heavy has been scrubbed from my soul.

Afterward, Billy comes to Number Ten, certain I'm dead or dying.

When he finds me alive and well, he grips my shoulders and gazes into my eyes. "What the hell, Minnie. You've been like a dog with a bone, nagging Homeland Security and 3 Peaks P.D. for months about arresting Eddie Morgan. I thought you'd be there pumping your fist in the air. What happened?"

I shrug. "Let's just say I took a little dip in the river of forgiveness and decided it was time to get on with my life."

His eyes crinkle with amusement. "No shit?"

"No shit," I repeat.

He wraps me up in a hug. I start to push him away, but change my mind and snuggle into his familiar body.

He strokes my hair. "I miss you so much, Minnie. Does that dip in the river extend to me?"

In the spirit of my new mind set, I murmur, "I'm working on it."

After he leaves, I call Kendra and tell her the news. She, too, cannot believe I missed the opportunity for gloating and revenge.

Before we end our conversations, Kendra says, "Hey, your mom called me about Paco and Aida's wedding. We have things to do, girlfriend. Get your butt out here."

I promise her I will. "Do I have to wear a hideous dress?"

"Of course. It's a requirement."

I groan.

She says, "And, we can talk about Billy."

I open my mouth to tell her there's nothing to talk about.

Too late, she's already clicked off.

Chapter Forty-Four

Fast forward one month. It's the Saturday after Thanksgiving and time for Paco and Aida's big, fat, motorcycle gang/Russian wedding. It will be performed in the back of the Godmobile and presided over by my stepfather, Abel. But first, some vital background information.

My mother, Sandra, and Abel arrived in the Godmobile a week ago. Since the truck is already outfitted for Abel's ministry, it's simply a matter of decorating for the wedding.

The problem is, nothing is simple when my mother is involved. First, we had to find a place to park the humongous vehicle. Temporarily tucked in next to the pub—Sandra, Abel, and I drove Buttercup around 3 Peaks looking for a parking space and appropriate venue for the wedding. Because it's a special occasion, Sandra said it had to be pretty, not a Wal-Mart parking lot.

"Pretty?" I exclaimed. "We're talking about a wedding in an eighteen wheeler full of gang-bangers, Russian girls, and babies. It's late November. Nothing's blooming, the trees are bare and snow is predicted. Plus, we'll need a place for people to park their cars and motorcycles. We need to go for space, not pretty."

It wasn't long before we'd escalated into an epic mother-daughter quarrel. God bless Abel, the peacemaker.

He clapped his hands to get our attention. "Ladies, please. Leave the location up to me. I promise I will find something both suitable and pretty."

At first, Sandra resisted. She wanted to be the decision maker. But, Abel, sweet Abel, took her hands in his and kissed the back of each one. "My dear love, you are the big cheese, the wedding planner, the engine, so to speak, driving this whole affair. Think of all the things you have to do. Order the wedding cake. Make decisions about floral arrangements. Order food for the reception. And, what about coordinating everyone's attire? Will you kindly allow me to find an appropriate location for this wonderful event?"

Never able to resist Abel when he's at his schmoozing best, Sandra reluctantly agreed. Fortunately, Abel delivered. While Sandra and I were knee-deep in pre-wedding hell at Kendra's house, Abel visited every church in the 3 Peaks area, looking for one to meet his requirements—namely, a pretty setting and ample parking. He found a beautiful, old church dating back to the early 1900s on the outskirts of 3 Peaks. Surrounded by towering pine trees, the church had been lovingly cared for. Its fresh coat of white paint and original bell tower satisfied Sandra's requirement for prettiness. The parking lot, though not huge, was adequate.

Abel sought out the minister. Though slightly taken aback by the notion of a semi-truck wedding with a number of motorcycle dudes as guests, he gave Abel permission to move the Godmobile to the parking lot behind the church. Abel assured him we would be like no-trace campers and leave the place in pristine condition. I'm pretty certain a large cash donation sealed the deal.

So now, the day has arrived. We all have appointed duties. It's complicated. Kendra and her husband, Craig have three children; three-year-old Aaron, nine-month old Andrew, and Dani's baby girl, eleven-month old, Destiny. Aida's baby, Larissa (named for her murdered sister) is three months old. All are vitally important to the wedding party.

Kendra is Aida's maid of honor. Craig is walking Aida down the aisle and handing her over to Paco. I am a bridesmaid/baby tender, neither of which fits my job description. Paco has two groomsmen, my former bodyguard, Chuy and Notary Public, Rocco. Mick is an usher and keeper of the peace. Abel will perform the ceremony. Sandra is overseeing the entire event and taking charge of music.

Yesterday, we practiced and all went well. The children were with a sitter, so we used imaginary babies as we walked through.

The procession will begin with Kendra carrying Andrew. I will follow, Destiny in my arms while I try valiantly not to trip on my puffy, pink dress. Next, comes Billy, holding the hand of little Aaron, the appointed ring-bearer and flower boy. Finally, Aida, the bride, will make her entrance. Accompanied by Craig, she will carry baby Larissa down the aisle. Sandra will turn off the boom box playing The Wedding March and take Larissa from Aida. Paco and his groomsmen will be waiting at the altar. What could possibly go wrong?

We abide by Sandra's strident command, "Be in the parking lot one hour early, people. Don't be late."

I ride with Mick. My dress is too big for Buttercup.

He's still in bad boy mode with a shaved scalp showing dyed dark roots, scruffy facial hair and tats. He looks scary but will fit in nicely with Paco's guys.

He tries, unsuccessfully, to hide his smile, as he looks me over. "Now, that's a dress."

"Sandra," I mutter.

We're the last to arrive. Aida is in the Pontiac with Larissa. Kendra is in the mini-van with Destiny and Andrew, both in their car seats. Craig and Billy are chasing Aaron around the parking lot in a futile effort to keep him clean. I see no sign of Sandra and Abel and assume they're inside the Godmobile getting it ready for the mother of all weddings.

Clad in motorcycle boots, white ruffled shirts, black bow ties, dark slacks, and their black leather *Los Habañeros* jackets, Paco, Chuy, and Rocco are standing next to the car, shooting the breeze. Paco's bushy mane has been tamed into a neat ponytail. His complexion, normally a healthy shade of tan, has taken on a yellowish cast. Though he's usually unflappable, it looks like Uncle Paco has a case of the nerves.

When I step out of the car, a sudden gust of wind dives under my dress and blows it straight up over my head. Blinded by yards of pink taffeta, I cuss like a lumberjack and bat frantically at my errant dress.

Whoops of male laughter and ribald remarks float on the wind as I try to get a grip on the slippery fabric.

"Oooeee, pretty mama, looking good!"

"Lookee there, matching pink panties! The girl knows how to color coordinate."

After what seems like forever and a day, Mick captures the billowing skirt and yanks it down.

I grip the skirt with both hands and check Mick's

face to see if he's laughing. He is.

"Took you long enough," I snarl.

Billy's back is turned, but I see his shoulders shaking. Little Aaron claps his hands as if I'd put on a public performance worthy of applause.

I muster as much dignity as possible and march back to the car. Now, I know why Aida and Kendra haven't ventured out. Mick joins the guys. I see a flask pass from hand to hand.

Had I known what was about to happen, I might have joined them.

Chapter Forty-Five

The guests begin to arrive. Fifteen of Paco's guys, accompanied by their old ladies, tool in on Harleys. Nick closed the bar so he could attend with the rest of the wait staff and cooks. My bio dad, Steve, arrives with his new boyfriend, Brad, who's the sous chef at a ritzy restaurant in 3 Peaks. Several carloads of Aida's girlfriends from Kazakhstan pull into the parking lot. Like a bevy of beautiful butterflies, they spill out of the cars, fluffing their colorful dresses, primping and positively giddy with excitement.

When the last of the guests are seated, the wedding party gathers at the bottom of the ramp leading into the Godmobile.

Kendra places Destiny in my arms and says, "If she starts to fuss, jiggle and rock. It usually calms her down."

Sandra lines us up, makes sure we're all carrying the correct baby, and then scurries up the ramp to manage the music.

Destiny looks over at Kendra, then back at me, her big, blue eyes clouded with suspicion as if to say, "What the hell?"

"Hi, baby," I chirp. "Remember me?"

Obviously, she doesn't. Her lower lip quivers, and she places both hands on my collarbones and pushes. She's amazingly strong for a baby. She opens her mouth and takes a deep, preparatory breath. I know what's coming.

"Kendra," I call. "This isn't working. She hates me."

Too late. The music is blasting. Kendra, with Andrew clutched in her arms, scampers up the ramp and into the cavernous truck. Destiny lets out an ear-splitting shriek, and my feet refuse to move, as if frozen to the asphalt.

Billy closes in behind me, gripping Aaron by the back of the collar. Aaron is already throwing rose petals even though we're not yet in the Godmobile.

Billy says, "Get going, Minnie, or the flowers will be gone."

Remembering Kendra's advice, I rock and jiggle Destiny while trotting up the ramp. She continues to howl.

When I step into the Godmobile, I look over my shoulder and see Aaron dump the contents of his flower basket onto the parking lot. A friendly gust of wind blows some of them into the truck. Billy cracks up laughing, lifts Aaron to his shoulders, and follows me down the center aisle.

I paste a phony smile on my face, carry the screaming baby to the altar, and stop next to Kendra, as prescribed by my mother. When Andrew sees Destiny's distress, he too, starts to cry. Despite the chilly weather, I'm sweating profusely.

"Kendra," I hiss. "Help."

But Kendra won't look at me. All eyes are upon Aida and Craig. Aida is sporting a serene smile as she strolls slowly down the aisle with baby Larissa cradled in her left arm. Larissa is sleeping soundly. At least one of the babies is behaving.

Sandra glares at me and turns up the volume on the boom box. I'm getting pissed off and glare back at her. Like any of this is my fault?

Craig and Aida join us at the altar. Beaming with joy, Paco steps forward, his gaze fixed on his new family. I see a tear slip down his right cheek. I bite my lower lip to hold back my own tears. Why, I don't know, since crying seems to be the order of the day.

Craig steps back and Sandra stops the music. This is where the baby transfer is scheduled to happen. From Aida's arms to Sandra's. Destiny's shrieks of anger subside a little. Andrew continues to whimper. Aida is gazing tenderly into Paco's eyes. When Sandra closes in, Aida thrusts the baby toward her before Sandra is ready, and baby Larissa is fumbled like a bad handoff between the center and quarterback of a football team. A collective gasp of horror reverberates throughout the Godmobile, but no worries…Billy the Kid is on the job. With a lightning fast move, he snatches the fumbled baby and places her in Sandra's arms. The crowd rises as one, clapping and cheering. Billy grins and sketches a bow.

Aida claps a hand over her mouth in horror and bursts into tears. Paco steps forward, wraps her up in a bear hug and pats her back. Larissa, who actually has a legitimate reason to cry, doesn't. Instead, she smiles and snuggles into Sandra's arms.

Abel steps forward and begins the ceremony. Kendra finally comes to my aid. She hands Andrew to Craig and takes Destiny from me. Abel, eloquent as always, does a magnificent job, speaking of God's love and the deep bond between Paco and Aida. After the bride and groom speak their vows and exchange rings, there's not a dry eye in the Godmobile. Except for the babies, all of whom have fallen asleep.

As Sandra would say later—she has selective memory—"What a glorious wedding!"

****

After the ceremony, the wedding party and guests head for the reception at Nick's. Except for me. I have an important matter to attend to, but first, I need a wardrobe change.

Mick drops me off in front of Number Ten. "Need any help getting out of that dress?"

I kiss his bristly cheek before I reach for the door handle. "I'm sure you'd be a big help, but I can manage. See ya soon."

"You okay going out there by yourself? Maybe I should I go with you."

I shake my head. "It's just the family and me. It's what they want."

I change into jeans and a sweater, leather boots and a parka. On the way out the door, I pick up Yasmin's *hijab* and, on impulse, Hope's red balloon. The *hijab* has been cleansed of my blood and carefully ironed by me.

I point Buttercup toward Red Ridge, reveling in the silence and beauty of my surroundings. A sense of calm steals over me, chasing away the pre-wedding chaos I've been immersed in for days. The brilliant blue sky is cloudless, the sun dipping low in the west. It will soon slip behind the mountains, touching the peaks with a fiery promise of its return trip at dawn.

The Rathjen family has already gathered at the spot where Yasmin's body was found. Bibi and family are not invited. I am honored to be present.

Riley walks to my car and opens the door. "Thank you for coming."

I hand him the *hijab* and step out of Buttercup, holding the string of the red balloon. When we join the others, I ask, "May I explain about the balloon?"

When they agree, I tell them about Hope, how she died, how she always loved red balloons. "For years, I pushed her out of my mind. Remembering her was too painful. But, not remembering her became more painful. A person close to me gave me this balloon and encouraged me to open my heart, to invite the soul of my sister to enter. For some time, I needed this balloon to remind me of her presence. I don't need it anymore because I know she's always with me. She would want me to give it to you. Where there's Hope, there's love."

Rachel begins to sob. Roxanne pulls her in for a hug, rocking her gently in her arms. Rick pulls them both into his embrace. Riley's eyes are dry as he takes the *hijab* and balloon from me. The sun touches the top of the mountain peaks as he walks to the grave marker. A flat stone embedded in the ground is engraved with Yasmin's name and the dates of her birth and death, a pitifully short span. At the head of the flat stone, a vertical granite butterfly reaches toward the sky. On the butterfly's left wing, is the inscription

EARTH HAS LOST ONE GENTLE SOUL

The right butterfly wing is inscribed with

HEAVEN HAS GAINED TWO SPECIAL ANGELS

Riley's hands are shaking as he fumbles with the scarf and balloon. I step in and help him crisscross the *hijab* around the butterfly wings. Once it is secured, we attach the balloon and join the rest of the family. I'm included in their circle. We face the west and watch the earth's slow turn as the dying sun illuminates the butterfly wings. Yasmin's *hijab* flutters slightly beneath the bobbing red balloon.

Riley takes a shaky breath and tries to speak, but his words dissolve in tears.

Rick throws an arm around Riley's shoulders. "I've got you, son. Let me do this."

Riley nods.

Rick's voice is choked with emotion, his words heartfelt. "We gather here to honor Yasmin Ayoob and her unborn child, I should say, our unborn child. Both were taken from this earth far too soon. We pray our small ceremony will be the beginning of healing for our family. I hope God will forgive us—especially me—for my wrong-headed thinking. May she rest in peace, and may that peace extend to my family. Amen."

Darkness descends like the falling of a midnight blue velvet curtain, and we walk to our cars. The Rathjens invite me to their home, but Sandra's words ring in my ears. "The opening of presents will happen at precisely 7:00 p.m., and you are in charge of writing everything down so Aida and Paco can send thank you notes."

Since it is now close to 6:30 p.m., and I fear the wrath of Sandra, I explain my situation and promise to visit soon.

On my drive home, I think about the Rathjens and the Ayoobs. I hope Rick and his family will get it together. Too bad it took the death of an innocent girl to wake them up. As for Ayoobs, despite Riley's act of forgiveness, Bibi will be in his own personal hell forever.

Then, my thoughts turn to my last conversation with Kendra, regarding my love life.

"You need to give Billy another chance," she said. "He loves you, and he's changed."

"As I said before, I'm with Mick, now. Do I have to repeat my mantra? One man at a time?"

"But Mick has secrets, and he's gone most of the time. He won't even tell you where his mother lives. Not good for a relationship."

"But, Kendra, he bought me snow tires and took me out to a fancy restaurant. He even cooked for me."

I see from the stubborn set of her jaw, she's not going to let it go. She says, "Billy is present, and his love is unconditional. And, he told me something you need to consider."

She now has my full attention. "Oh?"

"It's an issue his counselor helped him figure out. His mind was so screwed up, he didn't feel like he was good enough for you. The memories kept flooding back, all the horrible things he saw in Afghanistan. He killed people, Mel, and he feels guilty about it. He wants to be the hero you deserve. So he made bad choices and pushed you away. Now, he realizes how wrong his thinking was, how badly he blew it."

I heave a big sigh. "Geez, couldn't he just talk to me?"

She takes my hand. "Believe me, he knows he broke your heart. But I also know my brother. He won't back off until he makes amends. Promise me you won't give up on him."

She physically blocked the door until I promised to at least, think about it. And I will…someday.

Back in 3 Peaks, I park in front of Number Ten and

step over Thunder Paws who refuses my invitation to enter. I guess he has a hot date.

Another change of clothes, and I'm off to join the party at Nick's. The back door of the pub flies open, and my mother appears. A brilliant shaft of light and the sound of joyous laughter spill out around her. The celebration is in full swing. She peers anxiously across the parking lot until she sees me, then smiles and waves. I return the wave and then pause for a moment to wrap my hand around the open-heart necklace. I feel Hope's loving presence pour into my heart and soul. I silently vow to keep her there forever.

I scurry across the parking lot, knowing everyone I love is inside.

What more could a girl want?

A word about the author…

Marilee Brothers is a former teacher, coach, counselor and the author of nine books. Marilee and her husband are the parents of three grown sons and live in central Washington State.

After writing six young adult books, Marilee is once again writing romantic suspense for the adult market. She loves hearing from people who have read her books.

Feel free to contact her at:
      http://www.marileebrothers.com.

Her author page on Facebook is:
      www.facebook.com/marilee.author
and she occasionally tweets @MarileeB.

Marilee's blog is Book Blather,
      http://bookblatherblog.blogspot.com
where she features aspiring and published authors as well as some tidbits of her own.